David Burnell was born and bred in York. He studied mathematics at Cambridge University, taught the subject in West Africa and came across Operational Research as a useful application. He spent his professional career applying the subject to management problems in the Health Service, coal mining and latterly the water industry. On "retiring" he completed a PhD at Lancaster on the deeper meaning of data from London's water meters.

He and his wife live in Berkshire and also in North Cornwall. They have four grown-up children.

David is now starting work on the next "Cornish Conundrum".

i

Earlier Cornish Conundrums

Doom Watch: *"Cornwall and its richly storied coast has a new writer to celebrate in David Burnell. His crafty plotting and engaging characters are sure to please crime fiction fans."* Peter Lovesey

Slate Expectations: *". . . combines an interesting view of an often overlooked side of Cornish history with an engaging pair of sleuths who follow the trail from past misdeeds to present murder."* Carola Dunn

Looe's Connections: *"A super holiday read set in a super holiday location!"* Judith Cutler

Tunnel Vision: *"Enjoyable reading for all who love Cornwall and its dramatic history."* Ann Granger

Twisted limelight: *"The plot twists will keep you guessing up to the last page. This is a thrilling Cornish mystery."* Kim Fleet

Peter Lovesey *is winner of the Crime Writers Cartier Diamond Dagger.*

Carola Dunn *is author of Daisy Dalrymple and the Cornish Mysteries.*

Rebecca Tope *writes the Cotswold and West Country Mysteries.*

Judith Cutler *writes, among others, the DS Fran Harman crime series.*

Ann Granger *writes, among others, the Campbell and Carter Mysteries.*

Kim Fleet *writes the Eden Grey Mysteries.*

Sarah Flint *(back cover) authors the DC Charlotte Stafford series.*

For Barbara,

Happy reading!

David Burnell

June 2018

FOREVER
MINE

David Burnell

Skein Books

A Cornish Conundrum

FOREVER MINE

Published by Skein Books, 88, Woodcote Rd, Caversham, Reading, UK

First edition: May 2018.

ISBN-13: **978-1987522150**
ISBN-10: **198752215X**

The front cover shows the Engine House of Levant Mine, now a National Trust Museum on the Land's End Peninsula. A faint picture of Cape Cornwall is shown in the background. I am grateful to Dr Chris Scruby for taking and fine-tuning the main photograph; and also the photo of me shown on the back.

CAPE CORNWALL and ST JUST

THE CHRISTMAS HOLIDAYS

Land's End, seen along the coast from Cape Cornwall

i

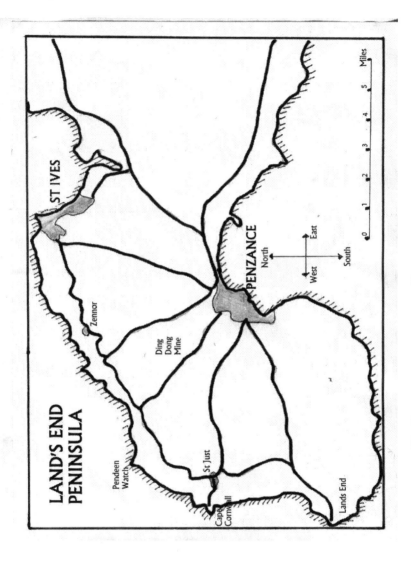

2

PROLOGUE

The Commanding Officer glared round the St Ives briefing room. It was June 1943.

'This is not just a training exercise. We're past namby-pamby play-acting now. And it's not an audition. You've all been hand-picked as Commandos for the rest of this ungodly war. Take a pride in that selection.'

He nodded as his eyes moved slowly over the twenty men in front of him. Even without their weapons they looked scary enough. But he needed to show his superiors that they would still look the part in the field.

'Yesterday was a tough day. Two members of this brigade drowned on the way to the exercise. But this is war. The question is how we respond when bad things, like a freak storm, happen.' He paused. 'I'm grateful for your unanimous support in repeating the exercise. We will remember our fallen colleagues; and this time we will succeed.'

'"Operation Brandyball" will set you down below Brandy Cliffs, ten miles along from St Ives. Like most cliffs round here, they'll seem to overhang as your landing crafts approach. That is a delusion. They are not vertical – not quite, anyway. And there are climbing routes up them. You'll be equipped with ropes and other gear. By the time you're up you'll be at a height of nearly

3

four hundred feet.

'At the top you will find just one stone, grey building with a slate roof; once part of a tin mine. I can assure you that mine was closed many years ago. For the purpose of this exercise that building is the enemy headquarters. You will have plenty of explosives. I want the whole place blown to smithereens.'

The CO went over the logistics and then invited questions.

'Can we use a radio link, sir?'

'Given this is a day-time operation and you'll be dropped close together, we won't waste time with that. But assume the enemy is listening and maintain operational silence.'

'What if we hit difficulties, sir? We can't afford to lose anyone else.'

'Do your best, all of you, to keep close to another team. But only signal for help if something has gone desperately wrong.'

'What if we come across non-military personnel, sir?'

'You won't. These cliffs haves been taken over by the Ministry of Defence.' But the Officer sensed his men weren't convinced.

'This is no parade ground exercise,' he went on. 'I want reality. Collateral damage is part of war. Act as you would if you stumbled over a local when climbing the cliffs of Sicily. Deal with them: make sure they can't disrupt the exercise. It has to succeed. Some very important people – including General Montgomery – will be taking note of what happens.'

The Commandos assembled at St Ives harbour just after dawn. It was close to high tide. A couple of Goatleys – small landing craft – were waiting. There was a thick mist and reduced visibility but not much wind. One of the Goatley skippers observed, 'Weather's *better than two days ago.'*

As they set off the men arranged themselves down the port side to study the passing cliffs.

'So this is your backyard?' observed Greg, the only Antipodean in the squad, to Don, his Cornish pair. A squat character, he might win a fight but never a beauty contest. 'It'd look even better in sunshine, mate; but it's attractive. Not many houses, though.'

'A lot of people left when the mines closed. I'm from Falmouth, the far side. That's a lot busier. Mind, the cliffs aren't as rugged.'

Two miles further on, they passed the remains of an old mine, shaft openings still visible on the cliff-tops.

Don tapped his partner on the shoulder and pointed. 'Look, Greg. There are lots of old mines around here. In the last century Cornwall was the world's leading producer of copper and tin.'

Greg smiled. 'Then the massive reserves in the colonies wiped you out.'

The voyage continued and Greg turned to the skipper. 'Mind if I borrow your glasses, mate?' The skipper nodded. Greg turned back to look at the mine, then at his map. 'That's Trevega Cliff, I reckon.'

Their boat continued; Greg noted an oddity in the tiny coves. 'I don't get it. There are tiny inlets but I can't see any stream. What caused them?'

'They're called "zawns". Like tiny chasms. It's some peculiar effect of the geology. It's mostly granite round here.'

Then there came a bigger headland. Greg consulted his map again. 'Zennor Head. Look, more shafts.'

The boat continued, past rugged Gurnard's Head and then a small beach. 'That'd be good for a swim if you could get down to *it, Don. Maybe once it's all over?'*

'There'd be a way, Greg, we'd just need to find it. But not today, I think. We're close to Brandy Cliffs now.'

The soldiers started final preparations. Layers of clothing came off and were stuffed into their rucksacks. They'd have to jump ashore and would probably get wet but there was no point in being completely sodden. Don and Greg would be the last to leave.

The plan was to drop the last pair in a zawn cut into Brandy Cliffs, scarcely wider than the boat. The rocky walls on either side were almost vertical, greasy, with no obvious holds.

Don looked up, saw an old lifebelt hanging on a post ten feet above. 'Someone must have put that there. If we can reach it I bet there's a path upwards.'

'So are you going on my shoulders, Don, or the other way round?'

'I'm taller but I reckon you're the stronger. You first. Leave your gear but take a rope ladder. I'll climb once you've attached it.'

The men looked incongruous, dressed only in boots and under-pants, but very determined. They told the skipper what they intended and he manoeuvred the Goatley to just below the lifebelt. 'Hurry lads,' he pleaded. 'I can't hold this position for long.'

Greg shinned up until he was astride Don's shoulders, then reached upwards. His hands inched up . . . stretched to the limit . . . but he was still a foot short.

A few seconds later he was back on deck. 'I can see how to do it, Don. I'll stand on your shoulders.'

'OK. Hope to goodness the boat doesn't move away.'

The manoeuvre was delicate but there was no alternative. Once again Greg clambered up Don's back. Then, moving slowly, he stood to balance on his companion's shoulders. He could sense the Goatley rocking beneath them.

Now the post was just within reach. The commando grabbed it with both hands, his legs scrabbled and then, with one final heave, he was onto the ledge and sitting astride the post. Don tottered, then managed to step back into the well of the Goatley.

A moment later a rope ladder snaked down towards him. Don slipped on his pack, leaned out and started the climb. As he did so he could hear the Goatley revving its engine, ready to reverse out of the zawn.

Seconds later he was up on the narrow ledge alongside Greg.

'Hell, that was hard work. Hope it doesn't get much tougher.'

Greg was looking quizzical. 'Hey, where's my pack?'

Simultaneously, horror struck, they looked down. By now the Goatley had reversed out of the zawn. It was being buffeted by waves as it headed as fast as possible back to St Ives. A moment later it was out of sight.

Greg swore but there was no point in blaming Don. He would have to complete the rest of the operation in his underpants.

An hour later, after some tough climbing, the pair had made their way almost to the top. Don's confident assertion that a path led down to the lifebelt turned out not to be true. There was a faint path but it ran almost level, into the zawn. 'Trouble is, Don, that won't help us with the climb.'

Instead they had battled a mixture of rock faces, gullies, bushes, bracken and thorns. Fortunately Don knew about Cornish *cliffs. By persistent effort he found a way over or through the various obstacles.*

It was as they'd reached the final section and were taking a moment to catch their breath that they realised they were not alone.

Don pointed to a dark shape, almost stationary, in the foliage on the far side. 'Greg, d'you see that?'

Greg followed his arm and watched for a moment. 'Well, I'll be blowed. It's a woman. Wait a minute . . . is that a gun?'

Trepidation followed by a moment of careful inspection.

'No. I reckon it's a film camera. The CO said we'd be observed. I thought he meant directly, but maybe he just intended to film us so he could show us off to his bosses. I bet she's been covering our efforts all the way up the zawn.'

Greg glanced down his almost-naked body and pondered. 'Don, I am not going to appear on an Army recruitment video in my underpants. I think we should take her out. Wipe that film before it gets seen anywhere.'

Don mused for a moment.

'Not only the film, Greg. If we handle this right you can take her clothes as well. At least you'd be dressed for the final assault.'

'Right. So what I want, Don, is for you to make your way towards her noisily. Take your time, thrash about, catch her attention, make her think we're both still on this side. Meanwhile I'll creep round behind her.'

Moving silently through rough terrain had featured prominently in their commando training. For some cultural reason that Don couldn't quite fathom, Greg had been particularly adept. He slipped away, moving so carefully that Don couldn't even see where he'd got to.

Meanwhile Don had to give the impression of being a double act. He pushed forward noisily for some distance. Then he left his pack, took off his beret and shirt, slipped back to where he'd started and came forward again, head visible above the under-growth, by a different route. With a bit of luck the camera woman was too far away to spot the deception.

Then he repeated the process, taking his time.

It was as he did it the third time that he heard a thump followed by a high-pitched cry. Looking across he saw that the film woman and her camera had disappeared. Don smiled to himself. He would give Greg a few moments to remove the woman's cloth-ing.

After longer than he'd expected, Greg appeared a short dis-tance further on and waved for Don to join him. He'd been successful – at least, he was no longer naked. The clothes he had borrowed were by no means a good fit but must have come from some sort of military store: they had a khaki base and were cov-ered in green camouflage patterns.

It was a pity, though, that the woman had been wearing a skirt.

Being once more fully clothed seemed to have reinstated Greg's self confidence. Now he was almost gung ho. 'We're not far off the old mine, Don. Enemy headquarters, remember. Come on. It's just over the next rise.'

The pair slipped forward more easily: the ground was almost level. Don glanced back apprehensively. 'Greg, what happened to the woman?'

Greg looked slightly embarrassed. 'Sorry, mate. Like the

Officer said, today is not just an audition. In any theatre of war there's always a risk of collateral damage.'

He sighed. 'Like you, I'm a man under authority. I had no choice but to follow the Officer's orders.'

CHAPTER 1

As a professional photographer I'd been to many weddings over the years but I'd never experienced anything as shocking as this.

It was New Year's Eve. The wedding was taking place in the church at St Just: that's a granite-coloured village on the far western tip of Cornwall. The last day of the year was trying to make up for earlier weather havoc by bowing out with a brilliant blue sky.

Mind, the biting wind meant it was still bitterly cold. I wondered how the bride would cope with the mandatory outdoor pictures at the end of the service: she'd steadfastly refused to buy herself a warm shawl, seemed to imagine that the status of being star of the day would protect her neck and shoulders from the icy chill. Or else that on this day of all days she simply wouldn't register air temperature at all.

Meanwhile the service was edging towards the close. The bride, my old friend Maxine Tavistock (strictly speaking, I suppose I should now be thinking of her as Mrs Maxine Travers) looked serene and utterly radiant in her flowing ivory wedding gown. Her new husband, Police Sergeant Peter Travers, stood tall beside her at the altar in his best light blue suit, looking like the cat that had finally got the cream. Hadn't scoffed all of it, mind, but made jolly sure it was firmly in his clutches. He wouldn't be letting go any time soon.

The local vicar, Father Giles, had been formally in charge of the event and had spoken to welcome us all at the start of the service but the bulk of the work, marrying the couple and then providing the sermon, had come from an old college friend of Maxine's, the Revd Esther Middleton. Any remnants of the local population who were still opposed to women priests would have been forced to think again by this bubbling live wire, exuding joy and wisdom in equal measure.

The church was several hundred years old and it did of course have a traditional organ. That had provided a striking theme from Vivaldi to welcome the entrance of the bride, but the rest of today's music was much more tuned to our generation.

I'd learned this week that Peter Travers sometimes played the guitar with musical friends from his village of Delabole, at the other end of Cornwall. He'd invited the band, "The Slaters", to come down to provide the musical accompaniment in the service and later to lead the dancing in the reception. They were a folk group, played a variety of instruments and had added verve and gaiety to the service.

I suspected Esther Middleton had chosen the songs, all written in our own lifetimes and with uncomplicated tunes the band could quickly pick up. The words also made sense. The effect had been to make the whole service fizz with life and cheerfulness.

Glancing around, as the congregation launched into the final song (it was hardly a hymn), I caught the eye of some of the individuals I'd got to know over the past few days.

There were Maxine's mum and dad, of course: Maria and Alex. They owned a guesthouse that faced out over the rugged coast, just down the road to Cape Cornwall. Maxine, in her early forties, was their only child and they'd risen to the occasion. They'd closed Chy Brisons straight after Christmas. Maxine had taken the chance to invite some of her friends (including me) down to help get things ready, at the same time as enjoying a few days' holiday on the peninsula.

George Gilbert, chief bridesmaid, looking gorgeous in a knee-length maroon dress, was standing behind the bride, ready to follow her down the aisle. She'd been with Maxine at Cambridge and was some sort of industrial mathematician. I'd no idea what that meant but she was certainly efficient and well organised.

There were three other bridesmaids. Two were Maxine's cousins and the third the bridegroom's niece. They were standing behind George, also in maroon dresses.

Peter Travers's best man, Brian Southgate, now stood behind him. He was also from Delabole, the local medical doctor. The two men went back a long way, I'd learned that they'd been at school together. Their roles had been inverted when Brian married Alice some years earlier. Alice stood further back in the congregation, slightly apprehensive: she would be chef for the main reception.

Brian had drunk lustily over the week. I didn't know if he had to keep the habit under wraps while he was in Delabole to avoid disturbing his patients and this was a chance to catch up; or had Alice's role as chef given him extra freedom? Perhaps he was drinking to steady his nerves, ready for the best man's speech?

13

Mercifully he hadn't needed to make much of a contribution before today. But I wasn't that worried. Brian looked the sort of man that could improvise an entertaining speech on the hoof. No doubt he and Peter had had many adventures over the years that would provide an embarrassment of material. The bigger challenge for the Master of Ceremonies might be to bring his speech to a halt.

On the row behind stood other (mostly older) relatives of the happy couple. Behind them were the friends of one or other who'd been down with me for part of the week, including the tubby, tousle-haired journalist who'd read the lesson. Then a bunch more guests that had arrived for the day. Some had come by taxi from Penzance station. There were also a number of St Just locals known to Alex and Maria; and regular members of the congregation with an informal invitation to the service and the subsequent cake reception.

Personally I hoped this wouldn't last too long. I'd been up early, taking pictures of Cape Cornwall at dawn and other background scenes, and was looking forward to the main reception, which despite various commotions would take place in the barn next to Maxine's parents' guest house.

Maxine had insisted that as well as the views of her outside she wanted a few pictures of the invited guests. I slipped round the side as the procession headed for the door and followed them out into the cold.

It was then that I saw the police car. It was parked at the end of the lane leading down to the church. The roads at this time of year were impossibly muddy and it didn't look as though it had been recently cleaned. What on earth was that doing? He might be a policeman, but surely Peter wasn't going to drive Maxine away for their honeymoon in a police car? Then I recalled that Land's End Airport was just down the road. Were the two planning a rapid exit?

Idiot, Kirstie, I told myself. There was the whole reception to enjoy first. The Slaters would be even better at encouraging the celebration party than they'd been at leading the service.

But the police car wasn't just parked and unoccupied. There was a policeman sitting at the wheel, in fact I recognised his face: he'd been around for some reason earlier that morning. He was chewing gum and stony-faced. It didn't look like he was here for the wedding ceremony.

And then it happened. Two members of the procession that were following the happy couple detached themselves from the rest and stepped over towards the police car. As far as I could see there were no goodbyes to the bride and groom. One of the pair opened a rear door and then both seated themselves inside.

After which the police car reversed back up the lane and drove steadily away.

CHAPTER 2

The whole tragic business had been completely unimaginable just a few days before Christmas.

A hoot of the horn marked the arrival of a smart four-wheel-drive hire car outside the Tavistock's guesthouse, Chy Brisons, on the road from St Just, out towards Cape Cornwall. A tall man, rugged but edging towards baldness, jumped out and headed for the front door. But his arrival had already been noticed. Before he'd even reached it Alex Tavistock strode out and gave him a massive hug.

'Ross. Back in Cornwall at last! Welcome, welcome. I'm so glad to see you here again.'

'It's been a while, Alex. Thirty five years, I believe.' He shivered. 'But I see global warming hasn't reached these parts yet.'

'It's probably a little colder here than Sydney, Ross. Mind, this is our winter and your summer, so it's not really a fair comparison. Come on, let me meet your family.'

The two men made their way back to the car, where the three other passengers, stiff from travelling halfway round the world, were starting to climb out.

'Alex, this is my wife, Lisa. Of course, you two met when you came over to Australia to mark the millennium. I'm not a man to boast, but I don't think she looks a day older.'

Alex saw an attractive, honey-blond woman in her fifties and gave her a welcoming hug. Lisa was pure Australian, he remembered, so took it she would have no emotional inhibitions.

Ross turned to the other passengers. 'Alex, these are my daughters, Shelley and Frances. Fortunately they take more after Lisa in appearance. I admit they looked younger when you last met, but fifteen years ago they were scarcely teenagers. They're so looking forward to being Maxine's bridesmaids. It's an unexpected honour.'

Shelley and Frances each gave Alex a polite hug. He noticed that they, too, looked a little cold.

'Do come inside, all of you. Maria and Maxine are busy with the baking. We hadn't expected you till tomorrow, actually.'

Half an hour later introductions had been completed and Ross's family were seated in the guest house lounge with mugs of coffee and a plate of biscuits, alongside Maria and Maxine.

For Maxine this was the first time she had met her Australian cousins face to face, though they'd had plenty of email and Skype conversations over the past few months. She noticed, though, that coming half way round the world didn't seem to cause the pair to be lost for words.

They hadn't even learned the art of speaking in turn. Both gushed away simultaneously, giving their views of air travel from Australia in the run up to Christmas, the busyness of motorways in the UK and the oddity of Christmas decorations on dark days. It was relentless. Maxine wondered for a moment whether she had been wise inviting them to be bridesmaids.

'The thing is, Alex, my firm needed me to come to the UK around this time in any case. It was a happy coincidence that I could arrange it to tie in with the wedding.'

'And even that wouldn't have worked if you hadn't brought the event forward in mid November,' added Lisa. 'It was very considerate but didn't it cause a few problems at this end?'

Maxine felt she was being treated as an extra in the main production. It was, after all, her wedding. It was time to assert herself.

'Actually, the change of date wasn't anything directly to do with us. You see . . .'

She stopped for dramatic effect. Rather a pity as it gave her mother chance to take over. 'The hotel that Maxine had booked for the wedding, over in Bude – that's the far side of Cornwall – had to go into administration so it cancelled all its bookings.'

As she drew breath Maxine took over. 'My fiancé, Peter, declared that he couldn't face the whole process of finding somewhere else and probably losing another few months as we did so. If he was going to change the date, he said, he wanted it brought forward.'

'Good man,' said Ross. 'I like the sound of him.'

Her mother continued. 'Meanwhile Alex and I had been musing over the whole thing. We realised that with the guest-house and a bit of adjustment we had the facilities and contacts to hold the whole thing in St Just. Alex and I had attended the local church here for years, you see, and that's quite large - it would hold a couple of hundred, though of course the typical congregation is only a couple of dozen.'

Alex could see the dangers of a diversion into church tradition and hastened to take over. 'Besides, Maxine's our only daughter. Once the opportunity had come up, we realised how much we wanted her to be married from our home – even if she'd not been brought up here.'

Ross intervened. 'So this is just a wedding for family and close friends – a couple of dozen guests in total?' He looked around. 'That sounds nice and cosy. I can see that's about all you could squeeze in here.'

'Oh no, Ross. We've got a Barn, you see.' He pointed out of the window. 'It's the far side of the lawn, with a huge window down one side that overlooks Cape Cornwall. We use it in summer as an afternoon tea room, so we've plenty of tables and so on.'

'But if you only use it in the summer do you have any heating in there? I mean, you locals are used to arctic weather but it'll be a bit chilly for some of us.'

'Don't worry, Ross. I've ordered a set of heaters from Truro. When they come, I thought perhaps you could help me fasten them to the cross-beams?'

'Be glad to make a contribution, mate. It shouldn't take us too long. We're both pretty tall.'

Maria didn't want the whole thing to sound too easy. She glanced at her daughter. 'Mind, it would have been better if we'd had more notice. Trouble is, if you're starting in November, Christmas is the next obvious time for a wedding. After that the bleakness of winter makes it a lot harder, at least until you get near to Easter.'

With some difficulty Maxine managed to hold back her frustration. It was her wedding. If she and Peter had realised how complicated it would become to accept help from her parents, what their idea of style would involve and how far they would want to take over, they would have been tempted to slip into the Bude registry office and marry without any ceremony at all.

It was a temptation that would recur over the coming days.

CHAPTER 3

Christmas Eve.

They were all free of jetlag now. Today Ross had taken his family off on a tour of the Land's End peninsula. Alex had enthused about the open-air Minack Theatre at Porthcurno and the Telegraph Museum next door. 'Even if there's no production, just seeing the location, with Logan's Rock to one side and the sea beyond, is fantastic.'

His brother had seemed happy enough to take his family out to have a look. Or maybe just to escape from Chy Brisons.

It was early afternoon when Maxine, newly-arrived for Christmas from Bude, found herself alone in the kitchen with her mother. Maria was in a state close to panic.

'Maxine, we've got twenty five guests booked in for a special Christmas lunch tomorrow.'

'Mum, that's exactly like you had last year – and the year before.'

'Yes but the chef sloped off yesterday with food poisoning – or so he says, it's probably a surfeit of alcohol. Then this morning your Dad got called away to help the coastguards.'

'I've come down to help, Mum. What d'you want me to do?'

Her mother eyed here dubiously. Maxine was no super chef, she was more thinker than woman of action. 'How are you on

21

peeling potatoes?'

A few minutes later Maxine found herself standing at the kitchen table with a massive bag of King Edwards and a large bowl of ice-cold water.

'Don't cut them too small, dear. Ideally I'd want them all the same size. Then they'll cook at the same rate and be easier to dish up.'

'Right.' It was a mindless task but that was a relief after the recent pressures of work.

Maxine kept the fact as quiet as possible but she worked as an analyst and decoder at the Cleave Camp Listening Station, a remote part of GCHQ, just up the coast from Bude. It was a recurring question in Security whether terrorists were more active close to public holidays because they hoped they wouldn't be spotted or because they themselves wanted to mark the occasion with a bang.

For the next few weeks, at least, that was a challenge she could leave to others.

Her mother seemed slightly more relaxed now she wouldn't be completing the Christmas lunch preparations on her own.

'We're closed after tomorrow, thank goodness. Alex insisted. Said we couldn't do justice to the wedding if we were still trying to run the guest house and restaurant as well. That's why we had room for his brother's family. Trouble is, dear, it's all been so much of a rush.'

Maxine could see her mother needed some Tender Loving Care. 'It's wonderful you could fit us in, Mum. After that wretched hotel in Bude went bust. Peter and I couldn't face going round and round to find somewhere else, then waiting more months for the wedding itself.'

'If I can't put myself out to help my only daughter get married it'd be a bit sad.'

There was an agreeable silence. Maxine plodded on with the potatoes while her mother dealt with a host of other vegetables.

'When's Peter coming?' her mother asked.

'He'll be in St Just on Boxing Day. He's spending Christmas with his brother and family in Padstow. Of course, that will give him time with my youngest bridesmaid, Katrina. They'll follow later.'

Her mother was still fearing the worst. 'Mind, I imagine with policemen there's always a chance of something nasty coming along to mess up their annual leave.'

'Now we are being cheerful.' Maxine smiled. 'As far as I know there's nothing urgent happening at the moment. It's not as bad in Cornwall, you know, as in places like London. And he's got a strong team working with him in Bude. They're all excited that he's getting married, happy to cover his absence for a week or two. It's good he's got two weeks off. If Dad wants, Peter can help get the Barn ready for the reception.'

'Hm. As long as he doesn't spend the whole week drinking his way round the pubs of Land's End with your Dad and Ross.'

'Even if he does that'll help with family integration, Mum.'

Maxine's dad, Alex, arrived back at Chy Brisons an hour later. It was only half past four but already dark. He barged in through the kitchen door, looking extremely fed up. His face lit up as he saw his daughter, still peeling potatoes and concentrating hard to make each one the same size.

'Maxine. Thank goodness you're here to help.' He strode over and gave her a big hug, then returned to the doormat to prise off his walking boots. Maxine could see that the loop had added mud to the slate floor.

'Good to see you home, Dad. Mum told me you'd been called out to help the coastguards. Is everything OK?'

'Well, not really.' He was reluctant to say more but Maxine was not easily fobbed off.

'Did you find whoever you were looking for?'

'It wasn't search and rescue, I'm afraid. Just as well this time of the year. It's perishing cold out there. If someone had fallen down the cliffs they'd likely be dead from exposure before we got anywhere near them.'

'So what was it?'

He peeled off his high-visibility waterproof jacket and scarf, hung them behind the door, then turned to face her. 'The police had asked the coastguards for help. Our chief coastguard, Colin Trewern, called out everyone who was around. As you'd expect, a lot of the regulars are away visiting their families over Christmas. That's how I got drawn in.'

Maxine laughed. 'Sounds intriguing. Breaks up your week, anyway. Mum tell me you've not got many residents at the moment – apart from Ross and his family.' She looked at him carefully. 'You can't stop now, Dad. Tell me more.'

Alex wasn't bursting to say but he knew his daughter was persistent and could see no way back. He gave a gulp. 'Somehow or other the police had learned about a dead body at the foot of a mine shaft. Presumably he'd fallen down. They were after help from volunteers who were used to outdoor rescue work.'

'So between you, you had to carry the body on a stretcher back to a road?'

'It was worse than that. Two of us had to climb a hundred feet down a rope ladder, tie the body securely to the stretcher and then guide it with ropes we'd attached. Meanwhile the ones at the top struggled with the hauling.'

Maxine stopped peeling for a moment. 'That sounds rather awkward. Was the shaft wide enough?'

'About eight feet, could have been worse. Fortunately it's a procedure we practice regularly: it has to be done very slowly so the body doesn't get caught on the rocks. From the bottom of cliffs, I mean. I've never had to do it from down a mine shaft before.'

'So you've been beavering away with that for most of the day? No wonder you're cold. And now you've come home you've got to be host, brimming with Christmas spirit, ready to entertain your guests.'

Alex shrugged. 'I didn't mind. I don't much like staying indoors and I was with colleagues. It's the victim you should be sorry for.'

Maria overheard the last sentence as she returned to the kitchen. She'd been all set to blast her husband for being out most of the day but she could see that in this dismal context that might not be appropriate.

'So there was a victim, Alex. Was it a man or a woman? Anyone you knew?'

Alex turned toward her. 'Hello, dear. I was just telling Maxine, we were asked by the police to help extract a body from an old mine shaft. I was one of the volunteers who climbed down the shaft. It was a man, but he wasn't easy to recognise: he'd smashed his head in the fall. As you might expect, the police weren't very forthcoming. They just needed help on the logistics.'

Maria wasn't easily fobbed off either. 'Was it a local mine shaft?' she probed. 'Was it deep?'

'It was one of the shafts on Ding Dong Mine.' He turned to Maxine. 'That's five miles away, a couple of miles in from the coast.'

He paused to collect his thoughts. 'Once we'd convened in St Just we drove round the coast road, up from Morvah towards Madron, parked at the top and then walked in over the moors. It's six hundred feet up and pretty bleak. It wasn't helped by the mist, either.'

He looked at them both carefully. 'Now listen. I don't want this to interfere with the preparations for the wedding. To be honest, I'd rather you both forgot all about it, at least till that's over. And for goodness sake don't tell Ross. He's told his family that nothing significant ever happens in Western Cornwall. It's in all our interests to preserve that impression.'

Now she'd learned the core facts, Maria was less concerned with the perceived need for secrecy and more worried about the cleanliness of Chy Brisons.

'If you've been handling a dead body, Alex, you'd better go

26

and have a long bath and put all the clothes you've been wearing in the linen basket. The whole lot, please. Once you're fully decontaminated you can come down and give me a hand. Remember, we've got to rearrange all the tables in the dining room and then squeeze in more for all those guests we're expecting tomorrow.'

Her mum couldn't be faulted for lack of focus, thought Maxine. Though maybe she could work on being more empathetic.

CHAPTER 4

Although Dr Brian Southgate would regularly tell his patients in Delabole to watch their weight if they hoped to live into their eighties, he did not apply the advice to himself or his family on Christmas Day.

'You know, Alice,' he remarked, as he confronted the duck with the oven, 'we ought to do something to encourage George and Robbie to get closer.' These were two of the guests who'd been invited to lunch later. George Gilbert would be chief bridesmaid at the forthcoming wedding. Robbie Glendenning was a friend of longstanding.

George had once studied maths alongside the bride, Maxine Tavistock. The two had reconnected over a security-based crime in Bude, which was how Maxine had come to meet Peter Travers. Solving the crime had put the women in some jeopardy, so it was no great surprise, later, when George had been invited to be chief bridesmaid.

Robbie Glendenning was a senior journalist with a respectable national newspaper and a former historian. As chief South West reporter he covered events all over the Region. 'My job,' he would claim, 'is helping write the first draft of history.'

Robbie didn't know Maxine at all, he'd been invited to the wedding as George's friend. There was potential tension between

Maxine's need to keep her security activity out of the public gaze, while Robbie's instinct was to make everything open and transparent.

Robbie and George had combined resources over several mysteries in Cornwall, starting with a flood in Looe. When harnessed to solving a crime they were a good combination. George's incisive logic would guide the way forward while Robbie contributed more practical investigative skills, for example tracking down elusive witnesses.

'They'll get there in the end, if that's what they both want,' replied Alice. She knew from talking to George that their relationship had had its ups and downs. But she was a schoolteacher, not a counsellor. She was not going to match make for two friends of her own age.

Brian gave the duck one more heave, which pushed it into the oven. 'I reckon the core problem, Alice, is that both of them are extremely busy.'

'All of us are busy, Brian. The problem is that they're not just busy, but in different places – half the time in different continents.'

Brian considered. Robbie was based in Bristol but George's home was in London. She did, though, own a cottage in Treknow, between Delabole and Tintagel. This provided a base when her work fell in Cornwall.

'It could be made to work. They seem fond of each other. The thing is, Robbie needs to be more decisive, say "no" to being sent abroad.'

'The trouble is, Brian, he's so good with people. They'll always

29

tell him more than they'd intended. That's a rare gift, invaluable for a journalist.'

'Yes, but he's been in China for too long.'

'It's no wonder his friendship with George is becalmed.' Alice glanced at the kitchen clock. 'Look, he'll be here soon. Why don't you take him for a walk over the cliffs, give him a gentle nudge? But make sure you're back by three. We don't want that duck overcooked.'

Robbie turned up soon after eleven. On Christmas morning traffic had been non-existent coming down from Bristol. He was happy enough to drive down to Trebarwith Strand with Brian and take a scramble over the cliffs.

'How's life with you these days?' asked Brian, once the two had toiled up the first headland.

'Can't complain. These days anyone with a full-time job has to be grateful. Mine's more interesting than most. China's quite intriguing.'

'Aren't you fed up with spending so much time abroad? Don't you ever want to settle down?'

'That's what my mother keeps saying. Between ourselves, Brian, if George was more enthusiastic it might all be different.'

'You sure it's George that's diffident?'

'Well, when we first met she was coming to terms with losing her husband in that plane crash. I could see she needed space.'

'That was years ago, Robbie. I'd say she's had all the space she needs. She's coming for lunch too, you know. Maybe this next week in Land's End will give you more time together.'

When they got back to the Southgate's, after a short stop in the Port William, overlooking Trebarwith Strand, they found George had already arrived. She hadn't changed much, thought Robbie, with her slender figure and dark curly hair. But there was another woman with her.

'Hi guys,' said George. 'Good to see you both. This is an old friend of mine, Esther Middleton. She's a vicar over in Bideford. We were both at Cambridge together. Esther's going to take the wedding service next week. Esther, these two rogues are Brian and Robbie.'

Robbie didn't habitually study clergy too closely but he'd never met a vicar who was so easy on the eye. He could imagine that any male member of the congregation would find it hard to take in much of her message when she was preaching – though they might be keen to discuss it with her afterwards. 'Pleased to meet you,' he stumbled. 'It's great that you're with us. But . . . shouldn't you be leading a Christmas Service somewhere?

Esther smiled. 'I did. It was an All-Age Service with kids roaming everywhere and I was the preacher. But it started at ten and was over by eleven. Christmas Day isn't the time for long sermons. Bideford's not that far, you know. And now I'm off clerical duty. Are you coming to this wedding too? Tell me, are you a friend of Peter or Maxine?'

Half an hour later Alice invited them all to take their seats. Esther was invited to say grace. She remembered those around the world who were less well-fed and also prayed for all those preparing for next week's wedding.

Then everyone started on their sliced melon and ginger, while Brian fussed over what they wanted to drink. Esther and Alice had fruit juice, the rest preferred the special Merlot he'd acquired for the occasion.

'I haven't been that close to Maxine in recent years,' said Esther. 'And of course I don't know Peter at all. I'd be happy to hear any stories you felt you could tell me about them.'

'And I'd be particularly interested in memories of Peter,' said Brian. 'Remember, I've a best man's speech to put together. People might expect it to be funnier than your sermon, Esther.' He saw a puzzled look on her face and hastily added, 'Of course, that might not be possible. Anyway, this is the best chance we'll have to swap notes without either of them around.'

George found herself in the odd position of being the key source on both characters.

'Maxine and I studied maths at Cambridge,' she began. 'I was always more interested in practical applications but Maxine was an outstanding theoretical mathematician. I'm sure she wouldn't want it broadcast widely, but that's why she ended up decoding for the government on security issues. That's where I came across her again.'

She could see questions crossing minds for both Robbie and Esther. 'I suppose, since that was the case that brought Peter and Maxine together, they wouldn't mind me telling you something about it.'

'I'm very used to keeping secrets,' said Esther.

'You know I never publish personal stuff without permission,' added Robbie. 'And then only if it's in the public interest.'

So the next half hour, as the meal progressed, George re-counted the events around Bude which have been recorded in "*Twisted Limelight.*"

There were many interruptions and tangents and several points of divergence. It wasn't bad as an ice breaker.

BOXING DAY

MONDAY

DECEMBER 26th

Zennor Village, between St Ives and St Just

34

CHAPTER 5

Nifty footwork by Brian Southgate led to Robbie offering George a lift down to the Land's End Peninsula on Boxing Day.

'I don't know how much space Maxine's family have got for parking,' he said. 'But the fewer cars we have down there the easier it will be to manage. I expect we'll mostly be doing things together anyway.'

With the windy December gale blowing ferociously George hoped they'd all be spending most of that time indoors but she didn't want to argue. Esther was no driving addict. She was equally happy to leave her car at the Southgate's and travel down a little later with Brian and Alice.

'Robbie, d'you know the far end of Cornwall very well?' asked George, as they set out along a minor road which crossed the old Trelill railway tunnel – a key location on an earlier case. 'I've only been there once in recent years. That was to meet Maxine's family.'

'I hardly know it at all. It's the far end of my beat. But I may know it better over the next few months. I'll be spending more time down there, you see. I've been asked to update my paper's economic assessment of mining in Cornwall.'

'I don't want to disillusion you, Robbie, but is there anything to update? Every mine was closed down by the end of last century, wasn't it?'

'That's what I thought. "I'll give you a historical perspective," I told my bosses. "Too late, we've already got someone on that," they replied. "A woman called Siobhan Hitchen".

'That was a surprise. I knew Siobhan at Bristol, you see, we were history students in the same year. But she's heard that something new is being looked at. They want me to poke around, find out more about it.'

'But anything that brings new money to Cornwall must be welcome? After all, it's one of the poorest parts of the UK.'

'I'm not sure. Have you seen the disruption caused by mining? The spoil tips and so on. It's not just the noise of the shaft itself. There's all the processing and transportation that goes with it.'

As their journey continued, George asked Robbie about his recent trip to China.

'It's a really amazing country,' he said. 'Vast, of course. Very different to the UK, it's growing at an incredible rate.'

'How d'you mean?'

'Currently China's GDP is expanding at 7% per year. Puts our 1.5% pa into the shade. Even a casual visitor can see it. They're building high-rise offices and flats at a tremendous pace. They don't just work in the daytime. Oh no. The builders lodge in the first rooms that they build. From then on they're always on site so they can work through the night. It's twenty four hour production, not just nine to five like the UK.'

'You were there a long time. What were you looking at?'

'My newspaper wanted to know what the Chinese were doing to generate new energy sources. They've hundreds of coal mines and until recently they relied on coal fired power stations. But that's an old technology and leads to vast amounts of atmospheric pollution.'

Robbie mused for a moment. 'In Shanghai there's smog all the time. It's a bit like a Cornish sea mist but much more deadly. Half the population go about wearing face masks, though I doubt that does much good. So now the leaders are pushing for nuclear power, also taking more interest in renewable energy.'

'Like wind power and solar panels?'

'And the rest. There are lots of possibilities. The thing about the Chinese is, once they know they have to study something or adopt it, they do so in a madly wholehearted manner.'

He paused to collect his thoughts. 'When they want a high speed railway it's not like our HS2, with years of hassle that takes twenty years to complete and then knocks twenty minutes off the journey. The Chinese draw a straight line between the end-points and then build directly between them. If there are houses in the way they'll knock 'em down. So now they've got bullet trains, faster than anything we'll ever have. Hourly between Beijing and Shanghai, going at hundreds of miles an hour.'

He sounded very enthusiastic. 'So will you be going back?' she asked.

'One day. I might even learn Mandarin. But not yet. I told my bosses I wanted to spend more time in the UK. That's when they suggested this Cornish mine investigation.'

Once they'd joined the A30 they could travel faster. There were no lorries and even the car traffic was light. The weather was almost sunny.

'We're in no particular hurry are we?' asked Robbie.

'Don't think so. Maxine said she wouldn't start the final wedding preparations until tomorrow. Why, have you thought of a detour?'

'Well, you know we were pulling together a tasty crime mystery for Peter and Maxine, for when they got back from their honeymoon?'

'Trouble was, Robbie, we'd had too much Merlot. Schemes running wild. Hercule Poirot would have struggled with our final challenge.'

'Probably. Well, out of interest, I looked up the Penzance Police web site. Had they got any crime at all?'

'And you found . . .?'

'Among the dross was one announcement I thought was interesting. It said the police had found the body of a middle-aged man at the bottom of a mine shaft on Christmas Eve.'

George mused for a moment. 'Did they give any more details - the bloke's name, for example? Or how long he'd been lying there? I assume he was already dead.'

'The notice didn't say much. Perhaps they couldn't until the next of kin had been informed.

'And I bet they'd be short staffed, most local staff on leave. I don't suppose they do extra shifts in Penzance.'

'Huh. That's just an excuse. It did give the name of the mine, it was called "Ding Dong". Have you heard of it? Five miles from St Just.'

George frowned. 'Never. It doesn't sound remotely Cornish. Are you suggesting we could go and have a look?' She considered. 'Presumably it's off the beaten track. I'd be happy to walk off yesterday's lunch. But can we find it?'

'It's marked on the map of Land's End in the glove compartment. I had a look before we set off.'

After they left the A30 they dropped down to a winding road with stone walls on either side that followed the north coast from St Ives. A mile or two further on they came to the delightful village of Zennor.

'How about a coffee?' suggested George, pointing to a sign advertising an all-purpose village store.

They went in, taking Robbie's map with them. The main room was a former chapel, warm and comfortable, with plenty of Cornish artefacts on the walls and specialist books about mining and so on for sale.

While Robbie was ordering coffees George took a soft chair at the far end and studied the map. Zennor was easy to find, with many mine shafts on the coast nearby. It took a while, though, to find Ding Dong.

'I've seen several old shafts around Ding Dong,' she reported, when Robbie returned. 'It may not be easy to tell which one the man fell down.'

'That's alright,' he replied. 'I talked to the girl at the counter. She said there'd be some police tape at the top. Apparently a team of coastguards brought the body up to the surface, including one man who lives in Zennor. He wasn't back till after dark. I've got his name by the way, we could find him later if we need to.'

George reflected with a tinge of regret that Robbie the journalist was never fully off duty.

Twenty minutes later they set off again. Two miles later they turned inland on a road signposted for Newmill. Once that was reached they turned onto a single track road which led past occasional farms, almost bereft of signposts.

'These places have got unusual names,' noted George. 'One's called "Break my Neck Farm". Another one's "Bay of Biscay"'.

'Farming round here must be very tough,' Robbie replied.

The analyst had to focus hard. They turned this way and that, steadily climbing the moor, to reach as close as possible to "Ding Dong". George could see at least a dozen shafts nearby.

Eventually Robbie spotted a tall old stone engine house close to the road, its roof long gone. They pulled into a grassy lane to take stock.

'Surely the police will have left some trace behind,' said George hopefully. 'There's only a mile between them. We'll just have to go round them one by one. We should have found the coastguard in Zennor to get more details of the recovery operation.'

Robbie shrugged. 'From now on we've no alternative.'

They put on their walking boots and Robbie reached for his binoculars. Now they were sitting outside, six hundred feet up on the open moor. It was bitterly cold, even though there was still a glimmer of sunshine. The moors dropped away too gently to see either coastline.

Robbie examined the nearby landscape carefully. 'If you were going for a brisk walk on Boxing Day you'd probably prefer the Coast Path,' he observed. 'The views would be far more dramatic.'

'Wouldn't that make this spot ideal for murder?' asked George. It wasn't that she was ghoulish, but all earlier adventures with Robbie had involved unnatural death.

'Yes, but you'd have to get the victim up here in the first place. How on earth would you do that?'

They set off along a grassy lane between gorse and bracken. There were more ruined buildings half a mile ahead.

George pointed. 'Is that the hub of the old mine?'

'Maybe,' said Robbie. 'When we get to St Just we need to look up the mine's history – assuming there's anything written. I'd like to know how long ago the workings began and when it closed for good.'

They strode on in companionable silence until they reached the scattered buildings. Another ruined engine house stood at the centre.

Robbie looked at it thoughtfully. 'I reckon, you know, one of us might be able to climb up to that old window space. That'd give us a better view of the surrounding area.'

'I'll have a go if you can help me get started,' responded George. 'I used to rock climb in my student days.'

It was a shock to realise how little they knew each other. 'You do surprise me. Is it still a regular hobby?'

'Well, I don't get much free time these days and most of that is

41

spent in London. Besides, I had rather a nasty experience that put me off.'

The two clambered over the stones around the engine house, looking for a way up. Round the back was a massive high stone wall that finished halfway up the main building. 'That'll do.'

Robbie steadied himself beneath the wall and clasped his hands together. Next George put an arm round his neck and placed one foot into his hand. Then she heaved hard. There was an old hawthorn bush growing in the wall. Her hand grasped it and she pulled hard, scrabbling at the same time with her feet.

A minute later she was perched on top of the wall. Then, after a pause for breath, she headed for the engine house. A delicate manoeuvre – the rock was greasy – and she was standing inside the shell of the window.

Robbie didn't like her position but knew he mustn't fuss.

'D'you want the binoculars?' When George nodded he clambered round to beneath the window, stood on tiptoe and held them up. She could just reach them. Then, slowly, she stood up and started to scan the nearby landscape.

'Most of the shafts don't stick up far,' she observed. 'I'm not sure I can see all of them. But there is something . . . over there.'

She pointed away from the way that they'd come. 'It looks like a length of ribbon. I reckon that's our best hope.'

George had one more inspection and then started to climb down. Once she was on the wall she took her full weight on the bush and lowered herself slowly into Robbie's arms. There was a short pause before he released her to the ground.

'It's too cold for this sort of thing here,' she rebuked. But she didn't struggle to get free with any speed.

Ten minutes later the two had found a grass path leading from the engine house towards the shaft which was adorned with ribbon. As they got closer they could see the blue and white colours of police tape.

'He's come a hell of a long way,' said George, looking back.

'He might not have come this way,' said Robbie, unfolding the map. 'Look. There's another road here. It's nearer than the way we've come.'

He adjusted the focus on his binoculars and scanned the horizon. 'In fact I can see a car parked over there. It's not that far.'

Once they were close there were other signs pointing to this being the fatal shaft: boot marks in the mud and a huge boulder that would have provided a good anchor for a rope ladder.

The shaft itself was covered with a large metal grill. It looked heavy and would need more than one person to move it away but there was no padlock holding it in position. The shaft itself was roughly hewn and more or less circular.

'Blast. I should have brought my torch,' said Robbie. 'I've got one in the car. Then we might have been able to see how far it goes down.'

'What a lonely place to die,' said George, glancing around. 'Either he came to explore the shaft and something dreadful happened on his way down; or else he came to this remote spot to commit suicide.'

'Yes. There wouldn't be much point in the police conducting a search of the surrounding area. With this wind at this elevation, at this time of year, it wouldn't take long for anything to blow away.'

George took a series of pictures of the shaft and the surrounding area to show Peter Travers. Then they turned to walk back to Robbie's car.

'It's good to be back inside,' said George, huddling into her fleece as they set off on back via Newmill. 'I've had enough exercise for one day.'

'It's not the exercise that's the problem, George. It's coping with the cold.'

CHAPTER 6

This year Peter Travers had had a special Christmas with his brother in Padstow.

In a week's time he'd be married to Maxine. He could hardly believe it. The anticipation, when he allowed himself to muse, sent shivers down his spine. Once he'd reached the age of forty, the policeman had assumed he was going to be one of life's bachelors.

Peter did have a social life in his home village of Delabole when pressures of work allowed, even played his guitar with the local folk group. But there were few unattached women of his age in the mix and he'd been out with those that were.

Maxine, a security analyst based in Bude, was the first woman he'd met whose forensic instincts came anywhere close to his own. He remembered meeting her the first time: honey blond, shoulder length hair, slender and slim, with piercing blue eyes. She'd dazzled him the first time they'd met.

Best of all, she seemed to feel much the same way towards him as he felt towards her.

Before all the disruption of the rearranged wedding, Maxine had invited him to spend Christmas in St Just. Peter, though, hadn't wanted to change his routine of spending the time with his brother. Tony had a hard life as a fisherman and this was a rare chance to spend time together.

Peter also needed to make sure sister-in-law Celia and niece Katrina felt part of the action, especially as the teenager was one of the bridesmaids; there'd been tussles over her dress. The two women and Tony would be travelling to Land's End later in the week.

Once the wedding had been rescheduled to take place in St Just, the policeman had booked himself into the Kings Arms, a pub on the main square. Partly he wanted to avoid bride and groom coming to church from the same location. He also gathered from Maxine that her mother was awash in wedding detail. Physical detachment might keep them all sane.

Peter was on annual leave for the next two weeks and had no interest in notices from the Penzance police. He was unaware of the recent fatality when he arrived in St Just.

The locals were not so ignorant. A death on the moors over their village was big news at any time, even more dramatic over the Christmas period.

When he first signed in the landlady gleaned that he was a policeman. He would have been happy to talk about his forthcoming wedding to the daughter of a local couple, surely an event of general interest? But instead the landlady linked the police to the recent fatality.

'But I've nothing to do with the police in Penzance,' he protested, 'I know nothing about the case.' The only comfort was that in the end the woman insisted on buying him a drink to welcome him to the village.

As she gave him his pint she nodded down the bar. 'If you

want to know more, Colin will tell you. He's in charge of the local coastguard.'

Peter could see no escape, though he resolved that it would not take too long. He was down here for the wedding, was due to see his fiancée in an hour. She at least would have other things to talk about.

Colin Trewern was a burly, bearded man of around fifty, wearing a thick fleece, sturdy trousers and strong walking boots. He was happy enough to chat.

Peter started off by explaining what he was doing in St Just.

'Ah, so you're the one that's marrying the Tavistock girl.' Colin had a distinct Cornish accent.

'Yes, I reckon I'm the luckiest man in the world.'

'Well, I'm pleased for you. Good to see an older man satisfied. Let me buy you a drink to welcome you to Land's End.'

Peter found himself with a second pint lined up behind the first. He'd have to watch this, he thought: wouldn't do to turn up drunk at the Tavistock guesthouse. Not on the first day, anyway.

'I'd heard nothing about this death until the landlady started telling me. I gather you played a key part. What happened?'

Colin was obviously pleased to be asked. 'Well, the first I knew of it wuz two days before Christmas: early evening. I wuz at home, putting up decorations, when the phone rang. It wuz the Penzance Police.'

Peter Travers decided he wouldn't admit to being a policeman for the time being. Colin was launched and it would be a pity to distract him.

'They said they'd just been contacted by a local woman in Penzance. She wanted to report that her husband had gone missing.'

Peter frowned. 'She must have some idea where he might have gone. You'd need some clue.'

'I don't know exactly what she told them, of course. But the police had an interest in Ding Dong Mine. That's an old mine up on the moors, about five miles from here. They thought he might have fallen down one of the shafts.'

'How many shafts are there?'

'Oh, at least a dozen.'

'But it was evening, you say. He might simply have stopped somewhere for a drink on his way home. And they couldn't expect the coastguard to help them check each one, working through the night, surely?'

'That's more or less what I said. As politely as possible. I told them I'd be happy to put a team together to haul out a body – we do all sorts of exercises like that. But it was a police job to be sure there was someone there in the first place – and to work out which shaft he was in.'

'How did they take that?'

'They weren't too pleased, I'd say. No doubt they were short staffed and Christmas made that worse. Anyway, I told 'em the first time I could get a team together would be the next morning. "Tell me at once if we're not needed," I said, "say if the bloke's turned up." Then I left my baubles and spent the rest of the evening phoning my regulars. Then, once I'd tried them, I called the stand-bys.'

'I bet they weren't too pleased.'

'None of us were. It wasn't just that it wuz Christmas. It wuz also that we felt taken for granted – and only being given half the tale.'

'Anyway, what happened next?'

'Were you here on Christmas Eve?' Peter shook his head. 'Well, there wuz a thick mist everywhere. I rang the police at daybreak: did they want us or had the bloke turned up?'

'But they did?'

He nodded. 'The sergeant and I agreed a location to meet on the road from Morvah to Madron. I said my team 'ud be there in an hour. Then we'd go round the shafts, see if any were open.'

'How many were in your team?'

'There were ten of us. And two police officers, Percy Popper and Mary Jelbert. We were all cold but my men were better dressed for the task than they were: we'd been to rescues many times, knew it might take hours.'

'And did it?'

Colin mused for a second as he sipped his drink. 'We were fortunate, I think. We happened to start on the right side of the mine.'

'You mean, the crucial shaft was the first one you reached?'

'That's right. The grate wuz moved aside on the first shaft we came to. That's when the police needed our expertise. We fastened a rope ladder to the top. Then a couple of my team, Alex and Sid, put on helmets with torches attached and climbed down to see what they could find.'

'Didn't the police want to go first?'

'Neither of 'em were keen. Popper wuz on the plump side and the woman, Mary, looked scared stiff. The poor kid was so young. To be honest, I don't think she'd been down a mine before.'

'Mm. How long was the rope ladder?'

'About thirty metres. I told 'em to take care not to step off the bottom. But it was alright, the shaft wuz only a hundred feet. They reached the bottom with a few feet to spare.'

'It's a gripping tale,' said Peter. 'You're sounding thirsty. Let me get you a drink.' More drinks were obtained. Better walk from here to Maxine's guesthouse, he decided.

'So what did Alex and Sid find?'

'There wuz a man's body at the bottom of the shaft. Stone cold, he'd been dead for hours.'

There was a pause for a few seconds of silent respect.

'So then Popper climbed down to check for himself?'

'You're joking. All he did was throw down a piece of chalk to my lads so they could draw round the body on the shaft floor. Any further work, he said, could take place once we'd got the body to the surface.'

Peter Travers thought for a moment. 'I guess if he'd been dead overnight – or even longer – then there wasn't that much hurry. Mind, his wife would be desperate for hard news. And she'd need to be shown the body to confirm his identity.'

Colin nodded. 'We moved as quickly as we could but it took us a couple of hours to bring the body to the surface. First we had to walk back to the cars for our equipment. Once we'd got that we could lower a stretcher and the lads below could strap the body on, as gently as possible, of course. Then ropes were lowered. Most of these allowed my team to haul from the top, a couple more helped the lads below to steady it. It kept drifting towards one of the walls.'

'Right. How wide was the shaft?'

'About eight foot. The stretcher only just fitted. I was very proud, mind. If the bloke had been alive and conscious he couldn't have had a steadier ride. Not that the police appreciated it. They just wanted to get back out of the cold.'

'So once he was up the police took over; your team could go home?'

Colin laughed. 'Not with these police. The shaft was half a mile from the road. We had to carry the body over there, once we'd managed to put the grid on. And at the end of the whole incident, d'you know what, our wonderful police colleagues didn't even say a proper thank you.'

Peter had many more questions to ask the coastguard but he suddenly noticed the time. He needed to shoot off if he was to reach Maxine's parent's guesthouse at roughly the time he'd promised.

Chy Brisons was on the western side of St Just, half a mile from the village centre, on the road down towards Cape Cornwall. Peter couldn't see anything in the dark but recalled the magnificent view of the headland he'd seen on his previous visit. He hoped there'd be some time for exploring while he was down here.

The policeman was slightly surprised by the number of cars nearby. Did these all belong to people staying at the guesthouse? Perhaps it was as well that he had chosen to stay at the Kings Arms. And explained why Maxine hadn't tried too hard to dissuade him.

Maxine herself came to the porch to let him in. Her radiant smile told him how welcome he was, as did her determined kiss. Finally she resorted to words.

'Happy Christmas, darling. Did you have a good journey down?'

'Fine. There's never much traffic on Boxing Day.'

She looked puzzled. 'So have you been here long?'

'I got to St Just earlier. I was slightly delayed at the inn by an encounter with one of the coastguards. He's an interesting chap, started to tell me about a local tragedy that's just happened at Ding Dong Mine.'

Maxine remembered her father's instruction to keep his role in the event secret. 'Right. I'd appreciate it if you didn't talk about that for now, Peter. I'll explain later.' Before she could say any more her father joined them in the hall and offered the visitor his hand.

'Peter, you're more than welcome. Happy Christmas. Come and meet some more elusive members of the Tavistock family.'

Peter had no idea what he meant but followed him into the lounge.

'Peter, this is my brother, Ross. He left Cornwall for the warmth of Australia over thirty years ago.'

'Great to meet you, Peter. Maxine was telling us that when the hotel went bust you insisted on bringing the wedding forward. She's a canny lass, I'm sure that's a wise decision.'

Alex knew his brother could talk the back legs off a kangaroo and swiftly moved on. 'And Peter, this is Lisa, Ross's wife. The two met in Australia. I've only met her once before myself.'

Peter noticed as soon as she started to talk that Lisa had a strong accent, obviously Australian through and through. This was going to be a really international wedding.

Finally he came to Maria, Maxine's mum. She too gave him a warm hug. 'Peter, it's great that you're here. It's all more or less in hand. We may need to cut a few corners but I'm sure it'll work out in the end.'

Peter remembered a few comments by Maxine over the phone about her mother having a dose of pre-wedding nerves. He gave her a big grin. 'Don't worry, Maria. I'm sure it'll all turn out just fine.'

Half an hour later George and Robbie joined the gathering. George was to stay at Chy Brisons for the week with Maxine; Robbie would be staying at the Kings Arms. It wasn't ideal but he knew George had a key role as chief bridesmaid. At least he'd have Peter for company.

Maxine was amazed that these guests too had a story to tell about Ding Dong Mine. She knew that news travelled quickly but this was ridiculous. But she persuaded them not to launch into the topic this evening.

Although they'd all eaten well on Christmas Day, Maria had prepared another sumptuous meal for them all. Alex produced more bottles of an Australian Shiraz, but Peter noticed it was he and his brother that took the lead in its consumption.

A riotous evening ensured, during which they learned a lot about social life across the planet. Anticipation of the forthcoming wedding meant plenty of discussion of differences in wedding etiquette between the two countries. And some wild and whacky new suggestions.

At the far end of the table there was a different discussion. Robbie made the most of his connecting skills to swap biographies with Alex's brother. He was interested to learn Ross was now involved in large-scale mining. He resolved to learn as much as he could while the man was here.

It was late when Peter and Robbie trudged back to the Kings Arms. Robbie was feeling slightly thick headed and decided he'd leave his car for the night at Chy Brisons.

Although each had information to share, neither felt like launching into a discussion on Ding Dong. That was an important topic but it would be best to let it wait for another day.

TUESDAY

DECEMBER 27th

Levant, one of many now-closed mines on Land's End

CHAPTER 7

Peter and Robbie had discovered that if they wanted a hot breakfast at the Kings Arms they needed to be downstairs by eight. Both, though, were used to early starts and met in the queue for bacon, sausage and eggs.

Once they had taken their sizzling plates to a table by the window, Peter was anxious to tell Robbie about his conversation on Ding Dong. He was slightly put out to learn that Robbie and George had actually visited the shaft where the death had occurred.

Swapping their separate perspectives took most of the meal.

'So you were satisfied with what the police did?' asked Robbie. 'Would you have done much more, starting at lunchtime on Christmas Eve?'

'It's not fair to judge. I mean, there were only two of 'em. That's not a full Scene of Crime team. They might have done more than the coastguard noticed. Or they might have been told more by the victim's wife when she first alerted them.'

Robbie frowned. 'Such as?'

'Well, suppose she'd found a suicide note. That would make it not a crime. Maybe she'd only just found it. In that case the

56

priority would be to recover the body as soon as possible.'

'So you're going to shrug it off? I guess you are on annual leave.'

'Well, the thing is, Robbie, I've came down to St Just this week to be with Maxine and help her prepare for the wedding. And I promised her, before all this Ding Dong business, that was all I would do.'

'In other words, you're stymied? And that's even before you're married.' The unspoken thought was, "this could easily get a lot worse."

The policeman mused. 'Well, it's hard to live with the fact that you and George have visited the scene while all I've done was to talk to a Sherpa.'

He paused. 'The thing is, I know from all my years policing that seeing a scene at first hand gives you far more chance of picking up insights than any amount of second hand knowledge.'

After breakfast Maxine and George left Chy Brisons out to catch up with their out-posted men.

As they walked Maxine explained how her father had been involved in the Ding Dong recovery team but wanted the fact kept quiet. 'Dad can see Mum is under stress. He doesn't want to say anything that will upstage the wedding.'

They shared what each of them knew about the incident. That meant they could join in at once with the conversation, once they reached the Kings Arms and found the men still on their toast.

'I'd love to visit the Ding Dong Mine myself,' said Peter. 'Trouble is, Maxine, I promised you a single-minded focus on the wedding.'

Maxine took a deep breath. 'Look, Peter, one thing I love about you is that you're such a wholehearted policeman. It's your passion, not just your profession.' She shook her head. 'Darling, I don't want to change that.'

She went on, 'I'm just as bad with my work on security. Whatever promises we made, I'm not going to stand in the way of some offline investigation. Especially if we can work on it together.'

Peter gave a sigh, a mixture of relief and pleasure. He gave silent thanks that it was going to be alright.

'If we want to see Ding Dong,' said George, 'it has to be as soon as possible after the death took place. Why don't we go now?'

'Yesterday,' added Robbie, 'George and I weren't strong enough to lift the grid off the top. It's made of iron and looked pretty heavy. But if all four of us went I reckon it'd be easy.'

So the decision was made. Robbie set off to walk back to Chy Brisons to pick up his car. Given Maxine's views on vibes from the kitchen, he wouldn't be going inside. George and Maxine decided to wait and ordered themselves fresh cups of coffee.

Meanwhile Peter found the address of the coastguard, Colin Trewern, from the Kings Arms landlady. It turned out he lived close by. By the time Robbie returned, he had visited Colin and borrowed rope and rope ladder in case they did want to go down the shaft.

Then they set out, Peter and Maxine heading for Ding Dong in Peter's car, following after Robbie and George in the other. The latter took the lead as they knew where to park, as near as possible to the fatal shaft.

'Have you been to Ding Dong before?' asked Peter as they headed for the moors.

'No. The thing is, my parents moved from Helston to Land's End soon after I had left for university. I made short visits to see them but never spent a long time in St Just. When I was here for more than a weekend, I preferred to spend any time outdoors on the Coast Path, rather than the interior. So I've never tramped the moors or been near Ding Dong Mine.'

So for both it was new territory. In front they saw Robbie turning off the coast road just after Morvah and climbing the moors towards Madron. Then he pulled over into a small car park. There was one other car there, a grey Skoda.

Peter parked next to them and they all got out. They were all sensibly dressed in fleeces, cagoules and scarves. 'It's certainly a "bleak mid winter",' said Maxine, jumping up and down to keep warm.

'Apparently it was even worse on Christmas Eve,' said Peter. 'My source said that as well as the cold there was also a really thick mist.'

'Ah,' said Robbie. He'd just had a light bulb moment. 'Mist. That might explain why no-one took any notice of that Skoda. It is grey, perhaps they just didn't see it. George and I saw it yesterday, I bet it hasn't moved. This is a very isolated spot. I reckon that's the victim's vehicle.'

The policeman looked pleased. 'In which case, my team in Bude can find out the name and address of the victim.'

He strode over to it, took a note of the number then called Bude. There followed a long conversation with one of his colleagues.

The other three discerned surprise from a fellow-officer that only two days after going on leave, Peter had found something new to investigate.

Finally he concluded and rang off. 'That was Holly. One of the pair I left policing Bude this week. She'll get in touch with DVLA, let me know the result as soon as she gets it. Right, let's take a look at this mine shaft.'

There was a rough path through the bracken heading in the right direction. It took just ten minutes to reach the mine shaft that George and Robbie had visited the day before.

Peter looked hard at the ten feet wide iron grid laid over the shaft. 'There are four of us. I reckon we can move that to one side.'

But George, looking at the shaft beneath as it fell away into darkness, had seen something else. 'You know, this shaft is off the vertical. Don't you reckon someone who fell in would hit the side on the way down?'

Peter stepped round beside her and looked carefully. Then remembered something Colin had said about the stretcher repeatedly touching one of the sides on the way up.

'I think you're right. Yes. Before we move the grid we ought to use Colin's rope to measure the offset angle. It's got markings on it, you see. Can we tie a weight to one end, push it through the centre of the grid and see what happens?'

60

The others were cold, eager for action of any sort. Robbie spotted a large metal bolt in the debris around the shaft and soon it was tied to the rope. 'But how are we going to reach the middle of the grid to drop it?'

'I'm probably the lightest,' offered Maxine.

'No way,' replied her fiancé firmly. 'We'll throw it into the middle hole.'

It took several tries. Then George got both direction and range correct and the rope end caught on the central hole.

'Well done, George,' said Robbie.

Slowly they lowered it down. It turned out George's observation was correct. Before it had gone forty feet the bolt was touching the side. 'It's about four foot from the shaft wall to the centre of the grid. So that's a gradient of about one in ten,' computed George. 'If you had to drive up a one in ten hill you'd notice. It's a significant angle.'

'No wonder they had a job pulling the stretcher back up,' observed Peter.

The discovery made Peter keener than ever to go down the shaft for himself and see where the body was found.

Robbie was dubious. 'They keep these places covered over for a reason.'

'Yes, but two coastguards went down on Christmas Eve – and returned. It can't have deteriorated much, that's only three days ago.'

'It looks a long way down,' said Maxine apprehensively. She looked at her fiancé with concern.

'It's alright darling. I borrowed a rope ladder from the coast-guard, plus a couple of caving helmets. That was all they used on Christmas Eve. There might be nothing of interest but I'd like to see the bottom for myself.'

George wanted to allay Maxine's worries. 'It'd be safer if there were two of us, Peter. I used to go caving in my younger days. I'll follow you down.'

Maxine looked relieved. 'Great. And Robbie and I will stay on guard at the top. You'll shout, won't you, if anything goes wrong?'

CHAPTER 8

'Let's start with soup,' suggested George. 'It'll warm us up.' It was two hours later. The four were sitting in the Lunch Box cafe at Carn Galver, on the road to St Ives. Peter had refused to divulge anything on the way about the mine, said the most important thing was to find lunch.

Four home-made chicken soups were ordered from the cheerful hostess. As they waited for it to arrive the conversation could begin.

'So what did you find?' asked Robbie, eager for news.

'Less than we'd hoped,' began Peter, as he opened his phone. 'I thought we might find the rope ladder the victim had climbed down on. Say if the ladder had come untied at the top. Or if it had broken, we might have found where it had frayed. But there was nothing down there at all. Look.'

He showed them a series of indistinct dark pictures.

'The only sign that anything had happened was the figure chalked out on the floor,' added George. 'But that was an odd shape, it hardly looked credible.'

'Yes, the figure was marked as lying straight out, not twisted up. If the chap had fallen down, his body would surely have been all crumpled – especially given that the shaft wasn't completely vertical, so he'd have bumped the side on the way down.'

Robbie and Maxine had also been swapping ideas as they jogged circuits around the top of the shaft to keep themselves warm.

'We didn't see how the bloke could have done the visit single handed,' observed Robbie. 'After all, it took four of us to move that grid when we started. Two strong men might have done it but the victim would never have managed the whole thing on his own.'

'But if he had come with a companion and they'd seen him fall, they'd have raised the alarm,' added Maxine. 'The police would have heard from his mate directly, not hours later from the poor, anxious wife.'

The soup arrived at that moment and gave them a breathing space. The owner also supplied a basket homemade bread. Sharing all this out brought the conversation to a halt.

'So where've we got to?' asked Peter, once the debate resumed. 'Let's go through the possibilities.'

George took the lead. 'The simplest option is that the death was the result of an accident. The chap had some reason or other – goodness knows what – to visit the old mine shaft. We should perhaps try to work out what that might have been. Maybe the shaft was already open –'

'Perhaps he'd been there beforehand with someone else and they'd left it open deliberately?' added Maxine.

'Possibly. So the victim peers over for a preliminary look and then trips and topples down.'

There was silence as the option was evaluated. Peter was the first to respond. 'You'd need to be pretty incompetent to fall down a mine shaft in broad daylight. Unless you had a heart attack or something.'

'Or were drunk,' suggested Robbie.

'Both of which are pretty unlikely,' the policeman concluded. 'After all, the bloke had already driven up here from somewhere and walked half a mile in over the moor. The other argument against the idea is the profile of the fallen body.'

'That's not conclusive, Peter. Maybe he did end all bunched up at the bottom. What if the coastguards had straightened up his body ready for the stretcher before anyone mentioned the chalk?'

'Well, we could find that out. We could ask one of the coast-guards who went down the shaft,' said Maxine. 'My Dad was one of them.'

The men were surprised. Maxine went on to outline her dad's return to Chy Brisons on the afternoon of Christmas Eve. 'I'd better be the one to ask him, though,' she concluded. 'He told me to keep his part secret so it didn't overshadow the wedding.'

'Right,' said Peter. 'So the chances of it being an accident, on what we know so far, seem pretty low. If it's an "unexplained death", there'll be a post mortem in the next few days. If that showed he was drunk or had had a heart attack that would make it slightly more likely.'

'If it was an accident, the post-mortem should also find signs where he'd hit the side wall on the way down.' George was still gripped by the off-vertical shaft. 'OK, if it wasn't an accident what are the alternatives?'

'Suicide,' said Peter succinctly. He'd been thinking about other options for some time.

'It's an odd place to choose,' said Maxine. 'And very remote.'

'Maybe he'd got some connection with the mine?' suggested George. 'Perhaps one of his ancestors worked there?'

'There's still the problem of how to lift off the grid on your own,' pointed out Robbie.

'It might just have been left open by accident. Maybe the victim chose the first shaft he found that had ready access.'

George had been thinking along different lines. 'There's one more thing. If it was a suicide, wouldn't you expect him to have left a note?'

Silence as everyone considered.

Peter sighed. 'Suicide notes are common but not essential. If we could talk to the wife she might have some comment on the notion of suicide. If he'd been very depressed, say. Or was facing some major challenge - maybe he'd just been made redundant. But unless that is the case, I'd say suicide doesn't look likely either.'

There was a longer silence. Each could see where logic was taking them.

'OK. Let's try murder.' Peter had been hoping to avoid this, even saying the word gave him a sinking feeling in his stomach. This was the last way he'd expected to spend the week before his wedding.

'Do we imagine that the murder took place at the shaft?' asked Maxine.

'Why not?' asked Peter. 'Let's think it through.'

'I can see two possibilities,' said Robbie. 'One: the murderer was a friend of the victim. The two knew each other, anyway. And they came to the shaft together. Between them they moved the grid and then they climbed down.'

'Perhaps they had a disagreement,' suggested George. 'Or even a fight. Sparked, maybe, by the business that had brought them to the shaft in the first place. During the fight the victim was hit over the head and keeled over. So the killer laid him out carefully, right at the bottom of the shaft. Then climbed back up the ladder to escape.'

'They'd have had to arrive here in separate cars,' added Maxine. 'The murderer drove away in his own and left the victim's by the roadside. Hoping, no doubt, that at this time of year no-one would notice it for days. They might not even come across the body for weeks. Long enough, anyway, for it to be unclear when or how the victim had died. That would make any further investigation very difficult.'

There was silence as the idea was considered. No-one could think of any reason to reject it.

'What's the other possibility, Robbie?' asked Peter.

'Well, the murder could have taken place somewhere else. The shaft was just a convenient place for the murderer to dump the body.'

'Hardly convenient, Robbie. Don't you mean obscure?'

'It's half a mile from the nearest road,' protested Maxine. 'That's a fair distance for one person to haul a body. They'd need to be very strong.'

'And once he got here, he'd still have to move the grid.'

'Well, what if there were two murderers – or the murderer had an assistant?'

'If they simply threw the victim down the shaft we're back to the unlikely profile of the body once it reached the bottom.'

'So maybe they'd throw him down and then climb down after him to rearrange the corpse.'

There was silence then Peter gave his conclusion. 'It's possible, I suppose, but it sounds very messy. There are easier ways of disposing of a body, especially with the length of coastline we've got around Cornwall. Unless, of course, the murderer also had some connection with Ding Dong Mine.'

'We've given it a good airing,' said George, half an hour later. 'What happens next?'

Maxine glanced at her watch. 'Crumbs. It's almost two o'clock. I need to get back to Chy Brisons, give my Mum some moral support. Try to stop her lapsing into a blind panic. Can one of you give me a lift back to St Just?'

'I need to go to see the Penzance police,' said Peter. 'Tell them what we've found. If they want to take over that's fine by me.'

'I'll come with you if you like,' offered George. 'After all, I've been down the shaft too. Two witnesses are always better than one.'

They all looked at Robbie. Which angle was he going to pursue?

'To make progress on most of these options we need to know more about Ding Dong Mine. If you wouldn't mind I'd like to look up an old colleague of mine, she's working somewhere down here on mine history.'

George had a moment of anxiety about Robbie with an old female friend but by now she'd already committed herself.

The party paid their bill and went their separate ways.

CHAPTER 9

It was easy enough for Peter and George to give Maxine a lift back to St Just en route to Penzance.

'You can drop me in the square, darling,' said the bride-to-be as the car reached St Just. 'The walk down to Chy Brisons will sharpen my mind.'

It was a slightly odd farewell but there was no time to argue. Peter drew in beside the "Best in the World" Pasty Shop and dropped her. Soon he and George were on the direct road over to Penzance.

'How are we going to play this?' asked the analyst. 'Do you want me to ring the police station, try and make an appointment?'

'I think it'll be best if we just turn up.'

'Catch 'em by surprise, you mean.'

The policeman sighed. 'The thing is, George, the coastguard I was talking to yesterday told me the name of the policeman on the case. He said he was called Popper. Sergeant Popper.'

George giggled. 'Slightly unfortunate.'

'Yes. That's why I remembered the name. He and I were on a course in Plymouth many years ago with a gang of other raw constables, we weren't the best of mates then. He was always looking for short cuts on the exercises they gave us. I remember a discussion at the bar one evening. Someone said that he would never make it to Sergeant because of the name and its association with the Beatles.'

'Well, let's be thankful he's done so. And not been over-promoted to Inspector to get past the embarrassment. I mean, you're only trying to help, Peter. You're not trying to take the case over – not this week, anyway. You're not even in uniform.'

Twenty minutes later they had reached Penzance. George had googled the address of the police station, it turned out it was close to the town centre. Inevitably, though, there was nowhere to park nearby.

But there was plenty of parking on the front. 'I reckon a couple of hours will be ample,' said George as she bought a ticket. The two walked back to the station and found a gnarled constable on duty at the entrance.

'Good afternoon,' said Peter Travers. 'Is Sergeant Popper around?'

The constable looked at him suspiciously. The name was a frequent butt of jokes in the town. But this man seemed serious.

'What are you wanting to see him about, sir?'

'It's the case of the body that was found down a mine shaft on Christmas Eve. I may have new information for him.'

The constable knew that the death had been mentioned in a press release and he'd been told to dampen down any media interest. News was in short supply in the week between Christmas and New Year. But these two didn't look like journalists. He pushed forward a pen and opened the visitors' book. 'Can I have your names and addresses, please?'

71

Peter and George complied, giving addresses from the other end of Cornwall. The policeman made no mention of his rank. The constable looked at the names and gave a sniff. Then turned away and used his phone.

A minute later he reported, 'Sergeant Popper says he'll be down in a few minutes. Would you like to take a seat while you're waiting?'

The two sat on one of the rather battered wooden benches in the foyer. In his mind Peter was making unflattering comparisons with his own station in Bude. But there was nothing to be done. And in truth he had never visited that station as a complete outsider.

After ten minutes the sergeant finally arrived. He looked older than Peter, was plump and had a florid face. He also looked rather irritated.

'Well, well, if it isn't Peter Travers. Finally stopped putting the world to rights in Delabole and come to where it's all happening. And this is?'

'I'm George, George Gilbert. I'm a friend of Peter's.'

The sergeant held out his hand. 'Pleased to meet you, George. I'm Percy Popper. Come through, both of you. I've only got a small office but we can squeeze in somehow. Don't suppose you'll need long. Fred, can you get us a pot of tea?'

They followed Percy down the corridor and into a small room which had just enough chairs for all three to sit down.

'So Mr Enterprise, what brings you to Penzance?'

'I'm about to be married; over in St Just on New Year's Eve.'

'Well, well, well. Many congratulations. And this is your

fiancée.'

Before George had chance to correct him the policeman had moved on. 'You'll need to keep an eye on him, George. Peter's full of enthusiasm but that gets him into one or two scrapes. D'you remember, on that course we did in Plymouth . . .'

The last thing Peter wanted to do was to go down memory lane with Percy. 'We were both much younger in those days. No, what I wanted to talk about was that dreadful business of the dead body down the mine. Someone I met in St Just was telling me about it.'

'Yes, it was a bit of a shocker. Especially just before Christmas.' He looked at Peter quizzically. 'My desk man said that you might have some additional information about it?'

Before Peter could respond the afore-mentioned desk man appeared with a tea tray. He dumped it on a small table and then disappeared. 'Can't leave the desk unattended,' he muttered as he hurried out.

The interruption, which continued as George poured the tea, gave Peter a few seconds to work out how he might begin. Given the fraught relationship with Percy he knew this would need some care.

'It all started when I met the chief coastguard in a pub in St Just yesterday,' he began. 'He told me the story of the recovery of the body from his point of view. It sounded like awkward timing?'

Percy agreed. 'Yes, it certainly was. I mean, Christmas is always a strain for policemen. The rest of society is far too busy and half our staff are on leave. The first we heard about it here at the station was when the man's wife got in touch the evening before. Said her husband was expected home for supper but he hadn't returned. Apparently that wasn't like him at all.

'Colin persuaded me there was no point in heading out for the moors in the pitch dark. He told me there were many shafts at Ding Dong Mine.'

'How did you know that was the place to look?'

'Oh, the wife told us her husband had mentioned the mine. It was where he was going when he left home two days before. Trouble was, as we all know, people change their minds. We couldn't be sure that was where he'd end up.'

Percy paused and glanced at Peter. 'But I'm sorry, I interrupted. Keep going. What's this new information about the case that you're bringing me?'

Peter decided that some challenge to the local policeman was going to be inevitable. 'According to the coastguard, the police hadn't themselves gone down the shaft. They'd been happy to leave it to the coastguards, he said. But I'm a curious chap. I thought there might have been something revealing left down there. So this morning George and I decided we'd go and have a look for ourselves.'

It was clear that this idea, visiting a potential crime scene to remedy perceived weakness, did not fill Percy with enthusiasm.

He turned to George. 'This is exactly what I mean, George: typical Peter. Don't let him bamboozle you once you're married. Lots of enthusiasm, easy for top brass to commend; but where does it lead? I'll tell you. It leads to more problems and further mishaps.'

Percy turned back to the other policeman. 'Go on, then, Mr Diligent. What did you find?'

George thought it might work best if she took a share of Percy's distaste. 'Actually, Percy, both of us went down the shaft. I didn't like the thought of Peter down there on his own. Especially the week before he was going to be married. Two would be safer than one. And what we noticed was that the shaft wasn't vertical, it leaned to one side.'

'You mean, when they dug the shaft a couple of hundred years ago, they got it skewed. Engineering was less precise in those days. So what?'

She could see Percy was upset now but there was no going back. George took a deep breath.

'What we realised, Percy, was that something was wrong. In short, the shape of the body which we found marked on the floor was far too regular. If the victim had simply fallen down then the shape was bound to have been far more crumpled. Especially as the poor chap would have hit the side of the shaft on the way down.'

With some effort Percy managed to control his temper.

'Well, thank you very much, both of you. I'll add your observations to the rest of the notes in the file. Give some thought to the possible effect of engineering failure two hundred years ago on the death last week.'

Peter had by no means reached the end of his questions and suggestions. For example, when was the relevant post mortem due? Would the pathologist be asked to look for any signs of the victim hitting the shaft wall? Or had he been killed at the bottom? But it was too late: he had run out of opportunity.

His opposite number stood up. 'Now, I won't take any more of your time. You're both busy people, and I'm sure there's a lot to do over in St Just. For a start, Peter's got to pull together a wedding speech.'

He faced them both. 'But don't worry. You don't need to do anything about Ding Dong at all. I can reassure you that the Penzance police will handle this particular case perfectly well on our own.'

CHAPTER 10

Robbie Glendenning had felt just the slightest twinge of concern, if not conscience, as he walked out of the Carn Galver cafe and sat in his car to use his phone.

Everything he had said in the teashop about the motive for his next actions was true. On the case so far there was a strong need to understand more about Ding Dong Mine. It was a bizarre question, but was there anything in its history that could possibly have led to someone wanting to revisit it just before Christmas? For whether the death was accident, suicide or cold-blooded murder, it seemed some reason was needed as to why the victim had come or been brought to this out-of-the-way spot.

It was also true that he had known Siobhan Hitchen since they were history students together at Bristol, twenty odd years ago. She was indeed on his newspaper's short-term payroll, with a commission to help the paper understand more about Cornish mining history.

What was also true, but was something he had not admitted to George, was that Siobhan was not just a friend, she had once been a bright flame. At one time, in their final year, they were almost inseparable. It was hard to remember now, it was so long ago, why the pair had split up. As far as he could recall through the mists of time, she had walked out on him.

A tangled history which would make the next phone call slightly tricky.

Robbie had been given Siobhan's phone number by his newspaper, after he'd accepted the remit to assess future economic prospects for mining in Cornwall. They said they couldn't give him Siobhan's address though, as the woman had no fixed abode: she was moving about Western Cornwall on her research.

Although he had Siobhan's number, it wasn't clear if the newspaper had also alerted her to him. She might not want to talk to him at all – could even be married and wary of old contacts.

Robbie sighed. Putting off the call wouldn't make it any easier. He tapped in the number.

'Hello,' said a warm Irish voice. He remembered now that Siobhan had an Irish background.

'Hi. I don't know if you remember me. I'm Robbie Glendenning.'

'Robbie! By all that's wonderful. I know you're a journalist, to be sure, but how on earth did you get my number?'

'Well, the thing is, on what I've been told, we both currently work for the same employer. I'm the newspaper's Southwest correspondent, you see. It's a job I've done for years.'

'You're right, Robbie. I'm a freelance history researcher, but I do currently have a project for your bosses. I'm trying to disentangle Cornish mining history.'

'I wondered if it was possible to come and see you.'

'Sure, I'd love to see you again. When are you suggesting?'

'Well, where are you at the moment?'

'I'm currently working in St Ives. I've just finished scouring the Museum on the headland, but it didn't help as much as I'd hoped. What about you?'

'I'm a bit further west, down for a wedding in St Just. But that won't happen for a few days. So what are you doing this afternoon?'

'Nothing that I have to do "dreckly"'. She sounded empathetic. 'It'd be great to see you again.'

Suddenly Robbie remembered the shop in Zennor where he'd been with George for coffee – was it only yesterday? The village was midway between the two of them. 'How about meeting me for coffee in Zennor?'

'That sounds great, Robbie. I can be there in about twenty minutes.'

It took Robbie only ten minutes to reach Zennor from Carn Galver. He parked at the far end of the car park, giving his hair a quick comb before heading into the cafe. While he was waiting he glanced at the booklets on sale, picked out one about mining tin and other ores and another about Cornish geology. They might give him some background on mining in the county, he remembered he'd be starting that project in the New Year.

He had his back to the door when Siobhan arrived. He couldn't have changed appearance that much, though, for she recognised his tubby figure and tousled hair at once and stood quietly behind him as he browsed.

'Both of those are well-written, to be sure,' she told him in a silky tone. 'And they've plenty of photographs.'

He hadn't heard the voice directly for two decades but it still touched a nerve. 'Siobhan!' Robbie turned and saw a tall, slim woman right behind him. She looked alert and energetic; and still had shoulder-length red hair. 'It's been too long.' Without thinking, instinct took over. He gave her an enthusiastic hug, to which she responded in kind.

Eventually they detached themselves. 'Robbie, do you not think we need to pace ourselves. Why don't we start with coffee?'

With some effort the journalist managed to pull himself together. 'You go and grab us a table, Siobhan – they've ones with soft chairs over in the corner. I'll go and buy these booklets and order our coffee.'

It seemed to Robbie that the woman behind the counter was eyeing him with suspicion. Then he thought, perhaps appearing with different close female friends on successive days was a little unusual. He made a note that he'd better not hug Siobhan again before they were outside.

'Well, tis a pleasant surprise to be sure,' began Siobhan, as Robbie joined her in the corner. 'When you didn't turn up at that Pizza Express for our final post-graduation meal together, I thought that you must have given me up for good. But I could never understand why.'

Robbie mused for a moment. It was a long time ago. 'But it wasn't like that,' he protested. 'I was waiting at the Pizza Express in Clifton for hours. It was you that never came. I assumed you'd given me up, though I'd no idea why. But I was booked onto a trip to go behind the Iron Curtain which started next morning so there was no time to chase it all up. And when I came back to

Bristol to look for you, it was September. All our student year had moved on.'

Siobhan looked at him wide-eyed. 'You were waiting in Clifton?' Her face crumpled in horror. 'No, no, no. I was at the Express in the town centre. Does that mean we've spent the last twenty years apart for no good reason?'

Robbie was spared a re-enactment of the earlier hug with even more passion by the arrival of the waitress with their coffees.

The next hour was spent in a hectic, if abbreviated, catch up.

Robbie learned that Siobhan was still making direct use of skills acquired from her history degree.

'It's hard work I can tell you, Robbie. I'll never make a fortune, but I've survived so far.'

'Where on earth do you find your sponsors?'

'If you look hard enough, Robbie, and you're reading the right journals, there are plenty of people around who'll pay for historical research. I mean, Cornwall's had a very long history. But not many have the time or the patience – or the know-how – to do it themselves.'

'Give me an example.'

'Well, I did a long piece of research on the slate quarry in Delabole for the latest owners, for example. They were dead keen to be learning what they'd bought, but they'd no idea where to start looking.'

'The quarry was producing slate in the thirteen hundreds, I believe.' Robbie still had a residual historical interest. He didn't want Siobhan to think she had a monopoly.

'So it was. And there are plenty of old houses whose past links in with other British events. I mean, you remember the Rotten Boroughs?'

'Not personally, but I remember the lectures. D'you recall? It was that skinny man who always turned up in a cape and goatee beard.'

Siobhan pondered for a moment. 'I don't think so. I remember it being taught by that plump man who always wore a nineteenth century three piece suit and a bow tie. Anyway, before 1832, the tiny town of Looe had two Members of Parliament. Two! Of course, you might say that was "corrupt" and in a way it was, but really, what does corrupt mean?'

'That's a question that's still with us today, Siobhan. Especially in certain parts of industry.' He could expand that topic at length – would do so when time allowed.

'We've obviously got a lot to catch up on,' concluded Robbie. 'All the time you've been beavering away uncovering the past, I've been working my way up the greasy pole as a journalist. Mostly with a respectable newspaper, I'm glad to say. One that's really interested in real-life people – fortunately that's my passion too.'

They continued to share details of their separate post-university lives for a long time, getting through several rounds of coffee as they did so.

Eventually Robbie noticed the time. And remembered why he'd tried to catch up with Siobhan in the first place. There was a present-day perspective to this conversation.

'I might be around these parts for a while, Siobhan. The thing is, I've just been assigned a special project of my own. My newspaper wants me to assess possible future developments of mining in Cornwall.'

'Sounds like a parallel study to mine, but looking forward rather than back. There'll be areas of overlap, to be sure.'

Robbie could see that there might. 'It'll run over the next couple of months. I reckon I'll best be based around here in West Cornwall.'

He looked at her hopefully. 'That'd give us plenty more time to talk, if we want to.'

'We can try and meet in the same restaurant, anyway. I'm currently staying in a bed and breakfast in St Ives. It's not very full. My landlady tells me she does nearly all her bookings in the summer. So her winter rates are quite reasonable. I'd recommend it if you were interested.

'In fact,' she went on, 'if you're happy to leave your car here, I could take you to have a look. Then maybe we could have a meal together this evening. I don't think I can take any more coffee for the time being.'

CHAPTER 11

Now he would have Siobhan's company for the evening, Robbie felt less inclined to raise his questions about Ding Dong Mine right away. Talking to her about a recent mine death couldn't help but darken the atmosphere.

But it would be useful to learn more about her current project. What was a "professional interest" in mine history? What sources had she managed to find and where else did she plan to look?

'I'd be very interested to hear about your current project,' he said as they headed along the coast road.

'Ah, you'll need to be more precise. I've got several things on the go, Robbie. Your paper is only hiring me on a part-time basis. There are other things I've taken on since, which I'm duty bound to keep confidential.'

Robbie considered for a moment. 'Fair enough. But you can talk about the mine stuff, surely? We're both working for the same paymaster.'

Siobhan laughed. 'That's true. Well, there's an awful lot been written about mining in Cornwall. I've spent a long time in the County Museum in Truro and then in other museums in West Cornwall. That's all given me a solid basis to start from.'

'When did you begin this piece of work, by the way?'

'Your paper got hold of me in September, I've no idea how.

Fortunately I'd just finished my previous project. I started at the beginning of October. And I've been at it three days a week or more ever since.'

Siobhan broke off. They'd reached the outskirts of St Ives and there was more traffic to deal with. Robbie halted his questioning to focus on where she was taking him. If all went well he might be doing this journey regularly.

It turned out that the bed and breakfast house where Siobhan was taking him was not in the town centre. 'I didn't want to be in the middle,' she explained. 'It's too expensive. And the traffic is mighty slow at rush hour, even at this time of year. I'm sure you won't be minding the walk?'

They drew up half way along a rising cul-de-sac of three-storey stone houses. 'These are some of the older buildings in the town, Robbie. But now they're too big for ordinary families. I've booked in for the week, my landlady's lent me a key so I can come and go as I please.'

Robbie followed her up the path. This was a sensible way to look for accommodation for the weeks ahead, he told himself. Whatever else it might lead to.

It turned out that the landlady was not in. Siobhan took the opportunity to give Robbie a conducted tour of the dining room and lounge on the ground floor and then her own guestroom, two floors further up.

'All the rooms are about this size,' she told him. 'And the beds are very comfortable.' Robbie could see that this was a working bedroom. Siobhan had a set of reference books by her bed, a tablet and post-it notes strewn all over the desk and a stack of A4-sized boxes piled up on the floor.

Siobhan followed his eyes. 'The trouble is, on a piece of work like this you end up with masses of notes. Otherwise it all blurs together.'

'So you're mainly assembling the key parts of a host of other records?' he asked. 'Can you augment that?'

'Oh yes. That's the interesting part, to be sure. But you have to know the context first. And most of that's already established.'

'So what sources haven't been tapped before?'

'My goal is "A social history of life in the mining villages". There's plenty been written, you see, about the engineering side of the mines and the economics of production. What's less well understood is how that impacted on village life.'

Robbie reflected for a moment. 'In Yorkshire there's plenty written about life in coalfield communities. The Miner's Strike in the 1980s and the need to understand what kept it going gave it a wider audience.'

Siobhan nodded. 'Yes, they're interesting accounts. But that didn't help with making sense of life among Cornish miners. For one thing, these mines were only making much of a profit in the century before. By 1900 most had closed. Those that were still open were never much better than struggling. And now, of course, there aren't any at all.'

'So I come back to my question: what are your extra sources?'

Siobhan sighed. 'You're very persistent, Robbie Glendenning. Alright, I'll tell you. But before I start, let's go downstairs and make a pot of tea.'

'Right,' said Siobhan, as she poured Robbie a mug of tea in the guests' lounge. It was spacious and light and they had it to themselves. 'I'll tell you a few of my professional secrets. But mind, this is only because we're old friends. It's what keeps me in employment when most of my fellow historians have moved on.'

'Journalism is said to be the first draft of history,' Robbie murmured defensively.

'Yes, but mostly it's a draft based on what is already known. What I'm after is the first draft of stuff that is otherwise unsuspected.'

This was like the repartee they'd enjoyed in student days. 'Go on then. Tell me.'

'What I'm looking for is not official histories. There are plenty of those. What I'm after is accounts that were never intended for publication.'

Robbie frowned. 'Like what?'

'Ideally first hand experiences of life as a miner or in a mineworker's family.'

'Except that most of 'em couldn't read or write.'

'There were schools in the late nineteenth century, Robbie. Even in Cornwall. They might not learn much more than a rudimentary skill in reading and writing, but that would be enough to keep a personal record if they were minded to do so.'

'But that wouldn't work in earlier times.'

'It might, would depend on the level of education in the household. Occasionally the mother, or perhaps an aunt or grandmother, would have had some education; and be keen to

87

pass it on.'

Robbie could see where she was heading. 'The miners doing the recording would also need to be receptive, to enjoy keeping a diary.'

'That's right. There would never be many, but I only need one or two.'

Robbie shrugged. 'I can see it might work occasionally. But Siobhan, there's only one of you. It could take a lifetime to assemble a decent body of evidence – not just a few weeks.'

'Yes. But the thing is, I'm not the first person to be chasing Cornish diaries. Social historians have been doing it for years, or anyone writing a television series set two hundred years ago. I start with sources someone else has identified. They're not on public display, but if you push the archivists hard enough and press the right buttons, then you can obtain access.'

There was a silence. Siobhan had admitted one of her secrets and Robbie needed to take it in.

'That's very interesting. I need to mull over how to link that to the work I've been asked to do. And there's another question that was in my head when I first rang you. But maybe we can talk about that over dinner.'

CHAPTER 12

George Gilbert and Peter Travers had just got back to their car parked on the Penzance front when Peter's phone rang. It was Maxine.

'I don't want to pressure you, darling. But is there any chance you could get back to St Just fairly soon? A couple more of my friends have turned up here earlier than I expected. I'm afraid it's put Mum into a flat spin. To be honest I could do with a bit more support.'

'We'll come right away, love. I've just met the local police. I'll tell you what happened when we see you.'

They got into Peter's car, drove off the front and headed along the road leading out towards St Just.

'Do you want to discuss anything about what just happened while it's still fresh in our minds?' asked George.

'Let's wait till we get back. I don't think we'll forget it in a hurry. We'll need to tell the rest the whole story, anyway.' In truth, both of them were still tense from an interview that had not gone according to plan.

Peter also needed to reflect, from a professional point of view, on how he was going to respond to the other policeman's intransigence. Dare he leave the whole enquiry to the local police? But what else could he do?

As he drove his phone rang again. George glanced at him, offered to take it but the policeman preferred to pull in at the next opportunity on the winding road. It was his colleague Holly, ringing from Bude.

'Hi, Peter. I've got the details from DVLA about the owner of that car you told me was parked near Ding Dong Mine.'

'Great. Hold on a second and I'll write it down.' He scrabbled for his notebook. 'Right, I'm ready.'

'The owner – or to precise the keeper – is called Jeremy Hocking. They say he's owned the car for several years. And Mr Hocking's address is in Penzance.' Holly cited an address which the policeman jotted down.

'Great, Holly. Thank you very much.'

'There is one more thing, guv. You know that these days MOT test results are linked in to vehicle licensing?'

'Yes?'

'Well, I quizzed the DVLA about that. They tell me that this car had its test just a couple of days before Christmas – December 23rd. At a garage in Penzance called Chinners.' Holly quoted a second address and contact details.

'You've caught me on the road back to St Just, Holly. Once I'm back I'll check where the garage is in relation to his home.'

'Already done, guv. According to Google maps it's just round the corner. Would you like their phone number?'

A few more pleasantries and the call concluded.

The policeman looked through the windscreen thoughtfully. It was half past four and dusk was falling. George could see he was torn between the plea to be with his fiancée and his urge to pursue the case.

It would be best to put him out of his misery. Maxine was a capable woman, she'd cope for a little longer. In any case, she wouldn't know exactly how long her fiancé would take to drive back from Penzance.

'Peter, why don't you ring the MOT garage right away? They might well close early this week. Once you're back in St Just you won't have much time on your own.'

The policeman sighed. 'You're right.' He picked up his phone again and rang the Penzance garage. This was a call where the experience of being a policeman, even one from over in Bude, might be very helpful.

'Chinners Garage. Joe Chinner here. How can I help you?'

'Good afternoon. My name is Travers, Police Sergeant Travers. I'm making enquiries about a car which I believe you put through an MOT test last week. The date which the DVLA gave me was Dec 23rd.' The policeman cited the registration number he'd taken from the car seen at Ding Dong Mine.

' 'old on a minute.' That was a relief. Mr Chinner was obviously not one to worry too much about data protection.

There was the noise of pages being turned.

'Ah, yes. That's Mr Hocking's car. He's a regular customer. He left the car with us the previous evening and we did the MOT first thing next morning. He picked it up, I reckon, about eleven o'clock.'

'No problems, then?'

'The car's only about six years old, Mr Travers. These days, most cars last a lot longer than they used to. Passed its test, no bother.'

George was catching the sense of the dialogue. Suddenly she had an idea. She leaned over and tapped the milometer on Peter's car.

The policeman blinked and then nodded. Then put his next question to Chinner. 'Did you by any chance take the milometer reading when the car was with you?'

'I've got the whole test record here, Mr Travers. Let me see. It's down here as 65,673 miles. That'd be about right for a six year old car.'

Peter wrote it down carefully and repeated it back.

'That's very helpful, Mr Chinner. OK, I've got one more question. It's a long shot, I know, but you say he's a regular customer. Can you remember anything about Mr Hocking's manner when you last saw him? I mean, did he seem upset or anything?'

'We 'ad a few minutes chat when he came for his car. I'd say he wuz no more gloomy than he usually is.' The man paused, then continued, 'He said he was wuz off for another of his days looking at old mines.'

Suddenly, it seemed, Chinner started to ask himself why the police were posing these questions. 'Hey, I 'ope nothing's 'appened to him. He's not the one that wuz found down a mine shaft on Christmas Eve?'

'I'm afraid I can't answer that question at the moment, sir. But what you've told us is potentially very useful. I'd be very grateful, though, if you could keep my enquiries to yourself for the time being.'

CHAPTER 13

Peter and George arrived at the Tavistock guesthouse in St
Just soon after five. The residents' lounge was rather
crowded: all Ross's Australian family were there and there were
several more visitors than there'd been that morning. There was
still no sign, though, of the guesthouse chef. Maxine whispered
to George that he was not even answering his phone.

One result was that Maria Tavistock was in a state close to
panic. She could run Chy Brisons capably when all was going to
plan but was thrown by events beyond her control. George could
see that, out in the kitchen, Maxine was trying to settle her nerves
but with only limited effect.

George took stock of the situation. She glanced round the
room. Two of the new arrivals were her old friends, Brian and
Alice Southgate, from Delabole. But if catering was a challenge,
she was sure they were part of the solution and not the problem.
All that she needed was a few minutes alone with Alice to explain
the situation and ask for her help.

The Southgate's had brought George's friend Esther Middleton, the vicar from Bideford, down with them. Her role would be
to conduct the wedding. The fourth new arrival, probably the
final straw as far as Maria was concerned, was someone George
had never met. She was a tall, athletic woman of around forty

with collar-length, chestnut hair. She saw George looking her way and came over to introduce herself.

'Hello, I'm Kirstie Conway,' she said. 'I'm a friend of Maxine from Cheltenham. We met playing the flute in a local orchestra. She asked me to take charge of the wedding photography and I was honoured to do so. That's the business I'm in, by the way.'

'Great. I'm George, the chief bridesmaid. The only thing is, I'm not sure that you were expected so soon,' said George diplomatically.

'No, I wasn't. But I decided to come down early so I could see where the wedding was to take place. I wanted to assess the lighting challenges and so forth: the position of the sun, the most scenic settings and so on. Also to explore this end of Cornwall, I've never been here before.'

Kirstie could see a sliver of doubt in George's face so she hurried on. 'Maxine threw out a general invitation to all of us who were going to help with the wedding. She implied her parent's guest house was quite sizeable. Trouble is, I think she may have miscounted.'

George counted for herself and pondered. 'I'm not sure yet where Brian and Alice are staying. You must meet Brian; he's Peter's best man.'

Brian overheard her and broke into their discussion. 'This week my job is to stay close to Peter. Say, if it turns out he's forgotten his tie, I'll drive back to Delabole to collect it. So Alice and I have decided we'll stay in the Kings Arms. That's the pub in the village where Peter is staying.'

George had noted the evening before that there were six

guestrooms in the house. That gave just enough room for present company, assuming that Maxine's Australian relatives took only two rooms. She hoped no more guests would arrive early and expect accommodation.

In the general melée as visitors introduced themselves George managed to get alongside Alice. 'Can I have a word with you in the corridor?'

'The thing is,' said George, once the two were out of earshot, 'they have a good chef here. He should be cooking this evening and he was scheduled to cook for the reception. Trouble is, he's disappeared, stricken down, won't or can't answer his phone.'

An hour later it had all been decided. George got alongside Maria and sold Alice the chef so thoroughly that the owner herself suggested that even if their chef reappeared he'd be told to stay away. 'We don't want him infecting the rest of us.' The next morning was booked for a full briefing.

Ross noticed what was happening. He was impressed that his brother's family could deal with the crisis at such short notice.

'But it's not fair to expect Alice to cater for the whole Tavistock family in their own kitchen on her first assignment. I'm sure she's competent. Even so, the poor girl needs the chance to find her way round the kitchen, cooking just for Maxine's friends. So I'd like to take Alex and Maria out for dinner in St Ives.'

Alex looked pleased. 'Thanks very much Ross. Maria and would be delighted to join you. What about Shelley and Frances?'

'Oh, they can decide for themselves.'

Maxine's cousins did not hesitate. 'We'll stay for a meal here.

Get to know the key members of the wedding party, anyway.'

Two hours later there was a mood of cheerfulness in Chy Brisons as Maxine, Shelley and Frances prepared for supper with their wedding colleagues.

Alice had been pleased to discover that none of the diners tonight had food allergies. She could have coped, would need to do so for the reception meal, but it made for a simpler life to begin with everyone on the same meal. After looking in the well-stocked kitchen cupboards, the stand-in chef started to prepare a tasty Spaghetti Bolognese.

The older Tavistocks, wives dressed in fashionable but flimsy dresses under thick coats, had made off for St Ives. Ross had reserved four places at a restaurant of high renown (according to the internet) that was open this evening. They were not expected back before midnight.

It had not taken Brian long, once they had gone, to discover that Chy Brisons had an unlocked cellar, well-stocked with wine, beer and cider. He left the best wines for later. Alice would need to find out at her briefing next morning which ones were for the reception. That still left plenty of wine that was highly drinkable.

He gathered a few selected bottles and put the white into the fridge.

Meanwhile Peter was having a private meeting with Maxine, the recordable part of which began with him outlining his encounter in the police station.

'So what d'you want me to do, darling?' he concluded. 'On the one hand we can do as Percy Popper asked, forget the whole thing . . .'

Maxine gave him a hug. 'Peter, I've been thinking about it all afternoon. It's a horrible thought, but it seems to me that we could well be looking at a murder. We'd never forgive ourselves if a sloppy policeman meant nothing was done. Even worse if that led to another murder. I mean, you and I will be away from here soon enough, but my parents live in these parts.'

Peter sighed. 'The thing is, love, we're off on our honeymoon in four days. Then back to Bude. If we're going to do anything it has to be now. I'd say that's only possible if we get all the help we can from our friends – especially Brian and George.'

Maxine frowned. 'What about Shelley and Frances? And what about my Dad's desire to keep it all secret?'

'They're more or less part of your family. They'll soon be part of mine. And they're also your bridesmaids. Can't we trust them not to blab everything we say to their dad? That's what Alex seemed most concerned about. He wants to create this daft illusion of Cornwall as being a place with no crime.'

'We don't have much choice. They've come halfway round the world, I can't just ignore them. If we present it carefully I think it'll be fine.'

When they sat down there were nine guests for the meal. George had been expecting Robbie but he'd not yet returned. The meal began with cheerful banter over slices of honey melon. Peter and Maxine had agreed it would be her call as to when to turn the conversation over to the body down the mineshaft.

The change in focus began once Alice and George had brought

in a large bowl of meat sauce, two dishes of spaghetti and a host of other vegetables, while Brian had made sure that those who wanted it had wine. 'It's one of my duties as best man,' he laughed. 'I need the practice.'

'Can I change the subject completely?' began Maxine, as the guests began to help themselves to the various dishes. 'One or two of us know about this but we'd like all of your help on it if possible.'

Brian looked at her shrewdly. 'This wouldn't by chance have anything to do with the body found in a mineshaft on Christmas Eve?'

'Did you see that in some local press report?'

'It's not reached that far. No, Peter mentioned it when I rang him to say what time we expected to be here. But that's all we know.' He glanced round the table. 'I'm sure we'd all be happy to help if we could. Why don't you and Peter tell us what you know so far?'

So, with various interruptions, cries of surprise and occasional invitations to have seconds, Maxine, Peter and George told the story as far as they had it to the rest of the guests.

Finally Peter summarised their experience in Penzance police station.

'So, you see, we've done our best to be helpful citizens but it's not done much good. And as a suspicious policeman I feel an urge to give it more of a push. So does anyone have any questions or suggestions?'

'Before we start, would anyone like more wine?' asked Brian. He knew that minds generally performed better after lubrication.

'Before we start to think about what else we could do, can we make sure we're abreast of the facts so far?' This was Esther. Peter hardly knew her at all. Then he remembered that she too had been at Cambridge.

Esther turned to Maxine. 'You say your dad was part of the coastguard recovery team and you were here when he came back. Can you elaborate? He must have told you something.'

'Dad didn't say much. Mind, as soon as she saw him Mum started nagging him to go and have a bath. But he asked us to keep it all quiet so it didn't overshadow the wedding – which we must remember, by the way.'

She paused. All eyes were on her. 'But I did manage to find out a bit more this afternoon. I was helping Dad in the cellar. I contrived to ask him if he'd seen anything else while he was down the mine beside the victim's body. He looked at me and said there was nothing at all. No frayed rope ladder and no other kit. He seemed pretty definite.'

'Did he comment on how the body was lying?' asked George.

'He said it was flat out. Made it sound like the chalk mark was accurate.'

There was a silence. 'Keep eating,' urged Alice. 'This meal won't stay hot forever.'

'It's quite hard thinking about a crime from the outside,' observed Brian after a moment. 'When you think about it, having an inside track does give the police a strong advantage. For one thing findings from the post mortem could tell us quite a lot.'

'Such as?'

'Well, if I was the police doctor I'd want to check if there were any signs of alcohol or poison in the body. That might be one way of committing suicide in a remote spot. Or a reason for the man to fall down the shaft.'

'It'd also be a way of bumping him off,' added Esther. Maxine was surprised at her comment, then reflected that her line of work meant she had more dealings with death than many.

'I don't suppose there's any way of tapping the pathologist on the Old Boys' network?' asked George wistfully.

'Well, I could make a few enquiries. I mean, they'll probably take the body as far as Truro. That's the nearest big hospital. If it does, I do have an old medical friend who works there. I could ask him, anyway.'

'Right. That's one line we might be able to take further.' Peter was starting to sound enthusiastic.

George feared this might be false optimism. But she had a different line of thought. 'Let's surmise that the grey Skoda that's still parked at the mine belonged to the victim – to Jeremy Hocking. And because of the MOT, we've got its mileage when it left the garage on Dec 23rd. Wouldn't it be helpful if we could find what mileage the car has now? That might tell us if he went straight from Penzance to the mine.'

'With modern cars you can only get the mileage to appear, you know, if the car is unlocked and switched on.'

'Well, can we think of any way to get the key?

'We know, because she rang the police in the first place, that Jeremy Hocking had a wife. She'd almost certainly have a key of her own. But do we have her address?'

'We got an address for Hocking from DVLA. In Penzance.

She's probably still there.'

Silence round the table as the problem was considered.

'Might she accept a visit from the clergy?' asked Alice.

'Possibly,' replied Esther. 'But she'd find it odd if I then asked her for the car keys. The only person whom she might expect to talk about cars with would be a policeman.'

Peter Travers had come to the same conclusion. 'It would all depend on whether the local police had found the car at the mine. I'm pretty sure George and I didn't mention it. If they haven't seen it and they've got the death down as an accident then they might not revisit her at all.'

'Why not phone her?' suggested Maxine. 'See if anyone else from the police has asked about the car. If they haven't, you could go round for the key and then drive the Skoda down to Penzance.'

There was silence for a moment. Then Brian spoke again. He'd been mentally conducting an overview of the whole case.

'Let's leave the keys for now. It seems to me that whatever the incident was, whether it was accident or murder, there's a need to understand what brought Jeremy Hocking there in the first place. It wasn't just chance. So what's behind the interest in Ding Dong? Has anyone got any suggestions?'

In the pause Alice saw her chance. 'I'm going to fetch the pudding. It's not very glamorous but I thought you'd prefer something hot. So tonight I offer you just a choice of crumble: either apple and blackberry or raspberry and blueberry. Add cream or ice cream to taste.'

'So what do we know about Ding Dong Mine?' asked Peter, once everyone had their choice of crumble. 'It's about five miles from here, on the top of the moor. The last tin was mined, I believe, in the 1870s.'

The policeman drew together the few other meagre facts in his possession. 'Maxine, George and I were up there this morning. There are a few old engine houses and a dozen shafts but the whole place is deserted: looks as though no-one's been there for years. So why on earth would Hocking want to go there?'

There was silence. Then Kirstie spoke, a suggestion coming from her photographic experience. 'You say the area is deserted. Is there any chance his interest was nothing to do with the mine itself? For example, is some rare bird nesting up there? Or maybe a rare plant?'

'That's a clever idea,' said George.

'Trouble is,' said Peter, 'I've been told me Hocking wasn't just interested in this mine, he'd been to others as well.' He reflected. 'Yes, that's right. It was the garage owner.'

Esther had thought of something else. 'You said Ding Dong was very old. Maybe that's the key fact here. Could this man be writing a history of old tin mines in Cornwall? And where he can, he likes to go down them. Maybe he's assembling a photographic record of their current state?'

'No-one's mentioned a camera being found with him, though.'

Another pause as the delicious crumble took their attention.

Then Shelley spoke for almost the first time. 'Guys, it's really good to be part of this conversation. Thank you very much for including Frances and me. We'd love to help. Trouble is, we know so little about mines in this country. Is there anywhere that might tell us more?'

'Hey, there is,' said George. 'Geevor Mine, it's two miles up the road. The mine's long closed but it still operates as a museum. We could go there tomorrow.'

CHAPTER 14

Robbie Glendenning and Siobhan Hitchen had had a splendid early evening walk around the winding streets of St Ives, both chattering incessantly and not just about history, before they landed up at the Alba restaurant. It was located near the lifeboat station. At this time of year the place was festively decorated to mark its place as a key point on the front and looked rather glamorous. It was as well, Robbie thought, that Siobhan had reserved them a table, the place was rather full.

The fact that there were so many diners meant the waiters were busy scurrying between tables and the meals, once ordered, were slow in arriving. That did not matter to them. They could even amuse themselves watching the chefs toiling away in the kitchens through interior glass windows. As they waited Robbie decided this was as good a time as any to move the conversation onto Ding Dong Mine.

'Can I pose a question about something odd that I came across yesterday?'

'Ask away. But I don't guarantee an answer.'

'Well, it's to do with Ding Dong Mine.'

Siobhan smiled. 'You're in luck, Robbie. I'm working my way down Cornwall, you see. I only got as far as the far western mines, including Ding Dong, last week. I might need to consult my notes, but since it's the last thing I looked at I'm remembering most of it.'

'Well, there's been a death at the mine. Someone was found at the bottom of one of the shafts on Christmas Eve. One of the friends I'm with for this wedding is a policeman, so we're trying to make sense of it.'

'I haven't got to that mine yet, I'm afraid.'

'I was there this morning. It didn't look like anyone except the victim had been there for some time.'

'So what's the question?'

'We were trying to work out what on earth the dead man might have been looking for. Is there anything special about the mine's history, for example? And that was when I thought of you.'

'Ah. So this encounter isn't a long-planned reunion then?'

Robbie couldn't see an easy way to answer this. 'Well, when I started it wasn't,' he conceded. 'But can we stick with Ding Dong for a few minutes? The thing is, whether the victim was peering down the shaft when he fell, jumped deliberately or was pushed, he must have had some reason to be there. And none of us had a clue what that might be.'

Siobhan was given a breathing space by the arrival of the waiter. Robbie ordered sea bass and Siobhan salmon en croute. To go with these they ordered, on Robbie's pick, a bottle of Sauvignon.

'Right. Let me start by giving you an overview of Ding Dong Mine. There's nothing secret, you could learn it all from the history books – or these days from the internet. Then we can see if that suggests any answers to your question.'

'That'd be great.'

The waiter brought the wine at that point and filled their glasses.

'Cheers,' said Robbie, clinking glasses with his friend.

'The area where you'll find Ding Dong,' said Siobhan, once they'd had their first sips, 'is reputed to be the oldest source of tin in Cornwall. The first tin was found before New Testament times. In the early days, of course, that meant scraps of tin ore being griddled out of the streams running down the nearby hillside. But gradually deeper mines were dug to get at more of the stuff.'

She went on, 'This wasn't an obvious spot to find tin. Most mines, you'll find, especially in Western Cornwall, are around the coast, starting from a much lower elevation. Whereas the Ding Dong Mine is on moors that, while by no means high, are at six or seven hundred feet.'

'Yes. I noticed that this morning. There was a strong wind blowing over the moors. It was very chilly.'

Siobhan paused to collect her thoughts. 'The mine you're interested in was at its peak in the early nineteenth century. By then, of course, they'd developed steam engines. They used them to pump out the floodwater and later to pull out the ore.

'All was going well until the builders of Empire found massive stocks of tin and copper ore in the newly-explored colonies, especially Australia. A long way from Europe of course, but these were massive reserves. Eventually the price that mine owners here could demand for their tin fell so much that all but the most productive tin mines in Cornwall could no longer compete. Ding Dong Mine ceased production, I believe, in about 1870. And I'm afraid it's never worked again.'

Their meals arrived at that moment. There was a pause while they settled down to eat, allowing Robbie to reflect on what he'd just been told.

'Siobhan, I can't see how the age of the mine, however old, can possibly be relevant today. The only chance, I think, would be something that happened while the mine was operating in its later years.' He paused for thought and then continued. 'For example, what if the place had mined a special ore – one which was worthless at the time but now turns out to have lots of potential?'

As he spoke, it occurred to him that this question might apply more generally to the Cornish mining industry. These mines had produced so much – tin and copper, arsenic and wolfram – what else might be down there? Was that one way that these mines might still have a future?

Siobhan responded. 'I don't know anything about special ores. But now I think of it, Ding Dong Mine did once have a very special Chief Engineer. He went by the name of Richard Trevithick.'

The name didn't mean anything to Robbie in a mining context. 'The only Trevithick I've heard of was someone in Redruth. He's supposed to have built the first steam-powered vehicle, around 1800.'

'Yes, that's the same one. He was an inventor, you see. Could hardly read and write, yet he found a way of making the Watt and Boulton steam engine far more efficient. He caused them to operate at a much higher pressure. That's what he introduced at Ding Dong.'

'Interesting, I suppose. But I don't know where it takes us.' Robbie had no idea where this conversation could possibly lead. He was happy, though, to listen to his friend. 'Tell me a bit more about him.'

'He was very tall, a gangling man, well over six feet. At school he was regarded as a complete dunce. But his father was a mining engineer and inevitably Richard followed him into the industry. There he found he had an instinct for making all sorts of machinery run better.'

'So was he at Ding Dong for long?'

'I don't think so. He moved onto other mines in South Wales and then took on engineering projects in London. His most famous remit was to build a tunnel under the Thames. But he was never much of a business man, to be sure, so it didn't make him any money. After that he went abroad. Bought and for a number of years ran a silver mine in Peru.'

'Amazing.'

'Huh. It was till Peru saw a revolution. Trevithick had to get out quick. His mine wasn't sold so much as taken over. He came back to Britain penniless. In the end he was buried in a pauper's grave in London.'

There was a longer pause while they cleared their plates. Robbie poured them another glass of wine. 'I'm assuming we are having a dessert?'

Choosing puddings took a few minutes. Cold and delicious or

hot and warming? Robbie took the chance to ask himself how Trevithick might have anything to do with the question he'd posed earlier.

'OK, here's a daft idea. Tell me it's stupid.'

'I'll do my best, Robbie. Go on.'

'Suppose for a moment that Trevithick didn't come back from Peru as empty handed as he always claimed. I mean, we know he was clever in a practical way. Say he managed to bring a hoard of silver back with him.'

'He might, I suppose. Go on.'

'Trevithick came from West Cornwall. In the UK that was the place he knew best. By this time he probably didn't trust banks at all. So he might just have wanted to hide his hoard away for a rainy day. If so, where might he have hidden it?'

'I'm finding it hard to guess, Robbie. You're talking about a game of hide and seek taking place two hundred years ago.'

'But don't you think that he might think of putting it down the mine where he'd first been Chief Engineer? It probably hadn't changed much, he would know it better than almost anyone.'

Siobhan considered for a moment. 'Well, he might. A mine wouldn't have much lighting back in those days – I mean, electricity hadn't yet been discovered. You'd have plenty of places to choose from. But you'd need to be sure it wouldn't be found by other miners.'

'Well, how about a passage that had been worked out and then closed off? As Chief Engineer, Trevithick would be able to arrange a way to get in even after it was blocked off.'

109

Siobhan was excited now. 'He might even have fixed it up while he was working there.'

The arrival of their puddings – both had chosen the warm option – gave them chance to muse further.

Robbie concluded, 'You might say it summed up his life: once it was hidden he never managed to get back to it. Maybe that's why he died a London pauper.'

'I'm not saying, Siobhan, that's what really happened. But I am saying that someone might think it could have. In that case, and if they'd found a way of getting down some of these old mine shafts, they could be motivated enough to go and take a look.'

They had no reason to hurry their desserts or their final cups of coffee.

Robbie had made progress on his original problem, was content to stop for the evening. He'd got one scenario for why someone might be interested, even today, in Ding Dong Mine.

'It's very late for you to be driving all the way back to St Just,' said Siobhan. 'Especially after half a bottle of wine. And to be honest, I'm not even happy to drive as far as Zennor.'

'I'll tell you what,' she said. 'My landlady keeps late hours. If we go back now we could ask her to give you a room for the night. Then I'll take you back to Zennor in the morning.'

It wasn't exactly what Robbie had been dreaming of but he could see it was a sensible suggestion.

As they made their way out, he noticed a table near the door whose occupants had obviously been having a good time. For the moment he couldn't place them; but he had some sense that he'd seen them before.

It had been a long day and by now Robbie was shattered. Maybe he'd have a better idea tomorrow.

WEDNESDAY

DECEMBER 28th

Entrance to Geevor Museum

CHAPTER 15

Wednesday Dec 28th. Peter and Maxine's wedding was now only three days away.

In Chy Brisons the bride, family and associates were having a light breakfast together and making their plans for the day. Making best use of the cars available made this trickier than expected.

'I've got an appointment at eleven with the local vicar,' announced Esther. 'First I must introduce myself to him. I don't think we've ever met. After that he and I need to carve up the service, decide who's doing what. I know I'm doing the sermon but all the rest is up for grabs.'

'I've known Father Giles for years,' said Maria. 'A bit stuck in his ways, perhaps, but he's very caring. I'm sure he'll let you do as much as you want.'

'He's happy to accept women priests, I hope?'

'"Happy" might be overstating it but he's accepted that's the way it is. Don't worry, I'm sure you'll hit it off fine.'

'I'll walk up with you,' said Kirstie. 'Remember, it was dark when I got here last night. I haven't even seen the coastline yet and it's supposed to be stunning. And I'd like to look at the church building, see the best angles for my photographs. Getting it clear in my mind beforehand is really important. You can't ask people to do the same thing more than once, simply to get the best pictures. There's only one entrance of the bridal procession. Within the wedding itself, anyway.'

The photographer turned to Maria. 'Is the church building normally locked?'

'Good gracious no. Not in St Just. Not in the daytime, anyway.'

'Good. So maybe, Esther, we can head up there about ten?'

So that was one plan made. Maria turned to her nieces. 'What about you two?'

Shelley responded, 'Someone suggested last night that there was a Mining Museum just up the road. It's supposed to be open this week.'

Frances added, 'Mining's a vital industry for Cornwall, or at least it was. It'd be good for us to learn about it while we're here. The only thing is, it's a way to walk and I don't think there are many buses.'

'That's alright,' said Alice. She had just joined them, having jogged down from the Kings Arms. She had feared they might be expecting her to cook breakfast but it seemed her duties applied in the evenings only.

'Brian would be happy to take you. He's never been to this museum and he told me he'd love to go. I'd come too, but I'll be busy today, learning the finer points of the kitchen and talking my way through the reception meal with Maria and Maxine.'

'Am I needed for that?' asked George. She was, after all, chief bridesmaid.

'I think that'd be too many cooks oiling the troth, if that's the phrase. Go with Shelley and Frances if you like.'

'I think I'll see what Peter's doing first. He might be glad of some company. Or do you need him to help put up decorations?'

When her world was as she expected, Maria was confident to issue plans for others. 'Alex and Ross are spending today on the Barn. They'll be happy working on their own, I'm sure. It'll take 'em a while to hang up the heaters and plug 'em in safely. Then they've got to sort the lighting and arrange the furniture. Most tables are tucked away for the winter in the garden shed. Mind, they might be glad of more help tomorrow.'

Half an hour later Esther and Kirstie, wrapped up warmly, set out from Chy Brisons.

It was a sharp, frosty morning with not too much wind. A wintry sun shone from a clear blue sky.

'Wow. Look at that,' said Esther. They'd come out onto the road and were facing down towards the coast. They found themselves looking down towards Cape Cornwall, a mixed grass and rocky headland which asserted its presence in a hostile-looking grey sea. There was a chimney of some sort perched on the top and a couple of white-painted cottages off to the side.

'When we come back, Esther, if it's still fine, I'd like a closer look. That would make a fabulous background for photographs of the happy couple.'

Reluctantly they turned away from the coast and headed up to the village.

'Bit deserted,' observed Kirstie as they tramped an empty street towards the main square.

115

'But remember, it's a holiday week for many. Lots of firms are closed down. Any tourists who are down here might be taking it easy.'

'Huh. They ought to be out, making the most of a fine day.'

'Maybe we're lucky, Kirstie, that the wedding gives us reason to do so.'

The women soon reached the central square, with pubs on three sides. Kirstie pointed out the Kings Arms, 'That's where Peter's staying', but Esther said it would be unproductive to go in. They could see the church beyond, both wanted to spend time there.

The church in St Just was built of stones hewn from granite. It had a typical square, Cornish tower with pinnacles on the top. From one of these a black and white Cornish flag fluttered in the breeze.

Their first sense as they stepped inside was of the slightly musty smell common to old churches. Was that from the hymn books or the kneelers in the pews? The church was a respectable size. The wood-lined roof was not especially high but the church was generously laid out. There was a feeling of space, with a couple of parallel aisles running down to the front. Esther counted the rows of pews and reckoned it could seat two hundred – far more than had been invited to the wedding, anyway.

There was a pile of blue guide booklets near the entrance. Esther picked one up and glanced through it.

'This building's five hundred years old, Kirstie. But there've been churches on the site here for eight hundred years before that.'

116

'Yes, I can believe that. It feels really old, doesn't it? But still very homely. I can see why Alex and Maria continue to worship here.'

The two wandered round for some time then Esther, glancing at her watch, noticed it was time for her meeting with Father Giles.

'I've plenty to be going on with,' responded Kirstie. 'I need to work out the best position to stand for each stage of the wedding and how I'm going to move from one to another. Take as long as you like.'

The vicarage was further down the lane from the church. Esther had talked to Father Giles once over the phone but not met him face to face. He had sounded cheerful and considerate and she looked forward to the encounter.

'Good morning, Father,' she greeted him as he came to the door.

'Ah, Esther. Welcome to St Just. Do come in, my dear, let me take your coat. Now, before we start, would you like a coffee? And by the way, my name is Sidney. Can't have you calling me "Father" in my own home.'

Sidney Giles was a tall, well-weathered man, probably in his late fifties. He looked fit enough, certainly not overweight. He was obviously used to living on his own: he could produce a cafetiere of high-quality coffee for them without any fuss.

'Now, let's go into the lounge. I'm afraid I can't afford to keep the whole house warm but I do my best with this bit.'

The room wasn't as warm as Chy Brisons but not too cold.

Probably Sidney coped by wearing a fleece. Esther was glad she'd put on a couple of jumpers and her warmest jeans.

'Have you been here long?' asked Esther. It was important to know the man a little if they were going to work together.

'I trained as an engineer. Then felt called to the ministry ten years later. My last parish was in Plymouth. The docks were hard work, Esther: drugs, refugees and smuggling. This is much quieter. My bosses think of this as a prelude to retirement. Not that I'm thinking of that yet, it's such a wonderful place to minister. Our church is a magnet for visitors. I'm not surprised Maxine wants to get married here.'

'So don't you find this too quiet?'

'The congregation is fairly small. Usually we get around thirty at the main Sunday service, so that's not too onerous.'

'But you'll have to look after other churches as well?'

'Several.' Sidney laughed. 'Cycling from to another is my main exercise.'

'So aren't you ever bored?'

'I play my part in the community. For example, I'm one of the reserve coastguards, called up when the main team are short-staffed.'

Suddenly a snippet of the conversation from the evening before came into Esther's mind. 'I was told the coastguard team were asked recently to recover a body. It was someone who'd fallen down a mine shaft. Were you involved in that?'

'My word, Esther, for someone who's only been in the village for a few hours you pick up news quickly.' Then he remembered where she was staying. 'Oh, I know, Alex must have told you.'

'Were you one of the ones that had to go down the shaft?'

'I was. They knew I wouldn't be thrown by a dead body. I was the first one down there. It was obvious the man was dead, he was all crumpled up. I did my best to straighten him out. Then they sent us down a stretcher to haul him back up.' He shook his head. 'Not a good event, especially just before Christmas.'

'Presumably he wasn't someone local – no-one you knew?'

'The police mentioned Penzance. But they were tight-lipped, not very forthcoming. In fact they weren't very friendly at all.'

There was a pause and Esther guessed that he wasn't going to say any more on the topic.

'Right. Anyway, let's get onto the wedding.

Forty minutes later it had all been agreed. Father Giles was very relaxed about Esther taking the bulk of the service as well as giving the sermon. He would simply provide the outer layers to the sandwich by providing the welcome and the final blessing.

'After all, you've known the bride for twenty years whereas I hardly know her at all. And even if you hadn't it's vital we try and make the church relevant to the younger generation. You've a much better chance of doing that than I have.'

Esther had cautiously broached the question of the bride-groom's folk group from Delabole, The Slaters, leading the singing in the service, using Christian songs that she would choose in collaboration with the bride.

Sidney was unexpectedly enthusiastic. 'That'd be great. As long as they're well-known tunes.' Then his face furrowed. 'The only thing is, we don't have one of those projector things to show

119

the words on a screen.'

He put his head in his hands. 'Come to think of it, Esther, we haven't even got a written order of service.'

'But you've a photocopier we could use to make copies? We'll probably need about sixty.'

'Oh yes. Then maybe another thirty for the regular congregation. They're all invited, Alex and Maria are well loved here.'

'It's a bit tight but we can make it work. I'll finalise the service sheet this afternoon.'

Esther glanced down her list of points to raise.

'Ah yes. Can we have a rehearsal in the church on Friday evening? That's Dec 30th. Let the couple make their mistakes beforehand, rather than on the day itself.'

'Of course. If you don't mind I'll join you.'

'I think that's it, then. It's been a pleasure to meet you, Sidney.'

Sidney glanced at his watch. 'You know, it's almost lunch time. Would you like to join me for a bite in the Star before you go back?'

'I'd love to. But could I collect Kirstie, the wedding photographer, to join us? She's currently assessing angles in the church.'

'Absolutely. We'll collect her as we go past.'

CHAPTER 16

The Star was another pub surrounding the main square. The warm greeting from the barman indicated that Sidney Giles was well known – maybe he had lunch there every day? He, Esther and Kirstie seized menus and found themselves a table by a window, facing out onto the square.

'Our main meals are provided in the evenings,' said Esther, 'so right now a toasted sandwich will do me fine.' Kirstie agreed and soon orders had been placed. With the women's agreement Sidney also came back from the bar with three halves of cider.

'Your church has some very old items mixed in with the recent bits and pieces,' began Kirstie. 'It was a joy to wander round, even if most of the items won't make the wedding photographs.'

'It's a very old church,' he responded, clearly delighted in her interest. 'Our present building dates from the fifteenth century but there have been other churches here for centuries before that.'

'Yes. I noticed a large stone on the other side, opposite the man door. It had a very old looking sign carved on it. A sort of fish shape, you might say, but with an extra pod sticking out the side.'

Sidney looked pleased. 'Ah yes. That's the "Selus Stone". It was found on the site by one of my predecessors, the Revd Buller, two centuries ago. It's called a Chi-Rho monogram and linked to

121

Celtic Christianity in the fifth century. The first church building in St Just might be that old.'

'Wow.' Esther's first degree had been in history. The Dark Ages were not her period but she understood that made the stone very old indeed.

'It's not the oldest evidence of Christianity in these parts, mind.'

Their sandwiches arrived at that point, prolonging the suspense. Once they had organised themselves Esther continued the debate.

'Go on then, Sidney. How old is the oldest carving here?'

'It's a stone with the very earliest form of the Chi-Rho. Buller found it down on the coast, somewhere on Cape Cornwall. It dates from early in the fifth century, that's the four hundreds. Only a hundred years after Constantine's Congress of Nicea, about when the Romans were being booted out of Britain.'

There was a pause as three sets of toasted sandwiches were munched and the facts considered.

'So you mean, Sidney, that Christianity reached this end of Britain very early indeed? About the time Augustine started to minister in Canterbury. But it can't have come that way? Not all the way from Kent?'

'I'm sure it wouldn't. No lorries in those days. But there are plenty of legends about Christianity reaching Cornwall very early. The Phoenicians were here even before the time of Christ. They were after tin to help them make bronze.'

'How did they get here?' asked Kirstie. She found herself being drawn into the story.

'By boat,' Sidney averred. 'Across the Mediterranean, through the Straits of Gibraltar and up the coast of Spain. Cornwall would the first part of Britain they'd reach and it was the part they were really after. The wider fame of our mineral wealth goes back a long way.'

Esther was still grappling with the find at Cape Cornwall. 'I don't suppose we know exactly where it was found?'

Sidney chuckled. 'They weren't so precise in those days. But I'd guess that it was found near the jetty at the foot of the Cape.'

'We haven't seen that yet.'

'Why don't you walk down this afternoon? You must walk up Cape Cornwall while you're here, anyway. There'd be good views to photograph, Kirstie – provided the weather holds. The jetty down the stony beach is a tempting place for a boat to land.'

Sidney paused, his eyes vacant, letting his dreams run wild. 'Once they'd reached sight of land, you can imagine the boats heading for Cape Cornwall. The headland can be seen for miles and it's highly distinctive. I'd say it's more special than other parts of the cliffs, or even the beach at Sennon's Cove.

There was a longer pause. Esther noticed that they had all finished their drinks. 'Will you have another, Sidney?'

'That'd be very kind of you, my dear.'

A moment later Esther had returned with three more glasses of cider. Maybe it was time for a change of topic.

'We've all been musing on the recent death at Ding Dong Mine,' Esther observed. 'We were trying to imagine what on earth the chap was doing there, just before Christmas.'

'Perhaps he had new information?'

Esther frowned. 'Information on what?'

'Well, you know I told you that Christianity came to these parts very early. One legend that's swirled about for centuries says Joseph of Arimathea – you know, the one who donated the tomb for Jesus – addressed the miners here at Ding Dong.'

'Sidney, I'm afraid that sound like wishful thinking.'

He shrugged. 'It might be. But Joseph must have been wealthy to have his own tomb. And the fact that he offered it for the burial of Jesus and the offer was accepted implies that he was some sort of distant cousin.'

'We've no idea how he acquired his wealth.'

'No. But in Matthew's Gospel it states Joseph had dug his own tomb, which suggests an interest in mining. Coming to Cornwall to buy tin might be how he became so wealthy.'

It dawned on Sidney that the women were looking at him open-mouthed. 'It's only speculation, of course. But it encourages my ministry at any rate. And it's possible that the poor chap that fell down the mine shaft thought he could turn wishful thinking into hard evidence. I've no idea what that might be, he never told me, but it would at least give him reason to go onto a lonely hillside in the depth of winter.'

It seemed this was as far as Sidney was prepared to go. He glanced at his watch, then put down his empty glass and rose from his chair.

'Now ladies, I'm sorry to abandon you but I'm afraid I have a sermon to work on. The first Sunday of the New Year is not far away. Thank you so much for your company. I look forward to meeting you both again in three days time.'

CHAPTER 17

Other plans had been made over a more substantial breakfast in the Kings Arms.

Peter had noticed that Robbie was not with them. He'd been to check that his friend wasn't still asleep after a late night and discovered that his room was empty, hadn't been slept in. But that wasn't the policeman's business. Maybe the journalist was staying in some place where phones were temperamental? It would be best to wait for a call saying what he was doing and when he'd be back in St Just.

Brian had made the most of the Kings Arms breakfast. At home breakfast was always a rush. His surgery started early and he rarely had time for more than a couple of slices of toast. Here he could wallow in bacon and egg, sausages, tomatoes and mush-rooms, with as much toast as he liked to follow; and with no Alice to challenge his consumption.

Brian and Alice had agreed, before she left for Chy Brisons, that he would take anyone who wanted to go to the Mining Museum. If there was no-one he would cheerfully go on his own.

'Don't forget, Brian,' said Peter, 'you've got to contact your friend in Truro, find out when that post mortem is scheduled.'

'Yes. But I'm enjoying breakfast first. And then I'm going to make the most of this museum. With a bit of luck I'll get some

125

quality time with an ex miner. Find out what the victim might have been looking for.'

Today's challenge for Peter Travers was the car they'd seen up near Ding Dong Mine. If it did indeed belong to Jeremy Hocking then the best way to obtain a key would be from his late wife. That would first require a carefully phrased phone call to make sure the Penzance police were not already taking care of it.

Once breakfast was over he knuckled down to the call.

'Good morning. Is that Mrs Hocking?'

'Yes?'

'My name is Peter Travers. I'm a police sergeant down in St Just and I'm trying to tidy up some details of the death of your husband.'

'That's good of you. I'm afraid my life's a bit of a mess. I'm not thinking very clearly. This is the first I've heard from anyone in authority.'

That was a relief, he wouldn't be muddling up any official inquiry.

'I've noticed a car parked near to Ding Dong Mine. It's been there for some days. I wondered if it might possibly be your husband's?'

'Ah.' There was a short pause. 'D'you know, I'd forgotten all about that. I've not been out the house, see, since Christmas Eve. That was when your colleagues came and took me to see the body.' She gave a muffled sob.

Peter felt a wave of sympathy for this poor woman who had lost her long-term partner. For the first time in his life this was not theoretical. He hoped it would be a long time before he was in a similar position.

'Am I right in thinking that your car's a grey Skoda?' He read out the registration number he'd noted the day before.

'That's right. That's the one.'

'Do you have a spare key?'

'Course I do. I mean, we both drive it. Jeremy a lot more than me, of course . . .' Her voice tailed off.

'Right, madam. What I was going to suggest was that a colleague and I came to see you, in, say, an hour. We'll pick up the key from you and then we'll go and pick it up, drive it back to Penzance.'

'That would be really helpful.'

Peter Travers did wonder, just for a moment, whether he should be putting so much energy into a parallel police investigation. He was, after all, on annual leave and getting married in three days time.

But the case had fascinated him. He drove down to Chy Brisons to check that all was well with Maxine and saw that she was fully engaged with her mum and Alice on the wedding catering. George, though, was less busy and happy to accompany him.

'We'll go to Penzance via Ding Dong Mine, make sure the car's still there,' he commented as they set off. 'It'd be a bit embarrassing to find that Penzance police had already removed it.'

'Is Robbie back in the King's Arms?' asked George as they passed through St Just once more. 'It would be great to have him with us.'

'He didn't come back last night. Obviously he's making progress of some sort.'

'Mm.' George would have liked to know the dimension in which he was progressing. But she didn't feel she could voice the thought to Peter. He had enough to worry about.

Soon they were up on the moor at Ding Dong Mine. It looked as though nothing had changed since the day before. 'Peter. Can you tell me our milometer reading? It might turn out to be useful.' Her friend didn't argue but peered at the dashboard and read out a number. George jotted it down.

'As far as I can tell the Penzance lads haven't been taking the case anywhere,' Peter remarked as they continued on towards Penzance. 'But I wanted to see Mrs Hocking as early as I could, just in case. It would be embarrassing to meet Percy Popper at her house, wouldn't it?'

It was only about six miles into Penzance and, in the week after Christmas, there was not much traffic.

'Mrs Hocking told me that she hadn't seen anyone official, apart from when she was taken to the mortuary on Christmas Eve. So she may be in an emotional muddle. I'm looking forward to meeting her, though. It's ridiculous, I have no idea how old she is.'

'It may be as well that there are two of us then,' George replied. 'I'll do my best to give you moral support.'

Soon they were through Madron and down into Penzance. It didn't take them long to find Mrs Hocking's house, a small, semi-detached residence at the far end of a quiet road.

'There's no-one official around as far as I can see,' observed Peter. He sounded thankful. They parked and headed for the front door.

There was quite a delay till someone came. They heard a chain being unfastened and then the door opened a fraction. A face peered at them from around waist high.

Peter wasn't thrown. 'Sergeant Peter Travers, ma'am. Here's my identification. And this is a colleague, George Gilbert.'

The door swung open properly and revealed a slender, grey-haired lady, probably in her early sixties, seated in a wheelchair. She was not wearing makeup and had obviously been crying buckets.

'Thank you for coming, Sergeant. Please come in.'

The hall was large enough for her to turn the chair back without difficulty. They followed her into the living room, pleasantly furnished though hardly posh. Peter deduced that the Hockings were adequately financed, better than "just about managing", but by no means wealthy. He decided to continue as he would have done in Bude.

'So all this began for you on the day before Christmas Eve?'

'That's right. Jeremy had been away for a couple of days, you see. He said he'd be back for supper that evening but he never showed up.'

'So when was the last time you heard from him?'

'I got a text the evening before. Everything seemed to be fine. He always did that when he was away, he was very considerate.'

'It was as well that he'd mentioned Ding Dong Mine, Mrs Hocking, or the police might have taken ages to find him. Had he

129

been there before?'

'Yes, it was unusual. I mean, going round these old mines was a bit of an obsession. There are so many, normally I couldn't tell you which one he'd gone to. Maybe he just thought I'd find the name Ding Dong amusing.'

'Do you know what he was doing there?' The woman was talking freely now, George felt she could join in without disrupting the flow.

Mrs Hocking frowned. 'Not really.'

'Do you know if he climbed down the shafts, for instance?'

'Might have. He used to work in some sort of mine a long time ago, over near Falmouth. That was when he had his accident. But he was over that. He'd been fit for years.'

George tried again. 'So was he on some paid project?'

'He acted as if it was. But he wasn't being paid much. We were getting by on our pensions, but money was tight.'

'And there was nothing that Jeremy said which might have suggested, looking back, that he was in a state of abject despair?'

'He would never have made it as a comedian but I'd say he was as cheerful as he ever was.'

Peter could see there was a question which had to be asked. 'I'm sorry to ask this, Mrs Hocking, but you don't think he would have thrown himself over the shaft edge deliberately?'

The woman looked shocked at the idea. 'Good gracious, no. He wasn't that way inclined at all. Besides, he'd have been worried about what would happen to me once he'd gone. I took it for granted that it was just some dreadful accident. That's right, isn't it?'

Peter shrugged but gave no answer. Ten minutes Mrs Hocking had handed over the car keys and they were on their way.

CHAPTER 18

George made sure they'd taken the milometer reading before they set off back to Ding Dong, though she had no idea how it might be useful.

As they drove Peter voiced a different anxiety. 'You know, George, with all the complications of counting days to Christmas, I think we may have made a blunder.'

'What's that?'

'Well, we've been told by various sources that Hocking died on Dec 23rd and was found by the police on the 24th. But how does that square with rigor mortis?'

George recalled the term from discussion on other cases. 'You mean, the way a dead body becomes rigid for a short time after death?'

'Yes. The rule of thumb is that rigor lasts for forty to forty eight hours. But in that case, if death occurred on the 23rd, the body would still have been rigid while it was being hauled up the shaft on the 24th. No-one's mentioned that, have they? Well, the chief coastguard didn't mention it to me, anyway.'

'But rules of thumb are meant to be broken, Peter. What happens, say, when it's very cold, as it was before Christmas?'

'That would slow the process. I suppose that, if Jeremy didn't die until late on the 23rd, and the recovery happened early next morning, the rigor might not start to take effect until he was en route to the morgue.'

George considered the problem, Peter himself didn't sound convinced. 'Alright, so what's the alternative? What if he died on the 22nd? Then his body would be relaxed again by the time the recovery team arrived on the 24th – whatever time they got there. Is there any reason why it couldn't happen like that?'

Peter had been musing. 'The only thing that really stands against it is the reassuring text message that Mrs Hocking received on the evening of the 22nd. But, you know, that's not watertight. It might not have been sent by her husband at all. It could have been sent by the killer, probably using Hocking's phone. That rules out accident, surely makes murder much more likely.'

'She seemed to rule out suicide, anyway. Abandoning a wife who's confined to a wheelchair would be a hard thing for anyone to do.'

Further thought dampened conversation for the rest of the way to Ding Dong.

'I hope the battery's not gone flat in the time it's been up here on the moor,' muttered Peter as they walked over to the Skoda. But that was one mishap which they'd been spared.

The door opened easily. The policeman squeezed into the driving seat, made sure the gear stick was in neutral and then turned on the engine. It faltered for a few seconds and then staggered into life.

'Before you start, what's the mileage?' asked George. To keep out of the cold she'd sat beside him. The policeman read out another sequence of digits from the dashboard and she jotted them down.

'Hm. This car has done just under twelve miles since its MOT in Penzance. Whereas when we drove to Penzance this morning the mileage was about six and a half. So why the extra five miles?'

'We'll get the car back to Mrs Hocking first then give it some thought. Which would you prefer to drive: this car or mine?'

Half an hour later they were once more in Penzance, parking next to the Hocking house.

'Shall we both go? If anything's said it would be good to have a witness.' After a delay Mrs Hocking let them in. She seemed less confused than on their last visit.

'Your car's parked outside, Mrs Hocking. As far as we know there's nothing wrong with it. It's still got plenty of petrol.'

'Thank you so much. You've had a busy morning. Could I offer you coffee?'

'I'll make them if you like,' said George, remembering her wheelchair. Mrs Hocking nodded and the analyst wandered into the tiny kitchen.

While she was busy Peter Travers decided he would see if he could learn more about the final text message.

'I've been thinking about your husband's death,' he explained. 'There's something odd that I don't understand. Could I possibly see the last text Jeremy sent you?'

Mrs Hocking reached to her side table and seized her phone. She fiddled with the options for a list of recent texts and handed it over.

134

'I assume it's this one?' He looked at it carefully. It had been sent on Dec 22nd at 18:45: "Project fine. See you tomorrow evening, love Jeremy"

'Mrs Hocking, is there anything unusual about this text?'

She glanced at his face and saw he was deadly serious. Took a moment to read it carefully.

'The only thing that's unusual is that it's signed "Jeremy". Normally he just puts "J". But the rest is much as usual. He's always referring to the "project" but I've no idea what he's talking about.'

'Right. Thank you. I guess I'd best just keep pondering.'

At that moment George emerged from the kitchen with a tray of coffees. They arranged themselves round the dining table.

'Mrs Hocking, have you had any peculiar phone calls in the last week or two?' asked Peter as they started to drink.

'When he's home Jeremy usually takes all the calls. I've had one or two when he wasn't here. But they weren't very informative, they just rang off.' She paused to consider. 'It's almost as though they didn't want to tell me who they were. And I haven't had any since Christmas Eve. You know, almost as if they knew he was no longer here.'

For a second they feared another bout of tears but she resisted. 'I'm sorry. I'm not much help.'

'You're doing fine, Mrs Hocking,' said George. 'One other thing occurred to me. It sounded as though you weren't surprised that Jeremy had been away and that sort of thing had happened before. Have you any idea where he used to stay?'

'D'you know, I did wonder from time to time. Even asked

135

myself, occasionally, who he was staying with. But I didn't like to ask him. It was all to do with this project, you see. It saved time, he used to say, if stayed near to the places he was interested in.'

A few moments later, coffees consumed, they were ready to leave. 'Now don't worry, Mrs Hocking,' said George, 'we'll keep chasing these bits and pieces up. Thank you for all your help.'

Peter and George sat back in Peter's car. They were about to drive off when they noticed another car drawing into the kerb ahead of them. A young woman dressed in a knitted hat and thick coat got out and headed for the Hocking household.

'I've no idea who she is,' murmured Peter. 'But she looks official. I think it's time to go.'

As they set off, George asked, 'Have we time to visit the local MOT garage?'

'If you want. Why?'

'Well, I've just had a thought. According to the DVLA, the test on Hocking's car took place on Dec 23rd. We need to see if it could have taken place a day earlier. Remember, Peter, he spoke to Hocking when he collected it. Chinnor is the last person we've found to see him alive. We might as well try and nail down the date.'

It turned out that Chinner's Garage was less than half a mile from the Hocking's.

'Good morning,' said Peter Travers to the receptionist in the front office. 'Is Joe Chinner in?'

'I'll see if he's available. Who should I say is calling?'

'Police Sergeant Peter Travers. We talked on the phone yesterday.'

A few minutes later they were ushered into a comfortable office and offered another cup of coffee.

'It's good to meet you in person, Sergeant. Does this mean you're still bothered about Hocking's MOT test?'

'It'll only take a minute. I've a query about which date the test was completed on. My source, DVLA, has it down for the 23rd and that's what I told you. But I wondered afterwards if that might be the date they received the notification, rather than the date you did the test?'

'That's easy enough to check. Hold on a minute, I'll get the records.'

Peter and George sipped their coffees as Joe Chinner disappeared. A few moments later he returned holding a large box file.

'These are the forms filled in by the mechanics as they tested. They're in date order. So what date are we interested in?'

Ten minutes later it was established that the actual test on Jeremy Hocking's car took place on the morning of Dec 22nd.

'I don't know how the DVLA lost a day. Either there was a delay in Swansea before it was entered into the system or maybe my admin girl sent it in a day late. Normally it wouldn't matter. I'm sorry if we've misled you.'

CHAPTER 19

George Gilbert and Peter Travers, chief bridesmaid and bridegroom to be, sat huddled together nursing bowls of soup in a cafe overlooking Penzance harbour. The cause of the squeeze was not some late emotional breakdown. They were both scrutinising a large-scale map of Land's End.

'So Hocking told Chinner he was heading for Ding Dong Mine. He had plenty of petrol, Peter, and he didn't go back home.'

'But there's five miles too much on his speedometer. Compared with the shortest route that we've followed twice this morning.'

'So that means two and half extra miles each way, on some detour from the fastest route.'

'Mm.' Peter reflected. 'That's not much. He couldn't go as far, say, as St Ives. That'd be more like an extra ten miles.'

'Well, what if he went to Ding Dong via St Just?' George traced out the route via the coast road with its multiple bends and gave a sigh. 'You know, I think even that's too much.'

There was silence. Each drank their soup and contemplated the map. Both saw a possible solution at the same instant.

'Just a minute, Peter. What if -'

'He drove as far as Ding Dong just like we did. Then he went on to Morvah, perhaps to pick something up.'

'Look.' George stretched her fingers over the distance involved. 'That's six inches, almost exactly two and a half miles extra each way. If he did that the distance would match exactly. Only trouble is, there's nothing in Morvah. I don't even recall a shop.'

Morvah was a gamble, a last shot in the dark, but further scrutiny of the map as they finished their soup yielded no other likely solutions.

'Wouldn't do us any harm to go home that way,' said Peter as they settled their bill. 'I mean, we're talking about Hocking's last ever journey. It'd be good to know where he went.'

The journey over past Ding Dong gave them a chance to pull together what they'd found out so far.

'Unless there's something else that no-one's told us, say Hocking was on a long bout of treatment at a local mental health clinic, we can rule out suicide,' affirmed the policeman.

'Accidental death's also doubtful, given the position of the body. And the absence of any equipment, like a rope, at the top of the shaft.'

'Or the bottom,' added Peter. He'd had another look at the notes which he'd made after his chat with the chief coastguard. Nothing had been mentioned about other items beside the body.

'But if it was murder, Jeremy almost certainly made his way to the shaft on his own. And we have no idea why.'

There was a pause as the morning's events were rewound.

'D'you remember, George, his wife made some mention of a project. She implied it involved visits to many mines.'

'And made it sound like it earned him some money.'

The conversation was inconclusive. They simply didn't have enough facts. Their best hope of taking it further seemed to be to find something new in Morvah.

Morvah was little more than a hamlet on the coast road consisting of small, stone-built houses with slate roofs. In the past, no doubt, this would be been home for many miners. For there were a lot of mines along the coast.

They drove slowly through the village. Nothing. Then Peter spotted a turning which led to a back road. 'Let's have a look round here.'

And there was something: an art gallery, halfway round the loop. There was no reason whatsoever, from what they knew so far, why Jeremy Hocking should take an interest in art, but it was somewhere that was open to strangers. Peter parked his car outside and they went in.

The gallery manager was pleased, even surprised, to see that he had visitors. Slightly less happy when he realised that they were not customers, not really interested in the landscapes which adorned his walls.

Peter Travers had decided, before entering, that he would use his status as a policeman investigating an unexplained death. It wouldn't matter here that it was unofficial. He fished out his warrant card and showed it.

'And this is a colleague, George Gilbert.'

The manager did not much relish police officers but he was willing to do his duty. 'How can I help you?'

'We're looking into the death last week up near Ding Dong Mine. We found the victim's car there. We were trying to work out where the man had last been.'

'It wasn't here, anyway.'

'No, I don't expect it was. But I wondered, had you ever seen his car?'

'It was a grey Skoda,' George added. 'I can show you a picture if it would help.'

She switched on her camera and flipped back a few pictures, then came to one of the Skoda. 'It's this one. Have you ever seen it around here? It's possible he came here on the day he died.'

The gallery owner found himself drawn in to the search. He reached for the camera then examined the picture carefully.

'Hold on a minute.' He went to the back of the gallery and called to someone in the room behind. 'Gladys, have you got a moment.'

A few seconds later a middle-aged woman appeared in an artist's smock.

'Yes?'

He showed her the camera. 'These two are police officers. This apparently is the car belonging to that poor fellow that died last week up on the moors. Have we seen it around here?'

The woman peered at the photo. 'I know where I've seen that. It's the car that's sometimes parked in the drive of the cottage nearly opposite. But it hasn't been around for a few days.'

George glanced at Peter. Success! Or at least, progress.

'Right,' said the policeman. 'So that might well be where the dead man was staying just before he died. In that case, it's important for us to examine that. Is there anyone around here who could let us in?'

'Well, I've got a spare key,' the artist replied. 'Visitors are told to pick up the key at this gallery, see.' She gave the policeman a careful glance. 'I suppose I can lend it to you, should be safe enough with a policeman. But you'll need to sign for it. I don't have another.'

Ten minutes later, the formalities of signing for the key completed, Peter and George crossed over towards the cottage. The gallery artist had offered to come with them but they had managed to resist the offer. 'We first need to see the place on our own,' explained the policeman. 'But we might need to ask you a few questions later.'

There was nothing wrong with the cottage. The paintwork was in a good condition, the rent must cover the costs of maintenance. The garden was tidy and the curtains drawn back. George was tempted to peer in but Peter restrained her.

'It sounds from what the artist said that this was Hocking's regular bolthole,' he remarked.

'One of them, anyway.'

The brass key they'd been given was a simple design and the front door was easy enough to open. The pair stepped inside and Peter closed the door behind them.

'We can relax now we're not under observation.' George realised now why he hadn't wanted them to peer in through the windows.

'Ought we to be wearing gloves, Peter? This might be a crime scene.'

'That's why I brought my scene of crime bag.' He opened a shoulder bag and fished out a couple of pairs of latex gloves. 'We'll be very careful not to disturb anything but it won't hurt for us to wear these.'

It was a very small cottage, with just one room downstairs that served as lounge and dining room, with a table in the corner. There was a small settee but no sign of a television.

'It's not lavishly furnished,' noted George.

'That probably keeps the rent low - at least in winter. In summer they might bring out a television. It would be a great little hideaway for a couple on holiday, would do fine for a honeymoon.' For a moment his attention faltered.

'We must ask the artist when we take the key back how long Jeremy's been coming here.'

They continued to investigate. There was a small kitchen behind the lounge, with some basic equipment. The breadbin held a loaf that had seen better days. George checked the cupboards and found a packet of cornflakes and a few food tins, enough for beans on toast. 'This is just a bolthole to stay the night, he only cooks basic meals.'

'But he obviously planned to use the place again. There's nothing here to suggest suicide.'

'He hadn't given back his key, anyway. That's why the artist only had one left.'

There was nothing else to study downstairs. Peter headed for a narrow flight of stairs that ran up the side of the lounge, with George close behind.

'There'll only be one bedroom,' she predicted.

She was right. There was just one room, plus a bathroom. Peter opened the bedroom door, they stepped inside and looked around.

'This was obviously his den,' said Peter.

A double bed had a duvet folded back. No bedside table but there was a wardrobe. Also a desk, with its own light.

But the most interesting item was the far wall, away from the wardrobe. For it was covered with fully-opened Explorer maps, not only the one they'd been using earlier of Land's End, but also the maps showing the next two chunks of Western Cornwall. One covered the Lizard and the other the north coast, including Redruth and Camborne. Between them the maps showed most of the mines in Cornwall.

'This is obviously where he planned his mine visits,' said Peter.

George had stepped closed and was examining the maps in more detail.

'The odd thing, you know, is the pencilled scrawls on these maps. All of them around old mine shafts. Whatever are they telling us?'

'No idea. But I guess this is the heart of his project. He wanted to keep it secret, never gave anything away to his wife. But he also needed a private space, to stretch the maps out where he could study them. That's why he needed this bolthole.'

CHAPTER 20

B rian Southgate had driven down to Chy Brisons to pick up Shelley and Frances soon after ten. He'd passed Esther and Kirstie coming the other way but they had no reason to recognise his car.

At the guesthouse his wife was deep in culinary discussion with Maria, so he kept out of her way. Alex and Ross were already at work in the Barn, installing heaters and extra lighting. Brian gave silent thanks that he hadn't been volunteered to help them. They'd be very cold out there until the heaters were working. He was pleased to see that Maxine's nieces were dressed in warm gear. They looked eager for their outing to the Mining Museum. Their mother had decided to join them.

'Thank you so much for taking us,' said Lisa as they got into the car.

'That's fine. I've not been to this Museum myself,' he told them as they set off. 'This is a long way from Delabole but it has a good reputation. I'm keen to see it too.'

For the time being the passengers were quiet. They knew that Brian was to be Peter Travers' best man but they didn't know him very well.

As they drove through Pendeen, Brian noticed a tall tower with colliery headgear mounted on the top, by the roadside.

'That's the place, I reckon.'

They bumped down a muddy side road and into a large car park, which was almost empty. 'Not many visitors today,' Brian observed.

They walked across a lawn to the entrance. There was a cluster of buildings stretching some way, all slightly well-worn and battered.

'Even the most passionate Cornishman wouldn't claim mining is a tidy operation,' Brian noted. 'You've got to remember, ladies, this was a working mine less than thirty years ago. That's only an instant in Cornish time. In the century before last you'd find this sort of cheerful confusion in a lot of places.'

As they bought their tickets Brian noted there was some sort of guided tour in half an hour, which they decided to join. In the meantime they looked round some rooms giving a general introduction.

Brian guessed from their opening reactions that the girls had come with no idea as to how far the place sprawled. The first room contained a model of the mine, set on a painted cliff-top. The building they were now in was a tiny piece of the whole operation. The main shafts were marked with LED lights and showed that the mine actually ran down under the sea.

'Wow. It's massive,' muttered Frances. A moment of panic crossed her face. 'We won't have to go under the sea, will we?'

'I don't think so. When the mine was working a lot of effort went into keeping it from flooding. Now it's closed they don't need to bother.'

Shelley found another poster. 'Hey, look at this. "The shafts go down two thousand feet," it says, "then the tunnels run a mile out to sea." '

'And there's a hundred miles of tunnel, and some ninety shafts,' added Frances, reading on. She scowled. 'That's surely an exaggeration?'

Brian and Lisa were slightly ahead and had come to another display in the room next door. 'Hey girls, come and have a look at this.'

They went into the second room. Brian pointed to an intricate three-dimensional model of the mine's shafts and tunnels, constructed using plastic tubing. The display took most of the room.

'The thing is, the tin ore is found in huge sheets that run almost vertically through the granite. They're known as lodes.' He paused to make sure they were all with him, and then continued.

'So to get at the ore, you need to construct a series of tunnels into each lode, one above another. The miners have to come down the main shaft, climb in and dig away at the area in between.'

Frances had a question. 'So what happens to the ore?'

'It's taken away in small railway wagons. Rails are laid along the tunnels and back to the main shaft. Of course, the whole thing changes over time as more ore is removed and new tunnels are built. It's a complicated piece of dynamic engineering.'

They all looked at the display for some time, growing in respect for the operation modelled. Then Brian noticed it was time for the guided tour.

The tour party that was gathered at the main reception was small. Just two more men, both from the depths of Yorkshire and old enough to be retired, joined them. The tour guide was a cheerful looking, tall man of around fifty. 'I'm Eric,' he told them. 'I wuz working here when the mine closed. That was 1990, I wuz just twenty five.'

Brian could see the guide was more interested in Shelley and Frances than the rest. The girls sensed it as well and seemed to blossom.

'Go on, then, why'd it close?' asked one of the older men, in a broad accent. 'Were there an accident or summat?'

'Nah,' said his companion. 'It were Thatcher. She'd done for t'coal miners in the eighties, then to 'er dismay she found some more working in Cornwall.'

There was laughter from the party.

'It was neither of those,' said the guide. 'It was a massive collapse in the world price of tin. In 1985 it started at £10,000 per tonne, by the end of the year it had fallen to £3,400.'

'What price did you need to make Geevor profitable?' asked Brian.

'Halfway between, about £6,500 per tonne,' he replied. 'So we went from being a viable enterprise with huge reserves to making a massive loss. And the price of tin never recovered. It was always cheaper to mine the stuff in other parts of the world. That's what did for us here.'

'I think we mine tin in Australia,' admitted Shelley, feeling a tinge of guilt.

'That's right: opencast sites with massive reserves. You drive the stuff away in lorries. It's a hell of a lot easier than digging it out from under the sea. Come on, let me show you.' And he led the party down the corridor.

Three hours later the tour returned to the main foyer exhilarated but exhausted.

They'd seen some of the tiny wagons on narrow track and heard about the battery-powered engine that pulled them around. They'd looked into the Victory Shaft, which Eric had told them was built in 1919, in the heady days after the First World War.

The party had walked through the extended process by which the tin ore was extracted from the rock removed each day from the mine. A series of angled trays sprayed with water separated the ore from the spoil.

'It's a massive reduction in volume,' the guide had told them. 'But that's the nature of tin mining.'

'I bet it was noisy to operate,' said Frances.

'It was horrendous. A continuous racket, twelve hours a day,' the guide replied. 'Mind, we didn't hear it, we were all underground.'

The tour had concluded with a short trip below ground. They'd walked far enough along a rough-hewn passage with a low roof, partial lighting and plenty of bends to get some sense of what it would be like to work underground. No-one had felt envious of those that once had to do so.

Now Brian was itching to ask Eric about the future of mines like Geevor but he judged he'd have a better chance once the main tour was over.

'Eric, would you like to join us for a pot of tea?' he asked, once the route had finally been completed. He hoped having Lisa, Shelley and Frances with him might lead to a positive response.

At this time of year the mine shut at four. There'd be no more tours today. In any case the guide was happy to take the weight off his feet.

Brian and Lisa went off to purchase the drinks and the girls were left to chat to Eric.

'So you ladies are from down under?' he began. 'Have you any connections with mining over there?'

'Our dad has some link. But I don't think its traditional mining. He's a bit mysterious about it.'

'So what's your connection with Cornwall? I mean, this isn't the best time to come. You wouldn't catch me swapping your summer for our winter.'

'Our cousin's getting married in St Just on New Year's Eve. We're both going to be bridesmaids.'

'Great. So your family has some connection with Cornwall?'

'Our dad was born and brought up in Cornwall. He left for Australia in his early twenties and his brother, that's the bride's father, stayed here. We've never been here before. We want to see as much as we can.'

Brian returned at that point carrying a tea tray. Lisa followed with a plate of cakes. Both were well appreciated.

'Eric, you've given us a fabulous insight into Cornish mining as it was in the past,' said Brian. 'Do you think it's finished for good, or is there some way it might continue?'

The guide considered for a moment.

'You saw the amount of effort needed to process the tin ore once it was extracted. I don't think mining for tin will ever happen again in Cornwall. But there are other things you can find underground that weren't much appreciated in times past.'

'Such as?'

'Well, I guess the most obvious one is geothermal energy.'

Frances broke off from eating her doughnut. 'I've heard Dad talk about that, but I've never understood what it really meant.'

'Well the basic idea is simple. The earth's surface is fairly cold – especially in a Cornish winter. But you don't have to go down very far to find hot rocks – I mean incandescent. If you can drill down in the right place and get at that heat, then you'd have access to another form of energy. It might last for thousands of years – almost forever. Save burning coal and oil, anyway, maybe slow down global warming.'

Eric was clearly an invaluable source. 'Eric, you know better than anyone that the world price of tin makes it unprofitable to mine here. Are there other things which could be mined which have a higher value?'

'You'd need to ask an expert. Maybe there are chemicals needed for high tech developments that you could find here. I mean, Cornwall's had dozens of mines for centuries. They found plenty of stuff alongside tin and copper. Arsenic, for example; and wolfram; different sorts of gems. Even China clay.'

Eric concluded, 'I'm not sure that any of those exist in big enough volumes to make a mine profitable. It would be nice to think so, wouldn't it?'

151

CHAPTER 21

That same Wednesday morning Robbie Glendenning found himself launched into a more serious discussion than expected with Siobhan Hitchen over breakfast in St Ives.

There had been no problem, the night before, persuading the landlady to give him a room for the night. She had a houseful of empty rooms.

Siobhan had supplied him with a spare toothbrush, already charged with toothpaste. The rest he would have to improvise. She had even banged on his door on her way down to breakfast, removing any temptation to have a lie in.

He was surprised when he got downstairs to find that Siobhan was the only other dining room occupant. Half a dozen other tables were empty. No wonder the landlady had been pleased to take another guest.

'Be helping yourself to cereal, Robbie,' she advised, nodding towards the side table. 'I told Mrs Humphries you were on your way. She'll be bringing the bacon and eggs in a couple of minutes.'

Robbie got himself a bowl of rice crispies, wondering for a second how long they'd been in the jar, and joined her by the window.

'Good morning,' he smiled. 'Thank you for waking me up.'

152

He peered out of the window. 'Looks like a fine day.'

'Eat first, talk later, Robbie.'

Their grilled course arrived a few minute afterwards and Robbie could see why he had been hastened along. It was delicious.

Apparently, Siobhan said, they could take as long as they liked over toast and marmalade. And there was unlimited coffee. In the quiet Robbie took the chance to challenge Siobhan's approach to her historical research.

'From what you told me, Siobhan, the heart of your method is to look for miners' diaries in likely places.'

'And what's wrong with that?'

'Nothing as far as it goes. But doesn't it mean that you just learn for yourself what historians before you have already discovered?'

Siobhan sighed. 'I don't have decades for this, Robbie. I was only given the remit in October and they want me to report in February. My report doesn't need to be exhaustive, just a good résumé. I'd say yours is the crucial one, outlining the future of Cornish mining. How are you going to do that, by the way?'

Robbie paused to draw his ideas together. 'That's only just started, Siobhan. There's lots of material on hand from around the world. Company reports, academic studies, international conferences and so on. I might ask the newspaper to fund my attendance at one or two.'

'But Robbie, if that's your plan I could say the same thing to you. All you're doing is drawing together what other people already know. That's an editing task; it's miles from front-line research.'

Robbie relished the debate. It was a refreshing change from working on his own. A different mindset gave a fresh perspective. He poured them both a third mug of coffee. Decided, in present company, to forego any more toast.

'Alright, I agree. And the distinctive thing that our newspaper wants from both of us is insights from Cornish locals. What each of us needs is well-informed, local experts. The question for us both, then, is where on earth we find them.'

Half an hour later the pair set out. As a professional journalist, Robbie had persuaded Siobhan that a good place to start their search for local experts would be the local newspaper, the Land's End Gazette. They'd looked it up and discovered that its office was located in the centre of St Ives. Robbie had made a phone call to the editor to prepare the way.

It was like a dream, he could still scarcely believe it, he thought, as he walked with Siobhan down toward the press office. They'd been so close at university and then the relationship had bizarrely come to a grinding halt. And now it might resume where they'd left off. He was tempted to skip down the road.

'You seem very happy this morning, Robbie.'

'Just glad of the company,' he replied with a grin. 'Very glad indeed.'

'I'm happy too that we can work together,' Siobhan replied. 'It's much more fun – like old times. Let's hope it continues.'

The Gazette office was close to the jetty, not far from where they'd eaten the evening before. They went in, introduced themselves. Soon they were being shown through to the editor's lair.

The editor was a man in his late fifties, wearing a well-worn suit and looking slightly crumpled from his regular battles with life. But he was cheerful enough and seemed pleased to welcome them.

'Ah, Mr Glendenning. I'm pleased to meet you. You write good stuff about us in the national press.'

'That's very kind. Please, call me Robbie. And this is my colleague, Siobhan Hitchen.'

'And I'm Sammy Tonkin. So what can I do for you?'

Convincing people he met that he was on their side was a regular occurrence for the journalist. He drew a deep breath. 'Well, Sammy, it's like this. Siobhan and I have a special assignment for our paper that you might be able to help us with. It's to do with mining in Cornwall – what happened in the past and what might happen in the future.'

Unsurprisingly, Sammy's initial response was one of doubt. 'You're not the first to ask these questions, Robbie. Thing is, if people have grand plans for mines, they don't normally start down here, they go up to the City of London and make big pronouncements. To get anywhere at all they need plenty of investment, see.'

'Of course. But my newspaper wants to help start the process a bit further back. Laying out the big canvas, so to speak. Drawing attention to possibilities for a wider audience.'

Sammy looked relieved. 'Oh, I'm happy to go along with that. Cornwall needs development alright. I mean, tourism is all very well but we shouldn't just be relying on the emmets.' He gave a sigh. 'You know, Cornwall used to be a hub of industry for the nation when our mines were in full swing. Did you know, we were once the world's biggest producer of tin and copper? So can you tell me a bit more about your project and what my paper could do to help?'

'Right. Siobhan's been working on the historical part since October.'

Siobhan took over. 'Part of this, Sammy, is setting the scene for readers who know a lot less than you and I. So I've been to the main museums in Cornwall, trying to find records, diaries and so on, that give a personal account of mining and what it meant for their community. Things that you could loosely call "human interest".'

Robbie added more details. 'I've only just got my remit, so I'm starting work next week. Obviously there's masses of material about mining from around the world. One of our research assistants is going to trawl through that. But I'd like to enrich that with ideas from locals around here about where mining could go. So what we both need is help identifying Cornish mining experts.'

He stopped. Sammy pondered for a moment.

'OK. Well, let me tell you what's on offer.' The editor paused to arrange his prospectus.

'You know, of course, that we're a weekly paper?'

Robbie nodded. He'd picked that up from the internet.

'In fact, Robbie, that's how we've always been. To be honest, not much serious stuff happens round here. Even on a weekly basis there's not much hard news.'

'So what on earth do you cover?' asked Siobhan. She'd glanced at the latest edition in the foyer, seen it comprised at least twenty pages.

'There are always lots of family events and so on, weddings and funerals. Then there are sports reports, puzzles and quizzes. Occasionally storms and flooding. Even more rarely heat waves. But we're often stuck for a substantial lead article. Which means that anything about mining, either development or difficulty, will always appear on the front page.

'I'd go even further. If something has happened that relates to any mine in Western Cornwall then we will have covered it. It might lag by a week or two but we'll get to it eventually.

'So I would say, Robbie, that the best chance of indentifying local experts would be for you to trawl the front pages of our paper.'

Robbie mused over the way he'd put it.

'"Trawl" is an odd word to use,' he commented. 'Couldn't we just do a search using the computerised database?'

'For recent events you could. Since 1990, anyway. But we've never had enough resources to retype our historic editions onto the computer. All we have from older times are the archive copies.'

'There won't be much for us after 1990,' said Siobhan. 'I mean, that was when the last mine closed.'

'And the Gazette only began in 1910,' he replied. 'So there's nothing before that either.'

'Wouldn't the best thing be for us to try browsing for a couple of hours,' suggested Robbie, 'say the rest of the morning. Then

157

maybe we could take you out for lunch and review how far we'd got?'

The prospect of a free lunch was always attractive to a newspaper editor, whether national or local. Robbie had made a good call. Soon they were being shown down to the basement where the archive copies were located.

CHAPTER 22

It was half past five before Robbie and Siobhan finally finished looking through the front pages and disentangled themselves from the Gazette's basement. They set off to walk back across St Ives.

'Now, Robbie, are you going to stay in St Ives for another night or do you need to get back to St Just?'

In the excitement of her company Robbie had almost forgotten he'd come down here to attend a wedding, indeed that many of his friends were down here too. Especially George.

'Um. You know, I think it would be diplomatic to get back there this evening. In any case I could do with a change of clothes and access to my razor. Could you drive me back as far as Zennor?'

'Sure.' They strode back up the slope until they were outside her guesthouse. 'You haven't anything to collect in here, have you?'

'All I had was my laptop and I've got that.'

As they set off through the light evening traffic a trace of anxiety passed over Siobhan and her face wrinkled. 'Robbie, I've been assuming that you have no emotional ties with any of these friends?'

'They're people I've got to know over the years. One of them,

159

that's the bridegroom, is a policeman. Peter Travers. He's the one that's got us into investigating this death at Ding Dong. Then there's the best man and his wife, Brian and Alice, and there's the chief bridesmaid. She's called George, spends most of her time in London.'

Something about the way he spoke about the last person mentioned, maybe a subtle change in his speed of speech or simply feminine instinct, caught Siobhan's attention. 'And there's nothing going on between you and George?'

'As I say, Siobhan, we're just good friends. I've known her for years, we've worked together on a couple of murders. Look, why don't you come to St Just with me, then you can meet her? I'm sure she'd love to meet you.'

There was silence as they set out from St Ives. Siobhan was concentrating on the traffic while Robbie reassured himself that there really was nothing between him and George. Could have been, he thought, but that boat had never quite left the harbour.

Once they reached Zennor there was a choice of car for the rest of the journey. 'Shall we take mine?' suggested Robbie. 'Then I'll bring you back again later.' Half an hour later he had driven Siobhan on to St Just.

'It's unfair for two of us to turn up at Maxine's family guest-house without warning,' said the journalist. 'I'm feeling quite hungry. Why don't we eat at the Kings Arms and reflect on what we got out of the Gazette. I'll introduce you to my friends after we've eaten.'

Down at Chy Brisons Maxine had reminded all her guests that

the death at Ding Dong was a taboo subject. Consequently they had enjoyed another of Alice's splendid meals with plenty of light conversation, much of it related to the forthcoming wedding.

Esther had outlined their visit to the church and her meeting with Father Giles, Kirstie adding her joy over the possibilities for photographs. 'It's a really old church,' she said. 'At least five hundred years old.'

Lisa, Shelley and Frances had shared impressions from their visit to Geevor Mine. The underground tour had gripped their imaginations.

After the meal Maxine had suggested an evening stroll up into St Just.

Robbie and Siobhan were just finishing their dessert when the group arrived.

'Robbie, we thought we'd lost you,' exclaimed Peter.

Robbie stood up to greet them. 'I'd better make some introductions.

'This is my old uni friend, Siobhan. She's another historian. And Siobhan, this is Peter the bridegroom; his best man Brian and wife Alice; the bride, Maxine and her cousins Shelley and Frances; the vicar for the wedding, Esther; the photographer Kirstie; and chief bridesmaid George.'

Siobhan followed the wave of his hand as he went round and murmured the names to herself. It was mainly a question of remembering which was which. But face recognition was a skill which she had long since mastered. 'I'm very pleased to meet you all.'

Peter took charge. 'Because several of us are staying here the landlord said he was happy for us to use the upstairs lounge. That'll be a bit quieter, I think. But it doesn't have a bar, so let's get our drinks down here first.'

Siobhan made good use of the time to talk to some of those that had just arrived. She made a point of shaking hands with George, who she could see was looking a little confused.

'Robbie brought me over here to meet you all,' Siobhan explained. 'Maybe there'll be chance to talk later about our research. He and I have made some real progress.'

George wondered about the direction of progress and where it left her. But it was hard to be cross with Siobhan, she seemed so enthusiastic.

Eventually they all had a drink and made their way upstairs.

'Right,' said Peter, glancing round the lounge. The place was comfortably furnished. There were several settees, each one better than any seating in the Bude police station. And for now, at least, they had the room to themselves.

'Last night, over supper, we identified several lines of inquiry relating to the dead man at Ding Dong. Despite the attitude of the local police, I believe this is an important piece of work. I know we've all been busy on it, one way or another. Thank you all for your efforts.

'Now, there are quite a lot of us – more than I have in my team in Bude. So I suggest we first go round in turn, saying the key facts that we've found, but being as brief as possible. After that we can have a wider discussion on where we might go next. Who'd like to go first?'

162

No-one rushed to take the lead. After a moment Esther, recognising the problem, claimed the floor.

'Kirstie and I have two interesting findings. Firstly, it turns out that Father Giles – Sidney – was one of the coastguards that went down the shaft at Ding Dong. His first instinct as a priest was to rearrange the body. So the tidiness we were talking about yesterday wasn't how the victim lay to start with, he started off very crumpled.

'The other thing is Ding Dong. It's very old, goes back to Roman times. There is a legend that Joseph of Arimathea once visited, addressed the miners of the time on the hillside. And there's hard evidence – carved stones – of Christianity here in the fifth century. So is it possible that the dead man had some new information about the olden times?'

'Thank you, Esther,' said Peter. 'That's beautifully succinct. Who wants to go next?'

Brian took up the challenge. 'Shelley and Frances spoke movingly over supper about Geevor mine. It was an impressive place in a sad sort of way. We had a very good tour guide who used to work there. I asked him about future prospects for mining.

'He agreed tin mining was dead in the UK, but mentioned various alternatives. One was geothermal energy, others were rare gems and alloys that might be more valuable in the future than they've been in the past.

'So it's possible,' Brian concluded, 'that the dead man was pursuing ideas for some new venture along one of these lines.'

'Thank you,' said Peter. 'We'll come back to these ideas later. How about the post mortem?'

'I rang my medical friend when we got back. He says the post mortem is scheduled for tomorrow morning. He won't tell me results over the phone but he's invited me to go over to Truro for a working lunch. So all being well I should have something by tomorrow evening.'

'Well done. Right, who'll go next?'

'Maybe, Peter, I should tell everyone what you and I found,' offered George.

'We took back the car – the grey Skoda – to the victim's wife in Penzance. It turns out she's confined to a wheelchair. She dismissed the idea of her husband committing suicide. She also talked about her husband's obsession with old mine shafts and mentioned a secret project.

George went on with the tale of the Skoda, culminating in an earlier date for Hocking's death.

'Finally, we had a breakthrough. A discrepancy over mileage led us to suspect he might have gone on to Morvah and then back to the mine. So we went to Morvah and landed up inside the dead man's bolthole.'

George paused for a moment to make sure they were all keeping up. 'You can't stop there,' said Brian.

'No, that would be unfair. The main item of interest was a set of maps on the bedroom wall. With scrawled markings around old shafts. We don't know what but it must be something to do with his project.'

There was a pause. 'Is there anyone else?' asked Peter.

'Siobhan and I have also been busy,' said Robbie. He turned to his research companion. 'Would you like to summarise?'

All attention went onto Siobhan. They had no idea what to expect.

'My remit is the human interest side of old mines in Cornwall. I've been working on it since October.

'We had one idea about Ding Dong. It concerns the Chief Engineer, Richard Trevithick, who was a very clever inventor. He later spent years running a silver mine in Peru before he was forced out, came home and died penniless. But suppose he'd kept some of the silver from Peru and brought it back home? If so, might he have hidden it somewhere down Ding Dong Mine?

'We spent all day today going through the archives of the Land's End Gazette in St Ives, looking for articles about mining in the last century. Unfortunately, though, the paper doesn't go back to Trevithick.'

Robbie took over. 'We photographed any articles we saw about mining. We haven't yet had time to go through them. They might give us local mining experts to contact.'

'Thank you, Robbie,' said Peter. 'And thank you Siobhan, especially coming into the investigation completely cold.'

He looked around the room. 'In fact, thank you everyone. You've all been remarkably disciplined at not interrupting one another. I wish my team in Bude could do half as well. I suggest we have a five minute break before we start on phase two, trying to make sense of what it all mean. If anyone wants another drink, now would be a good time to collect one.'

CHAPTER 23

Ten minutes later discussion resumed. Peter Travers, reflecting that he wasn't driving anywhere, decided to treat himself to a second pint of Doom Bar. Others exhibited a smaller thirst or tighter self discipline.

'OK guys. Let's give ourselves forty five minutes, that'll take us to half past nine. We all need a good night's sleep and a clear head for the next few days. And some of you need to walk back to Chy Brisons or drive over to St Ives. So what are the topics that anyone is itching to discuss?'

There was a pause as ideas were sifted.

'The phrase that jumped out at me, from what's been said tonight, is "geothermal energy"'. The speaker was Siobhan.

'OK, Siobhan. Let's complete the list of topics before we start to discuss them.'

'I love the idea of there being something hidden in Ding Dong,' said Kirstie. 'It sounds like something from Treasure Island. How can we take that further?'

'I'd like to know what ideas others have got to explain what Jeremy's scrawls might mean on the Explorer maps,' requested George.

Peter waited a moment for other ideas but no one else had anything to add.

'Right.' He turned to the professional historian. 'So Siobhan, what made you pick on geothermal energy?'

'Well, we've heard several ingenious ideas about what might be happening at Ding Dong. Can't rule any of them out, but a search that's related to geothermal energy sounds the most likely. If you could determine the right place to drill and you could get permission to do so then you could be onto a fortune.'

Most of the room knew very little about the subject. 'Can anyone give us a two minute guide as to how this might work?' asked the policeman.

'I know the rudiments,' said Brian. 'And I did more background reading on the internet after we got back. Basically the idea is to extract heat from the incredibly hot rocks far below the earth's surface. If you could do that then you'd have another source of energy that could supplement fossil fuels, probably for decades.'

'So what might that involve?' asked George.

'Well, one part of the problem is finding places where the distance down to the heat is not so huge. The deepest hole that's ever been drilled is about fourteen thousand metres. The deeper the hole the more it costs. You wouldn't want to go as deep as that. Another question is to assess where the geology may lead to fractured rocks that have broken up enough to allow the heat to be extracted and brought to the surface. They do it all the time in Iceland.'

'Yes, but why should anyone think that Cornwall is as promising?'

'The geology gives us some encouragement. You know that a

lot of Cornwall is made up of granite?'

'Yes. Well, I know Bodmin Moor is,' returned George. 'I've scrambled on the top of Roughtor often enough.'

'Granite runs right through Cornwall, and lies underneath most of the Land's End peninsula. The thing about granite is that it's an extrusion, it's been pushed up by molten rocks far below. So now those hot rocks underneath are nearer the surface than they were before. Maybe they're nearer here than in other places further from the granite.'

There was a pause then a new fact emerged. 'I read in the Museum in Truro that Cornwall's already produced geothermal energy,' declared Siobhan.

'Where?' asked several listeners.

'I can't remember what the place was called, but it was in some quarry over near Falmouth. An experimental rig, it ran in the 1970s. The thing worked, but not well enough to be kept going. But if it can be done once it can surely be done again. That's why I picked up on the term. We must know a lot more these days about geothermal energy than we did forty years ago. After all, it's been found in lots of other places.'

Peter glanced at his watch. 'Right, we've given that topic its allotted fifteen minutes. Next topic: something hidden inside Ding Dong. What do we think about that?'

A pause as the group switched focus.

'We've had two ideas presented this evening,' summarised Kirstie. 'One is Trevithick's silver hoard from Peru.' She turned to Siobhan. 'I assume it's a hard fact that that the man actually went there?'

'Oh yes,' said Siobhan. 'And that he was driven out and came back. The notion of a silver hoard is speculation but not impossible. Especially if someone's been up at the mine looking for it in the middle of winter.'

'The other idea,' added Kirstie, 'is something linked to early Christianity, maybe some specially-marked stone. Either of those would be well worth finding. And worth rather a lot to the finder.'

'Trouble is, there are at least a dozen shafts at Ding Dong Mine,' said George. 'Robbie and I walked past a couple on Boxing Day. We've no idea which one might hold the treasure.'

'If we had to guess, shouldn't we assume that Jeremy knew what he was doing? And was peering at the right shaft when the attack occurred?'

Nobody had much to add. The policeman glanced at his watch. 'So now that leaves us with the final question: what might the scrawls mean on the victim's Explorer maps?'

'Are the scribbles letters or numbers,' asked Esther, 'or hieroglyphics?'

'I believe they're all numbers,' George replied. 'I haven't had much time to study them yet.'

'Just a minute,' said Brian. 'Are the numbers about the same value?'

'From what I remember they're fairly similar.'

'Well, how about this for an idea? Suppose the victim was interested in the temperature at the bottom of each shaft. The man was used to climbing, managed to get down quite a few of them. And then, once he was down, he measured the temperature at the bottom. Maybe with a special sensor.'

'For what purpose?' George could sense where he was going but wanted it articulated for the rest.

'Well, we said earlier that the best place to drill for energy is where the hot rocks are closest to the surface. All these mine shafts around here make it possible to measure the temperatures at shaft bottom, and these will be at variable depths. If you looked at them as a whole, say a hundred data points stretched out across Land's End, might that not give a clue as to how the temperature varies down below? And hence which is the hottest place to try and drill for energy.'

'You might be right, Brian. It'd certainly be worth a few hours modelling the map data tomorrow, see if that makes any sense. I'd love to know where the most promising place turns out to be. Wouldn't it be odd if it happens to be Ding Dong?'

'Right,' said Peter. 'Our time is up.' He glanced round the room. 'So let's sum up. Where are each of us going tomorrow?

'I'm sitting in my room with my laptop, trying to build a Land's End underground temperature model,' said George.

'I've got to spend tomorrow in the guesthouse, polishing my sermon and finalising wedding service details,' said Esther.

'I'm off to Truro to meet my medical friend,' affirmed Brian.

'Robbie and I need to examine the data we obtained from the Gazette archive. Probably best to do that in St Ives,' asserted Siobhan. George was not ecstatic about the idea but she'd already made her choice and could see no way to prevent it.

'I've got to stay here,' said Maxine. 'I'm helping Mum produce cakes for the reception. Alice is needed in the kitchen too.'

She turned to her cousins. 'It would be good if you could find out what the dads are doing in the Barn. You've probably got more artistic talent in your little fingers than the pair have in their whole bodies.'

That left Kirstie. She looked beseechingly at the policeman.

'I don't suppose you've got any ambition to go down Ding Dong again, Peter? See if we can find Trevithick's silver hoard.'

'The thing is,' she went on, 'I'm used to rock climbing, it's my main hobby. If you could borrow the rope ladder again I'd love to come down with you. And if you wanted I could take some good quality pictures of the foot of the shaft. I have a thermometer that I use in my photography. We could measure the temperature at the bottom, see if that coincides with the figure on the victim's map.'

Peter did not take much persuasion. He wanted to avoid working on the Barn if at all possible. 'Good. All being well we'll have made a bit more progress by tomorrow evening. Let's convene here again after supper.'

THURSDAY

DEC 29th

Cape Cornwall and Priest Cove

CHAPTER 24

There was excitement in the air at the Tavistock guesthouse. The wedding was now only forty eight hours away. Maria's nerves over the event, once so fragile, were now more or less under control. Alice Southgate's presence in the kitchen had first reassured her, then impressed her, and was now taken for granted. The head teacher had proved that she was an excellent cook. Saturday's reception meal in the Barn was going to be fine.

Even Maria's husband had abandoned his usual dour countenance. Alex and his brother had had a good day of bashing and banter together out in the Barn. It now had plenty of heating and lighting. The rest of the preparations, setting the tables, decorating the walls and putting up the various signs and arrangements, could now be done in comfort. Alex was cheerful and looking forward to the day.

Life with Ross and his family, after a bumpy start, had settled down on a more even keel. Alex was no longer seen as answerable for every quirk in the United Kingdom. There were too many things wrong with the country for them all to be his fault.

Ross's daughters, Shelley and Frances, had grown into their new roles as honorary Cornish girls. The family were starting to take an interest in their Cornish ancestry. The visit to Geevor

173

Mine had been a landmark on that journey.

For Maxine, her habitual trump card of cold logic was dominating any wobbles in emotion. In a way the complications of resolving the Ding Dong death, while a distraction she would never have chosen, had given her a perspective on the forthcoming wedding. She could count her many blessings – a supportive family, good friends around her, a mysterious, almost magical, setting for the wedding itself and most of all her husband to be – and not take them in any way for granted.

Her chief bridesmaid, George Gilbert, was used to dividing her energies between competing priorities. Professionally these would usually mean deciding which troubled firm required her attention most. On the day before, a critical observer might have noted, she had given far more time to the bridegroom than the bride. Today she would be working at Chy Brisons and the priority would be reversed.

Once breakfast was over and the coffee consumed, the group stared to disperse. There were plenty of tasks awaiting them.

George recalled that she needed hard copies of the Morvah photos. She managed to grab Alex's attention before he and his brother disappeared into the Barn.

'Alex, is it possible I could borrow your printer?'

'Sure. Help yourself. The office behind the reception desk is never locked.' He thought for a moment. 'If you need to turn on my computer, the password is "Maxine73". I know, don't tell me – it's not the tightest security on the planet. But St Just is hardly a haven for terrorists, is it?'

Several responses crossed George's mind but she held them

back. Terrorism was not the only threat around here. 'Thank you. I'll use it later, once I've cleaned my teeth.'

Half an hour later, having set up a working area in her room, George came down to the office to print out hard copies of her photos. She had decided she would work just with the map of the Land's End peninsula. If there was any overall meaning to the scrawls there was most chance they would show up here. This, after all, was where Hocking had most recently been based.

The marked area of the map was mostly near the coast and she had recorded it with half a dozen close-ups. George slipped down to the office – it was, to her mind, ludicrously unprotected – and switched on Alex's computer. Not the latest machine but it would do all that she was after.

Ten minutes later cables had been attached and the relevant photos transferred. Was the quality good enough to be useful? She looked forward to seeing the images at full screen size.

George wished she'd got the photo editor from her own computer. One or two images would benefit from trimming and the scrawls were slightly faint. But she thought they'd be good enough to print out as they stood. She made sure the printer was switched on, set the print quality to maximum and began the process.

As she waited the analyst glanced round the office. It was tidy enough, with shelves of files on the far wall. Standing up, she saw that practically everything was linked to the business of the guesthouse: lists of customers, insurance, quality control and so on. Alex's bank statements and a folder covering tax returns were squashed in one corner. One large envelope was labelled "Tourist Honeypots". What was that? To George the whole coast line was the attraction, all accessible with a standard map. But maybe, these days, not all visitors were proficient in a map's use.

The printing was taking longer than expected. George pulled out the tourist folder and glanced inside, saw leaflets for places like the Minack Theatre and St Michael's Mount. There was also a brochure about the Scilly Isles. Tourists could fly there directly, she read, from the airport just up the road.

Was that where Maxine and Peter would be going for their honeymoon? Convenient but not exactly warm. The chief bridesmaid hoped common sense would prevail.

At last the printer had completed its task. George glanced at the prints, checked they were alright and then erased her photo files from Alex's computer. She, at least, could be security-aware.

Two hours later George's eyes were aching and she needed a break.

She had been squinting at map segments and jotting down each scrawl and its associated coordinates. The scrawls were all numbers, expressed to one decimal place. She'd used contour lines to estimate the elevation of the points and also recorded the mine-depth estimates. The heights varied considerably. Many places were around the coast but some were up on the moors, several hundred feet higher.

The actual location was always well-defined. Jeremy, or who-ever had augmented the map, had marked a small cross beside each scrawl. Most points coincided with mine shafts but by no means all. George decided not to worry about that for the time being. Thankfully none were anywhere near an urban area.

The Explorer map had one kilometre squares marked to show the grid so it did not matter when the printed out photos had distorted the scale. She used her own Land's End Explorer map as a reference when required.

George had been entering the values into her laptop as she deciphered them. But before she started grappling with modelling the values to see what they meant, she needed another coffee.

There was a fraught atmosphere in the kitchen. It did not require a psychologist to discern differing views over styles of cake. The time, thought George, for a chief bridesmaid to intervene.

'Maxine. I'm after a break. D'you know, on this visit I've not been as far as Cape Cornwall. That's a waste of fine weather. D'you fancy a stroll?'

Maxine could read between the lines. George was offering her an escape from the tensions in the kitchen. Only an idiot would refuse to take it.

Five minutes later the two had put on their walking boots and cagoules and were heading down to the headland.

'Seemed a bit tense in there?' asked George.

'It's mainly shortage of time. I mean, it's the day after tomorrow and there are so many things to get ready. I'm afraid my mum's about to freak out. She's not good at coping with pressure.'

'Best leave her to Alice. She deals with many stressed parents of the kids at her school. Anyway, I could do with a chat about temperature modelling from a limited set of data.'

Maxine immediately responded, as George had known she would. Mathematicians always responded to a logical challenge.

'Right. What can you tell me?'

'I've recorded all the marked data points, also their coordinates, height and what I'm guessing is their depth. I'm assuming for now that the values are temperatures at shaft bottom. They vary quite a lot and the effect is certainly non-linear. But there are only a hundred or so points. I want to interpolate so as to predict the most likely point for the maximum underground temperature.'

'Mm. Have you any idea where the hot spot might lie?'

'It wouldn't take me long to plot the temperatures on a graph. But the crucial point is somewhere around where we went for lunch on Tuesday.'

She paused to consider. 'I mean, a geology department will have advanced models of how underground temperature varies. I bet it's wildly complicated. But for a start I want something simple.'

'Well, if you want something really simple, George, would it work to model just the points running up the coast? You could fit it using some sort of optimisation. Then see where the maximum lies.'

'Mm. I could do that with the software I've got with me. And then try more complicated ideas. For example, what's the effect of the height of the top of the mine shaft? Is the hot spot near the coast or on high ground?'

By now they'd reached the end of the narrow road. There was

a car park over to the left but today it was empty.

'What d'you want to do now?' asked Maxine. 'Up to the top of the headland, or left to explore Priest Cove?'

'Let's go up.' Ten minutes later they'd reached the summit. The Atlantic Ocean stretched out below them. Looking south along the coast they could see the long beach of Sennon Cove and beyond that the crags of Land's End itself. In the other direction was an old engine house perched precariously at the bottom of a gentle slope, not far above the sea.

George pointed it out. 'For some reason that place looks faintly familiar.'

'You mean Botallock? That's because it's such a dramatic place to film. Recently it's featured during the Poldark series, you know, the one on television on a Sunday evening.'

'So although here is remote, there are times when there are loads of actors and film cameras?

'They use the locals as extras. They give 'em costumes styled for the early 1800s. Even my parents have appeared once or twice.'

There was a peaceful pause. George would like to have shared her anguish over Robbie's behaviour but could see that her friend had enough stresses of her own. 'I think, you know, my head's cleared now,' said George. 'I'd like to potter around Priest Cove, maybe tomorrow. But now I need to get back, make more sense of the data from Hocking's hideaway.'

The two took another route down the other side of the headland and climbed back up to Chy Brisons.

CHAPTER 25

L
ess excitement but more analysis was taking place over breakfast at the Kings Arms.

As they tucked into their mixed grill, Robbie Glendenning was being cross examined by two long standing friends, Peter Travers and Brian Southgate. The focus of their attention was his link to Siobhan Hitchen; and what that would mean for their mutual friend, George Gilbert.

Robbie did not much like this but maybe it was inevitable. If friends could not challenge one another then what was their point? And if a challenge was coming, it was much better faced in the relative privacy of the Kings Arms over a multi-course breakfast.

'So how long have you known Siobhan?' asked Peter. 'Last night, the way you shared the stage upstairs, it seemed like you were close friends.'

So Robbie launched on a potted history of the relationship. How he and Siobhan had been an "item" (though the term wasn't in vogue in the late 1980s) at Bristol, lost one another on a mix up over which Pizza Express they were to meet in, left university to pursue different careers and then not seen each other again for twenty years.

'Until my newspaper, nothing to do with me, chose Siobhan

to do some historical research on mining families in Cornwall. So I had her contact details and I thought it'd be worth talking to her about the history of Ding Dong Mine. To be honest, she was the only mining expert that I

knew. It was worth a try, anyway. But as soon as we met at Zennor the old magic started to come back. And that was for both of us. It seemed she'd missed me almost as much as I'd missed her.'

'That's all very well, Robbie,' said Brian. 'Great for you, in fact. I hope it all works out. But what about poor old George?'

Robbie looked a little troubled. 'The thing is, George has been a great mate. We are good friends. On any sort of investigation she's everything you could hope for: sparky, clear-thinking, logical. In one case her quick thinking saved my life.'

He paused, remembering, and then continued. 'But in truth, though we've known each other for years it's never got beyond us being good friends. We pass each other in a tearing hurry from time to time down in Cornwall, then she's back to London or I'm away in China. There's never been time for anything to develop.'

'Hasn't this week in St Just been a chance to build?'

'Well, if it might have we hadn't had a murder to investigate. But look at us. Without really trying we've ended up on different strands. And I think that whatever happens to me and Siobhan, that's how it's always going to be between me and George. So – '

The conversation was interrupted at this crucial point by the arrival of Kirstie Conway, who had walked up to St Just from Chy Brisons.

She sensed that the men had been in serious conversation. But she could hardly backtrack on her arrival or pretend she wasn't there. 'Don't want to butt in, guys, but I wasn't sure what time Peter was off to Ding Dong. I didn't want to miss him. This is my off-script excitement of the week.'

Kirstie had a mug of coffee with Brian and Robbie as Peter went off to get ready. He re-emerged a few minutes later wearing a fleece and padded trousers. He was glad to see that Kirstie was already dressed for a day on the moors.

'First thing we've got to do, Kirstie, is to go round to the local coastguard to borrow his rope ladder and some climbing gear. I hope he's not planning to be using it himself.'

They set out down one of the St Just side roads. A few minutes later Peter was knocking at a small, stone house with the inevitable slate roof.

Colin Trewern came to the door. He recognised the policeman but struggled to remember his name, they'd only met before briefly.

'Morning Colin,' said Peter. 'You remember me, I'm Peter Travers. This is Kirstie, she's going to take the official pictures at my wedding on Saturday. She'd like to take some pictures of the area here for background, so I offered to show her Ding Dong Mine. Is there any chance we could borrow the rope ladder again?'

The coastguard suspected the last sentence didn't quite follow but it didn't matter. 'Sure. Come in for a moment while I get the gear out.'

They followed Colin in to his living room. As they waited for him to fetch the gear from a garage at the rear, Kirstie glanced at his bookshelf.

'Colin knows plenty about mining in Cornwall, I see. He's even got a book about Cornish geothermal energy.'

Peter would have moved over for a closer look but the coast-guard returned at that moment, clutching a huge bundle of rope ladder, a pair of climbing helmets and a couple of pairs of leather gloves.

'Thank you very much, Colin. We'll bring them back by lunchtime.'

Peter carried the rope and Kirstie held everything else. They were both heavily laden. They walked back to the Kings Arms, dumped everything in the boot of Peter's car and set off.

Today was a fine day, no mist, glimpses of sunshine but with a fierce breeze. 'We'll be glad of those gloves, I reckon,' said Peter. They took the coast road as far as Morvah and then turned off on the minor road towards Ding Dong.

Kirstie was eagerly taking in as much as she could. In summer-time the whole scene would be a mass of colour, highly photo-genic. At this time of year there was less colour but still a raw beauty about the remote moors, the derelict engine houses and chimneys and the distant glimpses of the coastline.

She spotted a small parking area, a mixture of earth and peb-bles, off the road ahead. 'Peter, could we pull in there for a mo-ment? It'd be great to have a few pictures from here.'

'Sure.' As they stopped Peter glanced at the map. 'We could walk from here if you like. There's some sort of grass track over there.'

183

Kirstie got a tripod from her rucksack and set it up to hold a camera with a telescopic lens. Then she took pictures of the moors and a close-up of the buildings at Ding Dong Mine. Peter noticed the clouds forming a lively pattern above and the track to the mine making a good foreground.

He was right about the track, it had been used recently. There were footmarks in the mud, even a pair of cycle tracks. The mine was further away than where they'd parked a couple of days ago but the path was clear.

Peter locked the car and they set off. Once again the policeman struggled with the rope ladder while the photographer carried everything else. A good job it wasn't too far. Ten minutes later they'd reached the shaft where the body had been found.

Kirstie busied herself taking more pictures while Peter made sure the rope ladder was securely fastened to the boulder near the shaft.

'That'll hold us easily,' he said confidently. 'Do you want me to go first?' Kirstie was happy to let the policeman take the lead.

Five minutes later there came a call from the depths. 'Hi, Kirstie. I'm down now. Come on when you're ready.'

Kirstie was an accomplished rock climber, wasn't bothered by height exposure. She decided to leave the tripod folded at the top, it would be awkward to carry it any further. She slid the camera into her rucksack and made sure the lid was fastened. Then, holding firmly to the top rung, she carefully manoeuvred herself over the edge of the shaft and started down the ladder.

There was no difficulty with the climb until the ladder moved from the middle of the shaft over towards the side. This must be the non-vertical feature George had talked about.

Now the ladder wasn't so easy to hang onto, with the hewn rock of the shaft close to the rungs. But it wasn't impossible. Kirstie carried on slowly and five minutes later she, too, had reached the bottom.

'Well done, Kirstie,' said Peter. 'If you're still game for photos, I could do with a couple showing the chalk outline of the figure at the bottom of the shaft.'

Peter had been here two days ago. But this time the policeman knew he was at a crime scene and that sharpened his observations. Of course, any photos required flash. If he hadn't closed his eyes it would have left him temporarily blinded. But for some reason the residual glimmer as he reopened them give him enhanced vision.

'Wait a minute, what's that?' He shone his torch on the far wall. It was relatively smooth. And on it there was a pair of rectangular, faint marks, about six inches apart.

Kirstie mused for a moment. She was used to taping up photographs and titles at exhibitions. 'It looks as though something's been taped onto the wall. Why would they do that?'

Peter shone his torch round the space carefully. There weren't any more marks but there were a couple of low arches leading from the shaft bottom.

'Can we try them?' asked Kirstie, her eyes gleaming.

Peter had been told by Maxine that his companion was a skilled climber. She was as good a partner as he could wish for, a lot better than anyone else in Bude. 'OK. But we're taking it very slowly.'

Kirstie was eager to go first. She selected one arch, switched on her torch, ducked her head and clambered inside. Peter followed close behind.

But the passage didn't go very far. After thirty yards it petered out, or perhaps had been blocked off.

'Remember what Siobhan told us,' advised Peter. 'Richard Trevithick was very tall. If he was hiding a horde of silver he would most likely reach up high.'

Kirstie shone her torch upwards and moved it slowly over the blocked end. Then she saw some sort of ledge over in the corner. 'What's that?'

She reached upwards. At full stretch her gloved hands reached round some sort of black box. Slowly she drew it down towards her and shone her torch on it.

Had she found Richard Trevithick's silver hoard? For a second she could dream. And then her hopes were dashed.

'That certainly wasn't made by Richard Trevithick, Kirstie. Electricity hadn't been discovered then. This is some sort of meter. Look, there's a dial at the front and stubs on the side. Well done for finding it, anyway.'

She frowned. 'Does it . . . does it measure temperature?'

'I think so. We've found Hocking's sensor. I reckon this is what was taped to the passage back there.' The policeman felt in his pocket and produced a clear plastic evidence bag, then slipped the item inside. 'Would you mind putting that into your ruck-sack? We'll look at it more carefully once we're back on the surface.'

They searched the short passage for a few minutes but found

nothing more. Eventually they returned to the shaft bottom.

'Right,' said Peter, moving back towards the rope ladder.

'One more to try,' pleaded Kirstie. Her eyes still glowed in hope.

Peter could not bring himself to say no. 'Go on then.'

The second passage went steadily downhill for a long way. Peter counted his paces to keep track of how far they'd covered. He'd got just past four hundred when they came to an abrupt stop.

Kirstie shone her torch ever so slowly over the end wall but this time found nothing significant. 'Maybe the miners got so far, Peter, then decided that this was an unprofitable direction to explore.'

Peter though was examining the wall a little further back.

'Hold on a minute.'

Kirstie turned and followed the beam of his torch. There was a trace of another pair of tape marks, six inches apart. 'So it looks like Hocking came right down here as well.'

CHAPTER 26

Robbie Glendenning was feeling slightly battered as he drove over to St Ives. For years he had lived on his own, chased around from one story to another, never settled for long enough in one place to build a long term relationship. It wasn't a deliberate decision but he had come to assume, somewhat regretfully, that he was destined to be a lifelong bachelor.

Now there was a potential conflict of a different sort. For Robbie meeting Siobhan again had rekindled an old flame, made him recall how brightly it had once shone. He was resolved to push that as far as he could. But the breakfast conversation with his friends had reminded him that he wasn't completely on his own, he needed to take some account of George. At the very least he owed her a serious conversation and an explanation.

It was the week between Christmas and New Year and traffic along the coast road at nine in the morning was light. Most local firms were taking a week off and it was too early for the few holiday makers to be on the road. By nine fifteen he was in St Ives and parking outside Siobhan's guesthouse.

Siobhan had seen him from the breakfast room window and came to the front door to let him in. She gave him a penetrating look, saw the special look in his eyes and offered him a gentle hug.

'Welcome to St Ives, Robbie. Breakfast was a bit lonely on my own.'

He followed her back to the breakfast room, sat down and poured himself a mug of coffee. The landlady was nowhere to be seen.

'Right, Siobhan. We need to plan out the day.'

'Well I've been awake for ages. Started squinting at the photos we took yesterday at the Gazette,' said Siobhan. 'Even ran a couple of pages off on my portable printer. But the quality's awful. If we're going to do that for fifty pages and make sense of the details, we need professional printing.'

Robbie sipped his coffee before responding. 'D'you remember our lunchtime chat with Sammy? He was talking about some of his more off-beat sources. One place he mentioned was an old photography shop, not far from his office. It'd probably be easy enough to find. He said it had been around for years, at least since the war.'

'That's right. And he mentioned that it had modern kit there as well. They often helped the Gazette, he said, by taking some of the paper's photographs and by printing off others. They'll understand what we're after. Why don't we take our photos there and see what they can do?'

While Robbie was helping himself to more coffee Siobhan ran upstairs to get ready. She emerged ten minutes later wearing a dark green dress, cream tights and strong shoes, carrying a cagoule and scarf. She looked a lot smarter than was necessary for a day of historical research but Robbie wasn't going to complain. 'OK,' she said. 'I'm ready whenever you are.'

Soon they were in the centre of St Ives and searching the streets around the Gazette office. The "Traditional Photography Shop", established 1935, wasn't hard to find, it was in the next street. It didn't look particularly busy but that might have been because the whole town was quiet.

They went in and approached the counter. There was just one assistant, a short, rather musty looking man in a white shirt and dark suit. Robbie wondered for a second if he'd been serving there since the shop began, then realised he couldn't possibly be that old. But might he be a contemporary of Sammy? That might explain why the two worked so closely together.

'Good morning,' said Siobhan. 'We were talking yesterday to Sammy at the Gazette. He mentioned your name, or at least this shop.'

The musty man seemed to liven up, his face broke into a smile. 'Dear old Sammy, bless him, he's been a good friend to me over the years. How can I help you?'

'We spent most of yesterday in the Gazette basement, looking for articles about mines. We went right back to when the paper began. There were quite a lot and it would take us too long to note them all down. So when we found anything of interest we photographed the relevant articles. But now we realise that we need hard copies if we're to examine them properly. Would you be able to help us?'

At the prospect of a substantial body of work for his shop, Mr Musty seemed to shed at least a decade. 'I certainly can. Now, do you want black and white prints or full colour?'

Robbie smiled. 'The Gazette didn't print in colour until the

1980s, so I think black and white will be fine. But we'd like them scaled up to an A4 size and as legible as possible. For now we just want an overview of what sort of things happened. If there's anything really special we'll get a more detailed print later.'

'How soon could you do it?' added Siobhan.

'I can get my wife to start on it straight away. It might take an hour. You don't mind waiting?'

They had nothing else pressing so they handed over their cameras and showed Mr Musty where the relevant pictures began. At that point a tiny woman, presumably his wife, appeared and he handed over the whole package of work. She disappeared into the back office and soon a regular pattern of mechanical clunks could be heard.

Robbie recalled their original purpose in going to the Gazette, the search for material on mines. Maybe Mr Musty could help directly?

'Sammy told us that you often helped with his newspaper's photographs. Have you any pictures of mines we could look through?'

The owner beamed. These days so much of the shop's output was pictures of tourists on holiday. It was a pleasure to deal with some customers who had a longer perspective.

'Certainly,' he replied. He opened a drawer behind the counter and pulled out a couple of red, A4 sized boxes.

'This box is pictures taken before the Second World War. Cameras weren't so good in those days, of course, but there were a lot more mines operating. My aunt acted as the shop's camera woman when we were asked to send someone.'

191

He seized the second box. 'And these are the shop's pictures of mines taken after the war. There were a lot fewer mines by then, of course, but the cameras were a lot better.'

'Are those taken by your aunt as well?' asked Robbie.

The owner looked a little down cast.

'I'm afraid she was no longer with us. My mum, her younger sister, took over. She was competent enough but not so inspired. Later I took over from her. I wasn't as inspired as my aunt either.'

There were a couple of chairs at the rear of the shop. Robbie and Siobhan each took a box and sat down to sift through their contents.

They were professionally produced photographs, taken in good light. Each one was labelled on the back, plus a date, in light pencil.

'We might as well make a note of the mines they photographed,' observed Robbie. 'If, later on, we find any of them are of interest we'll know we can come back here for the pictures.'

For half an hour the pair ploughed through the boxes. There were certainly many excellent photos. Robbie had the box which had been taken before the war and could see what the owner meant. In all sorts of ways his aunt had managed to capture an impression of life in the places photographed.

The pictures were arranged in the order they had been taken. Further down the box he came to pictures that could only have been taken by someone who'd gone right down the mine. It was surely unusual, before the war, for a female to be allowed underground? The aunt must have been quite a character with huge powers of persuasion.

'I've just thought of something else,' said Robbie. He some-times thought his main journalistic skill lay in posing off-the-wall questions.

There were still no customers in the shop. It was a very quiet day. Mr Musty was looking bored.

'Excuse me,' said Robbie. 'We've really enjoyed the photo-graphs. I wondered if you had any taken during the war?'

Mr Musty sighed. 'Those were difficult times for everyone. The mines lost most of their workers, see. Many closed till the war was over. And a lot of those never reopened. Taking pictures of 'em was the last thing anyone wanted. Small personal photo-graphs, ones that would fit into letters to soldiers serving abroad, were the main thing that my family dealt with.'

Not every idea came good. Robbie shrugged, was about to turn away, when the owner had a flash of his late aunt's insight.

'Wait a minute. There was just one time.' He paused, wonder-ing whether the idea made sense.

'Go on,' said Robbie.

'My mum told me that the Army asked us to help them film a local Commando training exercise. It was a great opportunity for my aunt, or so my family thought.'

'But you won't have got that now?' asked Robbie. 'I mean, the Army will have taken it away. They like to keep anything like that secure.'

Mr Musty was looking animated. 'They did, of course. But we knew the firm that were processing the film, editing it and pull-ing it all together. Since my aunt had been one of the filmmakers, my mum managed to argue with the manager there that it was only fair we got a rough copy for personal use. The exercise had something to do with a mine, actually.

'Our copy's only about twenty minutes long. Would you and your friend like to see it?'

CHAPTER 27

'We used to have a dark room hidden in the space behind this cupboard,' explained Mr Musty as he wrenched open a panel close to the corner. 'Once upon a time we did our own developing, you see, but we don't do that anymore. That'd be the best place to see it.' He was obviously excited at the chance to show off his aunt's war film.

Robbie and Siobhan had no idea what they'd be seeing but they were still waiting for the prints off the Gazette so had nothing to lose.

'Can you bring those chairs in with you, please? I'm afraid we don't have any in here.'

The two pulled their chairs in after them. It was a bit of a squash, the room wasn't very big. Mr Musty was fiddling with an old-fashioned film projector on one side of the room, a roll-up screen hung down by the other. He produced a reel of eight mm cine film from a circular can and started threading it through the projector.

'I'm afraid there's no sound with this. There was some at the time but it was very poor quality. They hadn't worked out how to suppress the sound of the wind rushing past the camera and there was plenty of wind that day. The producers added new sound afterwards. So we're missing the odd bang, one huge explosion and some swish final commentary. But they said my aunt hadn't contributed to any of that so they wouldn't give my family the sound version.'

Loading of the projector was now complete. 'Right. I'll switch off the dark room light and let it run. There's no title screen, I'm afraid; it goes for about twenty minutes. We'll watch it straight through so you can see what it's about. Then, if you like, we can run it again, try and work out which bits of the coast we're looking at.'

Robbie regretted that they wouldn't have the tidy labelling they'd seen on the pre-war pictures, but they'd certainly be looking at something unusual. At least with no recorded sound in the background there was nothing to stop them discussing as it ran.

The light went out and the film began. Robbie and Siobhan recognised the opening shot as being St Ives harbour on a sunny day. It must have been very early in the morning as there were no crowds in view. Two boats were setting out, each laden with uniformed soldiers. This was presumably the start of the army exercise.

The next scene was taken from high on the cliffs. It showed the two boats out to sea, on course from right to left, parallel to the cliffs. All the soldiers were seated looking up on the shoreline side of the boats.

Next came a similar shot, taken further along the coast. By now, for some reason, the soldiers had stripped to their underpants.

Then came a series of scenes of soldiers being put ashore in pairs. A couple of them slipped and were completely immersed.

'You can see why they'd taken off their uniforms,' observed Robbie.

The last two to land were directly below a camera but a long way down. One had lost all his clothes apart from his underpants. Slowly they climbed up. They were almost at the top when one disappeared as the other came on more slowly. Then, suddenly, the film went blank.

A few seconds later a different camera showed the scene from a wider angle, obviously much further away. It began with a glimpse of senior officers, watching through binoculars. Then it zoomed in. Several pairs of soldiers had now reached the cliff top, dressed in a medley of clothing. Oddly, it looked as though one was wearing a kilt.

Finally, the soldiers started lobbing something towards a stone building just back from the cliff top. It had no obvious defence and after the third or fourth missile landed there was a massive explosion.

The final scene was taken a short while later. The smoke had cleared and the building was now completely flattened, nothing but rubble.

'Right,' said Mr Musty. 'Have you had enough or do you want to see it again?'

'The pictures are great but it's a pity there's no sound,' said Robbie regretfully. 'Yes please, I'd love to see it again. But this time can we take it in stages, see if we can work out where that building was which they flattened so completely.'

'I don't know how she knew, but my mum always said it was

the remains of an old mine.'

'The way the boats were moving right to left means it has to be somewhere on the north coast of the Land's End peninsula,' added Siobhan. 'But we don't know how far round they went. Can we see it again, please?'

The shop owner ran the film again, hand on the projector ready to pause it when requested.

'It's hard to tell which bit of cliff-top's being used for the filming,' observed Robbie.

'Yes,' agreed Siobhan. 'The trouble is, the editing that's been done means we can't just time the events and work out the locations from that.'

They let the film continue until it reached the point where the last pair started to climb.

'My parents said that was the best-filmed section,' said the owner. 'Given it was taken of moving men shot at a distance, it's very sharp. The camera must have been held very still and precisely focussed. Mum said it had probably been filmed by my aunt.'

'What's that blank fragment near the end?' asked Siobhan.

'They didn't know. Maybe something happened to the camera.'

The film ran on again until it reached the panorama of the coastline with the senior military men in the foreground.

'Stop there,' said Robbie. The film was stopped.

He got out his map of Land's End and studied it by torchlight. 'I reckon, you know, that's taken from the headland at Pendeen Watch. That's the far end of a concave section of coast. It's where

I'd choose for a long-distance angle, anyway.'

He turned to the owner. 'I don't suppose you can click the film on from there frame by frame?'

'You wouldn't normally. But we had this projector modified. At the changeover from cine to digital a few folk asked for it. Let's try.'

He pressed a button and the view zoomed from panorama to something closer in.

Another couple of presses and they were seeing the building which was about to be blown up.

Finally they saw the result of the exercise, a completely demolished engine house.

'I'd love to be knowing which mine that was,' said Siobhan. 'I've come across one or two that have disappeared from modern maps completely.'

Robbie turned to Mr Musty. 'Is there any chance we could get large-scale prints of the last few shots? So we could check them against the real coastline.'

'I don't see why not. That's the sort of thing we used to do with these old films. It'd take a bit of time, though. Could you come back for them after lunch?'

After a brief search they found a cafe open facing the harbour, serving tomato and basil soup with baguettes.

'D'you think we're getting too excited by this obscure Cornish war film? Is it distorting our priorities over Ding Dong?' asked Robbie.

'Well, it's justified in terms of my remit for your newspaper. If

I can find out anything about a mine that was bombed to destruction in the war, that'll make a good story. It'll be original, anyway.' Siobhan mused for a moment. 'But I'm not sure it has anything to do with the death at Ding Dong.'

For a moment both of them concentrated on their soup. It was piping hot and the baguettes had also been warmed, a good meal for a cold day.

'There's something odd about the bloke's aunt as well. What happened to her? The owner said she was "no longer with them". When did she die and what did she die of?'

Robbie paused, considering. 'You're right, Siobhan. I can't see a reason to link this mine to Ding Dong but it could make an interesting article for general publication. My newspaper always likes those. At worst they can use it in the Saturday magazine.'

'Anyway, Robbie, we've ordered the prints from the film now. We might as well take it one step further, go and have a look at Pendeen Watch. Let's see if we can work out from there where the mine was. A mine that's gone missing sounds at least as romantic as silver from Peru.'

CHAPTER 28

By three o'clock Robbie and Siobhan had had a busy couple of hours. Now, taking the chance to sit down, they were in the Lunch Box at Carn Galver, partway between St Ives and St Just. Robbie had remembered the place from a couple of days before. They had just ordered afternoon tea: a pot of tea and a plate of scones.

'Pendeen Watch was easier to get to than I'd feared,' commented Siobhan. 'I presume the road that runs right along it is the way to the lighthouse we saw at the end?'

'Yes. And it's definitely the place they stood to shoot that film. The final scenes, anyway. Even with the naked eye we could see the coastal skyline was exactly right. It's a good job we were comparing remote countryside and not an urban area.'

Robbie once more took out his slightly battered Explorer map and unfolded it across the table. He examined it for a moment. 'That means the army exercise must have finished somewhere in this section here. Close to where we are now, in fact.'

Their tea arrived at that moment, causing him to move the map away to make room for the tray. A word of explanation seemed necessary.

He looked up. The host was wearing a label which proclaimed his name was "John".

'My friend and I were looking into a mine somewhere round here, John, that was bombed during the war. Not by the enemy, you understand; blowing it up was the goal of an army exercise. A photography shop in St Ives had some film of the exercise which they showed us. Now we're trying to make sense of where the place was.'

It sounded complicated. The host was cautious but local expertise was supposedly his speciality. There were no other customers to serve anyway.

'There are loads of mines around here,' he began. 'This end of Cornwall's famous for them. There's a couple just off the main road, half a dozen more scattered along this bit of coast.'

'Yes. We noticed the marked shafts. We've just been over to Pendeen Watch to compare the actual coastal panorama with that shown on the film. Would you like to see?'

The host hesitated but he was too late. Robbie had reached into his rucksack and dug out the series of film prints they'd purchased in St Ives. He laid them out on the next table and the host politely stooped to examine them.

Robbie commented, 'Siobhan and I made that pencil mark you can see at the top, taking account of the various zooms. It's our best guess so far on where the mine was located.'

'Hm. So it was definitely on the coast.'

'Not far from here,' added Siobhan. 'I don't suppose you have any mining records from nearby mines?'

John looked uncertain but at that moment his wife, wearing a smart cream apron, joined him. Her label read "Sally".

'I've been here for years and my parents were here before me.

202

Exactly what's the problem?'

Siobhan repeated the introduction they'd given her husband.

'Ah. You're interested in a mine that was blown up?' said Sally. 'Not many people have heard about that. The Army stamped on the publicity. There'd be none at all if they could contrive it. Maybe they feared the incident would annoy local opinion.'

'Might have been right,' murmured John.

Siobhan explained how they'd come to hear of it. Then Robbie illustrated with the series of pictures of the coast taken from the film.

'We've got a remit from a national newspaper, you see, to delve into the Cornish mining industry – what happened in the past and what might be coming in the future.' He smiled. 'So any new sources of data that you could let us see would be really useful.'

Sally was obviously more taken with the idea than her husband.

'The mine you're talking about, like so many others, was closed in the 1930s. It was called Brandy Mine as it operated over the Brandy Crags. Sounded good, anyway. Made it sound a feisty place to work.'

'I haven't come across that name in my research,' said Siobhan doubtfully.

'The mine was only small,' replied the wife. 'Because it was so local my grandfather had become interested in their history. When he heard they were to shut it down he managed to acquire their records and a pile of miners' diaries. Then came the final destruction of the mine during the last war. That choked off his interest.'

'What a pity. So the records are lost?'

'Oh no, they're at the back of the loft. It's just that you're the first people to come asking about them. Would you like to see?'

This was a huge stroke of luck. The records were obviously well hidden. Accessing them took some time. Robbie and Siobhan managed to make their tea and scones last for half an hour. They were debating whether to order another pot and whether they dare go and make it for themselves when the owners returned. Each was carrying a large cardboard box.

Sally peered into the first. 'This one is the official Brandy Mine records: mine layout, output statistics, employees and so on.' She sifted through the contents. 'I think that includes a large-scale map of the surface layout. That'd show you exactly where it was anyway.'

Then she seized the second. 'This box is various diaries kept by the men over the years. I'd be happy to let you borrow both boxes for a day or two, but we'd certainly want them back.'

'The diaries would be great,' said Siobhan. 'That'd allow us to read about life in the mine as it really happened. Maybe give a clue as to why the place had to close. Thank you very much indeed.'

Ten minute later, contact details exchanged, they were outside and on their way.

'Can we go back to St Ives?' asked Siobhan. 'I'm itching to get into those diaries.'

'Fine. I'll take you back. Then, if it's alright with you, I'll go back to my friends in St Just. It'd be good to tell them what we've been doing and what we've found. Especially the mysterious Brandy Mine. You don't think that was what Hocking was really looking for?'

CHAPTER 29

Alice had produced another banquet in the Chy Brisons dining room for everyone connected to the wedding. After a starter of soup the main course was a rich venison casserole and roast potatoes, the dessert a huge Black Forest gateau. She didn't admit it but it was actually a rehearsal for the Wedding Breakfast which she would be cooking on Saturday.

There was a buzz of convivial excitement. Everyone had had a successful day and there was much laughter and cheer. More of the wine that Alex had bought for the wedding was consumed. Just as well, he thought, that he'd decided to over cater.

Alex declared that the Barn was now as ready as it could be, apart from the poinsettias and flowers due the next afternoon. It had obviously been good for him and Ross to work together. 'It's been like a renewal of brotherhood,' he claimed, 'a restoration of life from a bygone era.'

Shelley and Frances had also been busy with a host of decorations in the Barn. Maxine had been called in from time to time to advise or give a casting vote when her cousins had differing views but overall the effect was striking. A number of Australian features were particularly arresting.

Maria came to look from time to time and was starting to see that the younger generation could deliver huge benefits when given a chance. She was very glad that she'd entrusted them with the task.

Alice had run a thought experiment of cooking the whole reception meal to serve a guest list of around sixty. After that she'd assembled a cooking schedule to deliver the process. The process had identified various items that had either been forgotten or else ordered in insufficient quantities. She'd made a master list and had sent Lisa to buy them. Brian would go next day for any remaining items.

Esther later admitted, when pressed, that the wedding service had meant a few compromises, but it was now under control. The sermon had been completed and the lesson chosen. She had finalised hymns and songs with Peter and Maxine and run off the words for the service. 'I'll take the Order of Service to Father Giles to duplicate tomorrow morning.'

The Slaters, the folk group that would be leading the singing in the service, had been emailed the final song selection and had promised they would rehearse the items this evening. They were due in St Just late tomorrow afternoon. They'd have a longer rehearsal, inside the church building, early on Saturday morning.

The Slaters were also responsible for the music and entertainment part of the reception. That would draw on their regular repertoire, which had been agreed a lot earlier.

After supper a range of plans emerged. The older generation were happy enough to chill in the guesthouse. Shelley and Frances would also stay in. They wanted to catch up with their emails and Skype their friends back in Australia.

The rest walked up once more to the Kings Arms. Alice knew

207

she had to pace herself for the mammoth cooking session at the wedding and decided to have an early night. The others were eager to continue their review of the Ding Dong Murder and headed for the upstairs lounge.

'Welcome everyone,' said Peter Travers, glancing round the room. There were three or four less than the evening before but still a good number. 'Tomorrow evening we're all going to be involved in the wedding rehearsal at the church, so this is our last chance to review the case together. Thank you all very much for your interest, you've been a great team to work with.

'We'll follow the same pattern as last night. Round one to bring each of us up to date on what we've found out today. Then round two for ideas on what it all means and where we go next.'

'I'll begin,' offered Brian. 'I've spent most of today over in the Truro General with a medical friend. This morning he was performing the post mortem on Jeremy Hocking. I wasn't allowed to attend but he and I had a good lunch together afterwards while he told me about his findings.

'In a nutshell, guys, it's much as we thought. There were signs on the dead man's body of a scraping collision with a rocky surface. Also marks in the same places on his clothing. My friend said the two were entirely consistent with him having fallen down the shaft.'

'Was there anything odd about his blood or the contents of his stomach?' asked Peter. 'Do we need to consider poisoning?'

'Not that he told me. The only peculiarity he mentioned was that something must have happened to the man years ago. There were nasty marks on his chest. But that was nothing to do with his death last week.'

'So what was the cause of death?'

'A massive blow to the head.'

'Was that inflicted by something thrown at him on the surface?'

'Oh no, my friend didn't think so. He said it was almost certainly when his head hit the floor of the shaft.'

'So there's no hard evidence that he was murdered,' commented George. 'On the medical evidence it's possible but in theory he could just as easily have fallen down the shaft.'

'Let's hear all the findings before we start the analysis, George,' said Peter. 'What else have we learned?'

'Siobhan and I had an interesting day,' said Robbie. 'First of all we went to a photographer's shop in St Ives to run off hard copies of the front pages that I told you about yesterday. While we were there we learned about an Army exercise during the last war that blew up an old tin mine.

'To cut a long story short, we managed to show the mine was close to that teashop we went to on Tuesday. So we dropped in. The owners knew the place, said it was called Brandy Mine. They lent us two boxes of records and diaries, taken from the mine just before it closed. Siobhan's at work in St Ives now, looking through them.'

'OK,' said the policeman. He couldn't see how a long-lost mine fitted into anything. 'How did you get on, George?'

'With some help from Maxine, I've spent the day making sense of the data on Hocking's map that we found in his bolthole in

209

Morvah. 'I've managed to fit a computer model for what I believe is temperature data, probably measured well below ground. On the basis of this model, the point where the shaft-bottom temperature round here is highest is on the coast, not far from Carn Galver.'

'Well done. George. That sounds like a vital piece of analysis.' Peter Travers, remembering the awkward conversation he'd had that morning with Robbie, thought she needed some encouragement.

'So I think that just leaves Kirstie and I and our trip to Ding Dong. Kirstie, do you want to tell them about it?'

Kirstie glanced round, her eyes shining. 'It was a great day to be out. The moors looked forbiddingly dark but still beautiful. We got lots of pictures of the mine, first at the top and then down below. We also found marks on the bottom of the shaft that were probably due to an instrument being taped to the wall.'

She could see Robbie was trying to challenge but she ignored him. 'The reason I say "instrument", guys, is that we explored two of the passages leading away from the bottom. In one of them we found an instrument which Peter will show you in a moment. The other passage led downhill and Jeremy had been there too. Our evidence of that is more tape marks that we found on the wall at the far end.'

'This is the instrument we found.' Peter reached into his rucksack and brought out a clear plastic bag. It contained a black, rectangular box, six inches by nine inches and an inch deep, with a dial on the front.

'I've had a careful look at it after we got back, even found one like it on Amazon. They cost around £30, not wildly expensive. It measures the highest and lowest temperature over the period for which it's left to run. And various other quantities as well.'

He glanced round the room. 'Right. I think that's everyone? OK, let's have a break and refill our glasses. Then we'll consider what it all means.'

'I agree that it's a good guess that Hocking was measuring temperature but have we any hard evidence?' asked Robbie, once they'd resumed. 'For example, are there values on Hocking's map for Ding Dong? And do they match the temperature Peter and Kirstie found today?'

'I had a thermometer with me,' said Kirstie. 'I use it sometimes in my photography. The temperature at shaft bottom was about $11°$ C.'

George opened her laptop and checked the values she'd taken off the map. She'd made a special note of the values for Ding Dong Mine. 'Hocking had $10.8°$ so that matches pretty well. It must be temperature.'

There was a pause.

'Alright,' said the policeman. 'Let's take it that Hocking's project was to measure temperature in as many mines as possible. How many values were there, George?'

'Almost a hundred. Mind, not all of them coincided with shafts as marked on the map.'

'Yes, but we've found that he also went along passages leading away from the shaft and measured temperature there too. That might account for the non-shaft readings.'

211

'That's a huge number,' observed Robbie. 'And if he was leaving his meter down there each time, taped to the wall, he'd have to go down each one twice. Once to leave it behind and next day to pick it up. If he visited two shafts a day and did that more or less full time, say five days a week, that means he's done twenty weeks work.'

'We asked the artist in Morvah how long he'd had the cottage,' recalled George. 'She reckoned it was since September. That ties in roughly.'

'Perhaps that's why he had his bolthole?' replied Robbie. 'It would leave him free to work all hours. He could go down some shafts at night. I mean, you have to use a torch to go down, whatever the time of day.'

No-one felt inclined to argue or had anything to add.

'Let's leave that for now,' said Peter, after a pause. 'So we know more or less what he was doing. The key question now is, what does that tell us about why he was killed; and who might have done the killing?'

'I can think of one reason,' said Kirstie. 'As I saw this morning, this is a fabulously beautiful part of the world. Any sort of development would be very disruptive, wouldn't it? I mean, there must be a lot of work in drilling a geothermal mine, mustn't there?'

Brian recalled his internet research. 'The key thing is you have to drill a long way down before you get to hot rocks. The process of drilling is bound to be horribly noisy. I mean, think of the racket an electric drill makes when you have to put a plug into a brick wall. Drilling into granite would be much, much worse.'

212

'But there's an argument that Cornwall needs industry,' countered Robbie. 'It's one of the poorest counties in England, with rampant unemployment. It would depend where it was put. Once the access holes had been drilled it might not be that noisy to keep running.'

'The thing is,' said Peter, 'we're not saying it's logical to oppose geothermal developments. Or that it's a great idea. But it might be a motive.'

He glanced round the room. 'Suppose for a minute that is why it happened. What might that tell us about the killer?'

Silence. He'd forgotten that he was not dealing with his police team. Most of the room were not used to such a brutal question.

'It would have to be someone local, wouldn't it?' asked George. 'That's assuming the work, if it happened, would lead to a new venture on Land's End. Everyone else in Cornwall would just be thankful it was happening somewhere else.'

Peter nodded. 'And it'd most likely be a long-term local for another reason. That is, they'd have the best chance of knowing what Jeremy was after. They might have seen him at one or other shaft over the past few months, asked him what he was doing.'

'Or seen his equipment and guessed for themselves.'

There was another pause for reflection.

'Can anyone think of any other reason why Hocking's work might lead to him being killed?' asked the policeman.

Esther had been following the discussion carefully. 'Presumably, if you could establish a geothermal plant that delivered electricity reliably, week after week, it would be a profitable venture?'

'That's right. Evidence on where to drill is potentially a very valuable finding.'

'In that case, Peter, would it not be worth stealing? And if so, might not that in turn give someone a more tangible motive for the crime?'

FRIDAY

DECEMBER 30th

The Kings Arms on the main square in St Just

CHAPTER 30

On Friday, the day before the wedding, breakfast at Chy Brisons was friendly enough but signs of tension were not far below the surface. Almost unavoidably, given the preoccupations of those at the table, it became a planning meeting for the day ahead. Everyone, especially Maria, was aware that anything that was forgotten today would most likely be missing from the grand occasion tomorrow.

'I've never done anything like this before,' Maria said in a hollow tone, looking like she was about to face a particularly gruesome execution.

'All being well, Maria, you'll never do it again,' George reminded her. 'So you need to enjoy it, make the most of every detail. It's going to be a really special occasion, especially for your daughter. With lots of visitors, all supportive in different ways. We're all with you, playing our various parts.'

'Ross and I worked solidly on the Barn,' Alex reminded her, 'for two whole days – with help from Frances and Shelley, of course. The heaters are fastened to the beams and they actually work. Even turning 'em all on at full power doesn't blow the fuse. And we've managed to fit in ten tables, each seating six guests. The basic logistics are complete.'

A sudden panic struck his wife. 'But, Alex, what about toilets?

216

There's only a couple out there.'

Her husband sighed. 'What Ross and I have done, dear, is complete within our capabilities. We might both of us be engineers but we're not plumbers. You never mentioned fitting any toilets.'

'There'd be no room for 'em anyway,' added his brother. 'There's only just room for all the tables. The best we could do would be one or two portaloos placed outside, round the side. They'd give you a good view of the coast as you went out there, but they'd be perishing cold.' He was still getting used to Cornish winter weather.

Maxine said, 'They can use the toilets in the guesthouse. There are several in here. It's all going to be very relaxed. The guests will be roaming about here as well as in the Barn.'

'Oh my gosh, the place needs a final clean,' muttered Maria, glancing around. 'How am I going to do that with so much going on and so many guests already here?'

'In my opinion, Maria, the place is fine. They're coming for a wedding, not a Quality Inspection. But we might need one or two extra signs,' observed George. 'I can make some up if you like. Have you got some white card I can print them on?'

There was silence for a few minutes. Then Maria voiced another concern. 'What if there's so much snow and ice the guests can't get here?'

Maxine sighed and checked the latest weather forecast for Land's End on her phone. 'The weather's OK, Mum. There's high pressure over the southwest for the next few days: plenty of sunshine and blue skies. Mind, there'll still be a biting wind. The

217

ones coming by car will be fine. A few are coming by train. Peter's going to sort out a taxi from Penzance to bring them over.'

The forecast reminded her mum of another worry. 'Did you buy that white shawl we saw in Plymouth to go over your wedding dress?'

'I've lived in Cornwall for nearly half my life, Mum. I can cope with a cold wind for a few minutes.'

'By the time I've taken all the photos you asked for it'll be longer than a few,' asserted Kirstie. 'I expect you'll be frozen. The main thing is to make sure you're not so cold that you can't cut the cake.'

She mused for a moment. 'And there are also those pictures you mentioned, between the wedding and the reception, of you and Peter standing together on Cape Cornwall.'

But Maxine wasn't listening. 'Mum, you can wear as many layers as you like. Wear two coats if you want. This is my wedding day and I want to look my best. However cold it makes me.'

Silence reigned for a few minutes. Then Maria voiced another concern.

'Remind me, who did you say are going to be the ushers for the service?'

'A couple of Peter's colleagues are coming down from Bude. They should be here in time for the rehearsal. A couple of guests of mine will help if needed.'

Panic struck again. 'Who'll look after their coats when they all get down here? There's no space in the Barn.'

'We're going to use the cloakroom in the guesthouse. I'll talk to Peter this afternoon, make sure the ushers know that's part of their role.'

There was another moment of tense silence.

'So what jobs have to be done today?' asked George. She could see someone had to take the lead. Maxine was in a dream of her own. Her mother was in a state close to panic.

'There'll be the plants and flowers I ordered in Penzance coming later this morning,' said Maxine. 'I'll take delivery of those, I ordered them. Make sure they've sent the right ones. Maybe Shelley and Frances can take charge of arranging these in the guesthouse and the Barn?'

'I presume you've also got some to decorate the church?' asked Esther. 'Or are they coming separately?'

'Father Giles has a regular flower arranging lady at the church,' said Maria. He said she would sort those, so I'm leaving that to him. We'll give him a contribution for them afterwards.'

'I'm off to the church later to help print out the Service sheets. I'll double check on the flowers. When will the musicians get here?'

'They're coming after lunch,' replied Maxine. 'They asked if they could have a couple of hours on their own to set up their gear, test out the acoustics of the Barn.'

She sensed another ripple of fear. 'Don't worry, Mum, they're not planning to sleep here. They'll be joining Peter and Brian in the Kings Arms.'

There would be many other things to do over the day. Alice would be grappling with the known dietary specialisms, though she hoped there would not be too many, and that new ones wouldn't emerge at the last minute.

Maxine and her bridesmaids needed to spend time checking their dresses and practicing their processions.

Alex was still to finish off preparing his speech for the reception as the father of the bride. He'd already thought he'd finished that twice but Maria had voiced stinging criticisms. This time he did not intend to give her another chance.

And Esther reminded them, as breakfast concluded and they started to move away, 'Don't forget, you're all needed for the rehearsal in the church. That's this evening at half past six.'

CHAPTER 31

Meanwhile, in St Just, Peter Travers and Brian Southgate were making the most of another Kings Arms breakfast.

'You won't have many more of these, Peter, once Maxine takes charge.'

The policeman smiled. 'I'm not worried. There'll be compensations.'

Robbie Glendenning had already left for St Ives, possibly not wanting to risk further deconstruction of his emotional tangles. That left the two as the only ones in the dining room.

'Anyway, Peter, what do we need to do today?'

'My speech is more or less written, Brian. I might add one or two lines based on observations of life in the guesthouse.'

Brian laughed. 'Just be careful. I once went to a wedding where the bridegroom started his speech by thanking the parents of the bride for the wonderful reception. Then he added, wasn't it wonderful what you could get with Green Shield stamps these days.'

Peter smiled. 'I'm not that brave. I can see it's a huge strain for Maria, I don't want to make it worse.'

'Is that why you've taken such an interest in the death at Ding Dong? That's at least kept most of us away from the guesthouse.'

'Huh. That's not exactly worked, Brian, has it? Between us,

we've shown that the death was certainly murder, but made no progress on the name, or the motive of the killer. Not even persuaded the local police to take an interest.'

'Yes. I'd hoped the post mortem would be decisive. A blow to the head, say, that wasn't due to him hitting the ground. If it could be shown that it was murder, the lads in Penzance would need to get off their backsides and do something. But on what they know, the inquest can just be "death by misadventure". With no doubt dire warnings on the dangers of exploring old mine shafts on one's own.' He sighed. 'But to be fair, Peter, what could they do? What would you have done if it had been your case?'

Peter mused for a moment. 'It seems to me, given the back-of-beyond location, that it has to be someone local to Land's End who got to know exactly what Hocking was trying to do. It could hardly be a casual encounter at the mine, not at this time of year, anyway. They must have met somewhere else. And that wasn't in Hocking's home in Penzance.'

'So how would you take that forward?'

'For a start, I'd go into all the local pubs and teashops with a picture of the dead man, asking if they knew him. And if so I'd ask, was he ever seen with anyone?'

The policeman gave a sigh. 'As it is, I don't even have the bloke's photograph. In any case that'd take a team of professionals. Even with so many places round here shut for the winter it'd take some time. And right now, time is the one thing I don't have.'

Half an hour later the pair set out. Peter had various tasks to complete, mostly relating to vehicles.

First they drove separately to the hotel which would be the starting point of the honeymoon and left Peter's car there. Then Brian took over. He wanted to stay close on hand today in case his friend had any last-minute wobbles. Not that that seemed remotely likely.

As they drove on the policeman was still musing over the case.

'Even on what we've found, Brian, it's not straightforward. I mean, if we'd found nothing of interest at the bottom of the shaft, you'd think the killer had simply pushed him down then walked off with the rope ladder. But why bother to take away the ladder, it's not that light? And how does that tie in with the sensor?'

'Could Hocking have hidden it down there . . . say, on a previous occasion?'

'Why on earth would he do that? The sensor's not heavy. If Kirstie could climb back up the shaft with it in her rucksack then so could he. He might be older than us but he'd be more used to the weight.'

'But if it wasn't Hocking that hid it, it must be the murderer. Hey, he might have left his fingerprints – assuming he wasn't wearing gloves.'

'In that case, he must have pushed Hocking down first then climbed down after him.'

'Maybe he wanted to be certain that he was dead?'

There was silence. The jigsaw pieces they had could be made to fit but only with effort. Peter was coming to realise that he really hadn't got that far at all.

'Do you want to drop into the police station while we're here?'

'Don't think so. I haven't really got much more to say. My first task is to chat to one of the taxi drivers at the station. There's parking outside, I think.'

There were not many taxis waiting. Peter approached the driver at the front of the queue, who was in his early fifties and looked fairly dependable. He smiled optimistically as Peter approached.

'Hi. Sorry, I'm not after a lift today. I wanted to check, though, that you or one of you colleagues will be here tomorrow morning.'

'Don't see why not. New Year's Day might be a problem after a long night but tomorrow should be fine. So you want a lift in the morning then?'

'Not then either. The thing is, I'm getting married. One o'clock, over in St Just. Some of my friends who are coming should arrive on the train around eleven thirty. I wanted to make sure there'd be a way for them to get to St Just. The buses don't seem to go far this week.'

'Congratulations, mate. Tell you what, why don't you give me the fare now. I'll make sure I'm here in person and give them a guided tour of the peninsula as we go. I can even take them round by Land's End itself if you like.'

'That'd be great. Could I also book you in the evening. I'd like you to collect me and my bride from the reception in St Just and bring us back to the Gurnard Hotel, near Zennor.'

The cab driver got out his notebook. 'What time?'

'Around ten pm. The reception's in a barn on the road down to Cape Cornwall. You'll know where it is from the noise.'

'Fine. That'll be twenty five quid for the lot.' Notes were handed over and the deed was done.

'So what else d'you need, Peter?'

'One of the things Maxine has got lined up for us this afternoon is blowing up a couple of hundred balloons.'

'Right.' The doctor sounded dubious. He didn't smoke but he wasn't as fit as all that.

'What we need is a pump to help us along. I reckon the best place would be a bike shop. I'm sure there'll be at least one in the town.'

They set out towards the high street. There they quickly found a coffee shop, where they successfully quizzed the hostess for a bike shop location as they bought themselves mugs of coffee.

Fifteen minutes later, after a minor disagreement outside a barber's shop when Peter refused point blank to have a haircut, they reached the bike shop.

It turned out that it hired bikes as well as selling them. They had a huge range, from a tandem to a folding bike with small wheels that you could take onto a train.

'Hey, you could take Maxine away on the tandem,' suggested Brian.

'That'd be fine if we were marrying in Holland in spring time. I'm not so sure about it on the ups and downs of Cornwall at New Year.'

Eventually they bought a pair of pumps that the owner assured them would work fine on balloons and headed back to the car.

'We'd better get back,' said Peter. 'My folk group is coming down this afternoon. I need to run over their programme of songs and dance for the party after the reception. And make sure it includes Waltzing Matilda.'

CHAPTER 32

Robbie Glendenning reached St Ives by nine fifteen. But although the traffic was light there was no leisurely start for him today. Siobhan had long had her breakfast, had taken her second mug of coffee upstairs. He found her in her room, working on the papers and diaries for Brandy Mine which they'd been lent the day before.

'Hi, Robbie. Some of this stuff is dynamite,' she greeted him, glancing over her shoulder, not even getting up from the desk in her excitement.

'You mean, as used to blast out the mine?' he hazarded.

'No. I mean red hot. Take a look at this diary, written in 1937.'

The journalist took the diary off her desk. The handwriting covered many pages, it would take him a while to read. He wandered over to the easy chair and made himself comfortable.

The orange front cover showed that it was in an old school exercise book from Zennor School, written by one Josh Harvey.

The early pages, though neatly written, were fairly pedestrian. Josh was a new recruit, lived in Zennor, and had not long left school. At the start of the diary he was relieved that he actually had a full-time job. As in the rest of the UK there was plenty of unemployment in Cornwall in the 1930s.

In those days, Robbie inferred, most training happened on the job. For the first month Josh was assigned as an apprentice to an old hand, Bill, who taught him the rudiments of extracting tin ore. He read on.

"I was glad there was a mechanised way of getting up and down the shaft. It used a series of ladders, one below another, which moved repeatedly up and down. The motion was driven by a massive steam engine at the shaft head. We had to step on and off the ladders to go up or down as the top wheel rotated.

Bill was unenthusiastic. He'd seen a similar arrangement fail catastrophically at Levant Mine, just down the road, in 1919. By God's mercy he'd not been at the work that day, been smitten down by flu. Over thirty miners had been killed and many more injured.

It was sobering flashback but I still took the ladders. 1919 seemed a long time ago. It was better than toiling down the old static ladders for half an hour before the shift had started and another stint, climbing back up, after it had finished.

Brandy Mine was right on the edge of the cliffs, not far from Gurnard's Head. I had to walk down to it each day from the Tinners Path, an ancient inland footpath once used for burials.

I'd started work in July. On sunny days the view over to the coast was dramatic. But there were many days when sea fog made me take care. Once you'd finally reached the mine there was a spectacular view down nearly four hundred feet of cliff, to the pounding waves in the narrow zawn below.

Robbie skim read the opening pages. It was interesting stuff, would help Siobhan produce her social history of the mines, but he couldn't see why she'd said it was "dynamite".

He didn't want to appear stupid. In desperation he flipped towards the latter pages and started to read from there.

Josh had dated his entries. This was now four months further on. There was no further mention of Bill, presumably the youngster was now deemed to be fully trained. His daily routine, though, stayed much the same. Then, towards the end of the notebook, something new happened. He read on.

The main shaft had been dug deeper. A new tunnel was to be opened up leading out of it. I was one of those chosen to dig this new section. Youth and fitness counted for more these days than experience.

Soon the day came. The gyrating system of ladders didn't reach the new section of shaft so we had to climb down the final hundred feet. It was terribly warm at that depth.

The shift foreman had been given instructions on which way the tunnel was to go and chalked out a low archway on one side. In the near darkness I hoped it wasn't planned to head out underneath the sea. I'd heard tales from men at Geevor about the hazards of working beneath the waves.

Soon the leading pair started to attack the archway with their hammers and chisels while the rest of us took turns to move the spoil away. We were all sweating buckets. Twenty minutes later it was my turn to take the lead.

That was the pattern for eight long hours. No-one mentioned a break for lunch. By the end of the shift the tunnel was almost six foot long and I was shattered.

Robbie continued to read. The diary recorded that the work persisted in a similar fashion for many days.

Josh was young and fit and could cope with the workload. It was satisfying to see the tunnel growing longer and longer. Perhaps more capacity might increase the mine's life.

But there was a downside.

The tunnel was not only getting longer, it was getting hotter. Before long we were stripping to the waist before we started work. It got worse: after a month we all spent the entire shift in just our underpants.

Still the temperature rose. The heat sapped our energy. The foreman had to make the shifts shorter: he could see it was either that or else his men being too exhausted to climb back up at the end of the day.

A careful review of the entry dates told Robbie that the mine did not operate on a Sunday – or at least, if it did, Josh never spent time there. He couldn't tell what the young miner did on his days off; but whatever it was it didn't make the diary.

Finally came the entry for Monday, November 10th 1937.

We went down the shaft as usual. Even before we started on the last stage of descent the mine temperature seemed notably higher. And as we climbed down the final section, started stripping off, we were sweating like pigs.

As usual the foreman led us down the tunnel. But now the heat was intense. It was three hundred yards long by this stage but he couldn't even get to the end. The temperature must have built up over the weekend, it was sweltering.

"Let's go back, lads," he instructed. Of course we obeyed, be daft not to. But as I turned around I glanced back at the end of the tunnel. I might have been hallucinating, you'll have to judge. It might have been a foretaste of hell. But to me the end of the passage was glowing red.

Robbie hastily turned over the page of the exercise, wondering what on earth would happen next. But he couldn't tell. For the diary entries finished at that point. For some reason or other Josh had nothing more to tell him.

CHAPTER 33

Forty minutes later, Robbie and Siobhan were on their way to the coast where Brandy Mine had once operated, near the cafe at Carn Galver.

Siobhan filled in some of the journalist's questions as he drove. She'd come across Josh's diary the evening before, which had given her longer to ponder the information. Since then she'd managed to do a lot more background reading.

'I ploughed through all the monthly Output Reports for Brandy Mine, Robbie. Both on tons brought out and the tin ore they obtained. The place was going down and down for year after year. By 1937, it was blindingly obvious, the mine was making a loss. Putting it bluntly, the extra tunnel that Josh and his mates had been asked to develop was management's last throw of the dice.

'If it had boosted production, say found some rich new lode of tin, the mine might have carried on. When the new tunnel turned out to be unbearably hot and unworkable, the mine had to close.'

Robbie gave a sigh of relief. 'So you mean, nothing happened to Josh? He wasn't gassed or anything from the hot rocks they'd exposed in the tunnel? He didn't go down one more day and get killed by an explosion?'

'Not as far as I know. It was just that his job stopped abruptly.

The poor chap had nothing else to write about. Probably he was too upset to write anymore. He could have been too busy, looking for another job.'

The planned trip to Carn Galver, to tell the owners what they'd found and see if they could remember any more, wasn't just prompted by Josh's diary. For as they came out of the guesthouse, Robbie had remembered an aside from the editor of the Gazette: its weekly edition was published on Fridays. They'd passed a newsagent on the way out of St Ives and Siobhan had bought a copy. Of course, last week's death at Ding Dong was the front-page news.

The newspaper article didn't tell them anything new. It implied the death had been a dreadful accident. The police were praised for finding and recovering the body so quickly. But the article was accompanied by a photograph of the dead man. It must have been provided by his wife, it showed a middle-aged white man with short, greying hair and a barely-hidden air of anxiety. As Robbie observed, they now had something specific that they could discuss with the cafe owners whilst they were there.

Before they went to the teashop, Robbie wanted to investigate what was left of Brandy Mine. Siobhan had brought the large scale plan from the record box with her. Armed with that, they parked the car beside a sign pointing down to the Coast Path, donned their walking gear and set off towards the coast.

The map might be large scale but it was only black and white and had no contours. They would have had little chance of finding anything but for the mention in Josh's diary of the

233

narrow zawn, cutting into the cliffs just below the mine. Once they'd stumbled onto a view of that they knew they were close.

A few minutes later they came across a large collection of stones and slate, almost hidden beneath a tangle of bushes. 'I reckon, Robbie, this is all that's left of what was once Brandy Mine.'

Robbie thought about Hocking's quest for temperature data: had he been here?

'Would anyone have a chance of going down the mine today?'

'Can you see the top of the shaft?'

They spent the best part of an hour exploring the area around the ruin, doing their best to find the shaft. But either it was hidden under the rubble and totally inaccessible or else it had been so thoroughly blocked off that it was now gone forever.

'Maybe the army exercise finished it off, Robbie? Say, if some of the explosives went down the shaft and caused it to collapse.'

Whatever the reason, they could see no way that Hocking could have taken an underground temperature reading here.

Robbie took several pictures for future reference. Then they walked back to the car. 'I reckon, you know, we've earned ourselves a coffee.'

At half past eleven the Carn Galver Lunch Box was open for business, even had one or two customers. But by the time Siobhan and Robbie had ordered their coffees the other visitors had moved on and the place was once more as quiet as a grave.

'Can't keep you guys away,' observed John with a smile as he brought them their drinks. 'Have you had any time to look at our old records yet?'

'We found one diary that's very interesting,' said Siobhan. 'Written by someone that was working there when the mine closed. We'd love to discuss it.'

'Let me fetch Sally. She'd be the best person to talk to.'

A few minutes later Sally appeared, still encased in her apron. Robbie wondered if she ever stopped making scones. But now he had more important questions to ask.

Siobhan outlined the contents of Josh's diary. She went on, 'I've checked the dates against other mine records. It seemed that this low-level tunnel, where he reported an extremely high temperature, was the last thing he observed. The mine was closed the next day. And never opened again.'

'I started reading with the oldest diaries, never got as far as Josh's,' admitted Sally. 'But what you've just said confirms what my grandparents said were the rumours of the time. The allegation was that the mine had been dug too deep. It had got down as far as a spike of hot rocks. They're known to be lying below the granite in this part of Cornwall. But no-one could operate in those kinds of temperatures. It was the final straw.'

'Have other mines round here had similar problems?' asked Siobhan.

'I believe that Wheal Jane, over near Camborne, had one passage where the men worked stripped to their underpants. In the end they had to abandon it because of the intense heat,' said John. 'But in Wheal Jane they'd other parts they could move to so it wasn't so catastrophic. Mind you, even that mine had to close eventually.'

235

'What I don't understand,' said Robbie, 'is why finding hot rocks was taken as such a calamity. Shouldn't it have been an encouragement for the owners to change tack and start to search for geothermal energy?'

'Ah,' said John. 'That's a good question. I guess that in the 1930s few in Britain had heard of geothermal energy. The drills hadn't been invented that could reach through Cornish granite; and geology hadn't advanced that far. Tin and copper were pretty well all the mine owners of the day cared about.'

'But what about now? Isn't geothermal energy seen as the new renewable?'

John looked cautious. 'I suppose it might be. But I wouldn't want anyone drilling for it around here. Especially right on the coast.'

Robbie left the teashop owner's response unchallenged. He noted, though, that geothermal was not a universally welcomed energy source in this part of Cornwall.

'Can I ask you something else?'

John nodded.

Robbie unfurled the front page of the Land's End Gazette which they'd bought in St Ives earlier that morning.

'It occurred to me that this chap might have been taking an interest in mine shafts out of a passion for geothermal energy.'

John looked more closely at the picture of the dead man. 'He might have been,' he mused.

His wife seized the newspaper from him and looked at it carefully. 'You're right, John. He's dropped in a few times over the last month. Nearly always on his own. He never said much

236

but he was polite enough.'

'When did you last see him?' asked Siobhan.

'It was one day last week.' She frowned. 'Wednesday, I think.'

'Was he on his own?'

'No, this time he had someone else with him. They came in late morning, didn't stay long.'

'Did you happen to recognise who he was with?'

'Not one of our regular customers. I might recognise him if I saw him again. Why, d'you think it might be important?'

CHAPTER 34

'Where d'you fancy for lunch?' asked Siobhan as they walked out of the Carn Galver cafe and sat back in Robbie's car.

'We might as well go back to St Ives.' Robbie paused for a moment. 'Would you mind ringing Sammy? See if we can have lunch with him.'

Siobhan made the call. Now his latest edition was on the streets Sammy was in a relaxed mood and the meeting was arranged. 'Half past twelve, same pub as last time.'

As she put down her phone her face wrinkled. 'But why do we need to see him?'

Robbie got started on the journey before he answered. 'Sammy's been rooted into the Land's End grapevine for half a century. He knows I'm a fellow journalist and he trusts me so that'll be the fastest way to find new contacts. Besides, we need to challenge him about today's front page. It's way too complacent.'

Siobhan did not argue. She was starting to see that a journalist had a very different way of collecting information, compared to a research historian. More informal, anyway; often more challenging. It would be best to wait and see how well it worked before passing judgement.

Half an hour later they'd parked outside Siobhan's guesthouse in St Ives and were walking down to the Black Swan. As Siobhan had anticipated, Sammy was already in position, facing out onto the street from his favourite upstairs table. That didn't stop him letting Robbie buy him another pint of bitter along with a pint for himself.

Siobhan opted for bitter lemon, knowing that a stone cold sober car driver might well be needed after lunch. They each selected a toasted cheese sandwich to give them some sustenance then settled to exchange notes.

'We went to that old photography shop,' Siobhan began. 'In the end we got them to show us a film of an army exercise that was taken during the war. It led to a mine being pulverised.'

Robbie took over. 'And we found the name of the mine that was blown up. Brandy Mine. It's on the coast, near Carn Galver.'

'We can tell you why it closed as well,' added Siobhan. 'They dug so deep that a passage came close to some hot dry rocks. The teashop lady lent us a box of old documents, including a miner's diary. By the time the mine closed, he said, they were working practically naked.'

Sammy took a swig of his beer. 'Impressive,' he commented, 'just starting from the film. I doubt my lads could do as well.' There was a pause. 'Trouble is, I'm a newspaper editor, I live or die by the latest headlines. You can hardly class a wartime bombardment as news.'

'Talking of news,' said Robbie, 'we noticed your leading article this morning about the death at Ding Dong. Am I right in guessing that your source is someone in the police force?'

'We never reveal our sources.' The editor looked puzzled. 'But how did you guess?'

'It seemed to me extremely complacent . . . almost self con-gratulatory. Written to put the police in the best possible light. And it's by no means certain, you know, that it was just a nasty accident.'

Sammy frowned. 'Why ever not?'

'Well, if the bloke had just fallen down the shaft, what hap-pened to his rope ladder?'

Sammy shrugged. 'Dunno. Maybe it's still down the shaft. Or else the police took it away with them.'

Robbie took a sip of his beer as he arranged his arguments. 'I told you, didn't I, that I came down for a wedding? Well, one of the wedding party that's already down here is a vicar. She's come to take the wedding. She went to see Father Giles in St Just to talk over the details of the service.'

'Oh yes, I know Sid. Good man. He and I go back a long way.'

'Well, during their conversation, Sammy, it emerged that Sid was one of the coastguards who had brought the body to the surface. He didn't mention any sight of a rope ladder, either at the top or the bottom. Hey, if you know him, why don't you ask him yourself?'

'Maybe I will,' Sammy replied.

'And if there was no rope ladder, what on earth was a mature man doing, clambering about over the top of a mine shaft?'

'Perhaps he slipped?'

'But how on earth did that happen? Wouldn't it be worth asking the police if there were any signs that he was drunk or anything?'

Their sandwiches arrived at that moment, giving a moment for reflection. The waiter brought the cutlery and condiments were secured.

After munching a mouthful, Sammy was the first to speak. 'Robbie, for some reason I sense you're not telling me everything that you know.'

'Well to be honest I'm not, Sammy. But I am suggesting where you might start looking. After all, your team have got nearly a week to dig around before anything more needs to be published.'

'And somehow or other, you think this is connected to Brandy Mine?'

Robbie paused. He hadn't intended to join the topics so directly.

'I'm not sure about that. The hot rocks might be a link. The underlying question that Siobhan and I have been grappling with is, whatever was the dead man hoping to achieve in a long-forgotten mine like Ding Dong? What brought him there in the first place?'

'Mm. That's a good question. I'll add that to my list to ask the police in Penzance. What's your best guess?'

Siobhan could see Robbie had just taken another mouthful of toasted sandwich and responded on his behalf. 'We think it might be having something to do with geothermal energy.'

'Aha. That's one topic whose time might be drawing near.'

'Oh yes. Is it something your paper has intelligence on?'

'We haven't had much activity on the subject here on the peninsula. As far as we know. But there's been a lot of discussion over in Falmouth.'

241

'You mean, picking up from the geothermal plant that was run there in the 1970s?'

'Hey, that's right. Rosemanowas Quarry. It's closed now of course, but it ran for years.'

Robbie had finished his sandwich and was ready to pick up the baton.

'Sammy, have you got any contacts there that we could talk to? We're in a bit of a hurry, you see. The wedding is tomorrow; after that we'll both be busy on other topics.'

Siobhan furrowed her brow and added her Irish lilt. 'We're starting from a long way back, Sammy. If it'd make it easier for you to help us, we can surely agree to pass on anything we find.'

Sammy stopped eating, wracked his brain. Siobhan thought he was deciding whether to help them at all but it was more specific than that. Then his face cleared.

'There's Kevin Trezise. He used to work here in St Ives. I taught him everything I knew about running a local newspaper. He was my protégé. To be honest, I hoped that one day he'd take my place.'

Sammy paused to take another swig of beer then continued. 'But the lad was too impatient. Saw an opening in Falmouth and moved away. He's currently deputy editor of the Falmouth Echo. He's got sharp elbows and he's nosey enough. He'd know about anything that was going on. If you like I can give him a ring and ease your way to see him.'

CHAPTER 35

It took the combined skills of Robbie and Siobhan to wriggle away from Sammy without having to buy another round (or two) of drinks.

'If necessary Kevin will wait in the Falmouth Anchor all afternoon,' the editor claimed. 'He's always regarded Friday afternoons as wind down time. Take your time, you won't miss him.'

Robbie, though, wanted to be sure he would be cross examining a source who was sober. Siobhan caught his eye and stood up. 'We'll be out of parking in ten minutes, Sammy. Sorry, but we'll have to go.' Both had stood and were walking away before Sammy had dreamed up a riposte.

'You're right, Siobhan,' said Robbie as they walked down the stairs. 'Our time on this case is very short. If we're lucky Kevin might put us on to someone else that we can see this afternoon.'

This time they took Siobhan's car. The historian drove as fast as she could within the various speed limits. It was just after half past two when they reached Falmouth and found a space in the crowded car park behind the Anchor. Given that it was the last lunchtime of the working week, with New Year's Eve and its festivities ahead, the pub was fairly crowded.

'Our next challenge is to pick out Kevin,' observed Siobhan, glancing round a sea of grizzled men.

But as Robbie had suspected, Kevin was on the lookout for them; and as a pair they were an obvious target.

A well-built, suited man in his forties rose from a table near the window and approached them. 'Are you Robbie and Siobhan? Pleased to meet you. I'm Kevin.'

Robbie fought his way to the bar to buy drinks while Siobhan followed the Falmouth journalist to one of the quieter tables in the far corner.

'Sammy spoke very warmly of you both. Said you were onto something important. How can I help?'

Robbie had hoped for an uncontentious start, citing his newspaper remit to look into the future of Cornish mining, but it was clear Sammy must have passed on other parts of their discussion as well. Not what he wanted but it couldn't be helped. He gave a sigh and began to explain.

'I'm currently based in St Just, down here for a wedding. But there was a suspicious death last week, a body was found down an old mine shaft. Siobhan and I have got drawn into trying to make sense of it.'

'Yeah. It was the Gazette's lead story this morning. I saw it.' He frowned. 'Seemed straightforward enough.'

'It was at first sight. But we've been trying to make sense of what the poor chap was doing at the mine in the first place. One idea with legs is that he had an interest in geothermal energy.'

'And perhaps someone else hadn't? I suppose the idea is quite controversial. Someone might want to stop it. It all depends on whether you think Cornwall's future lies in new industry or in more tourism.'

'We learned from the County Museum in Truro that there used to be an energy plant somewhere near here that ran in the 1970s,' explained Siobhan. 'I'm a historian, looking for records and diaries. Have you any idea where we might find anything like that written about it?'

'I can tell you the basics. The place was called Rosemanowas. It was built in an abandoned granite quarry, just off the road from Penryn to Helston. It was an experimental project, run from Penryn. I guess it was prompted by the massive oil price rise in the 1970s.'

'But if it worked, why on earth was it closed? Oil prices have never gone right back down. Surely that energy would still be needed?'

'If you really want to know the detail you'd need to talk to staff at the University. The short answer to your question is that the plant produced plenty of hot water but they could never get it hot enough to power a turbine and convert the heat into electrical energy.'

Kevin stopped talking. Siobhan saw that he'd finished his drink. 'D'you want another?' she asked. Kevin nodded.

Robbie could see that the bar was even busier now. It would be a tussle to reach it, but it would have to be Siobhan that went. He'd have the better chance of making headway with a fellow journalist.

As his friend fought her way towards the bar, her red hair weaving though the crowd, Kevin nodded after her. 'You've got a

245

good woman there, Robbie. Been going out long?'

'We first knew each other years ago. Then we lost touch and now we've reunited. It's a bit complicated.' He stopped speaking, didn't want to spend time on this with the tenacious editor.

'Sammy said you were taking an interest in all sorts of mining ideas, Kevin. Or at least the latest ones.'

'Sammy's a good old-fashioned journalist who got me started. He's kept the Gazette afloat for decades but we can't stand still. I'm interested in anything new that might impact on Cornwall.'

Robbie frowned. 'So what does that mean in terms of mining?'

'The hope is that Cornwall, with its granite backbone, is so rich in mineral resources that you can find anything if you look hard enough. There were lots of minerals dug out while they were chasing after tin and copper. Arsenic, for example, and wolfram. Lead and silver.' He grimaced. 'But they're probably not there in big enough quantities to be worth chasing on their own. Not from the old mines, anyway.'

'But there must be new elements that spark interest, ones that no-one cared about, or even knew about, two hundred years ago?'

'Well, there are traces of radium and uranium in Cornwall, Robbie. There's also lithium.'

Robbie pulled out his notebook. 'D'you mind if I write this all down, Kevin? You've obviously spent a long time studying it.'

He scrawled for a moment or two and then looked up. 'Right. I can understand the radioactive ones. But why should lithium be so valuable?'

'Oh that's easy, Robbie. With all this effort going into electric and self-drive cars, there's bound to be a huge explosion in demand for rechargeable batteries. Right now most of these batteries are made using lithium. Its price has quadrupled in the last two years and might go up a lot further. There's also an argument that, if it is so special, Britain needs to make sure it has its own supply.'

Kevin broke off as he saw Siobhan returning with a tray of drinks. She smiled as he unloaded the tray and shoved it against the wall. Then seized his pint like a man who'd been battling through the desert.

'When I left, Kevin, you were telling us about the geothermal plant,' she said. 'Is there any chance you could arrange for us to meet one of the experts at Penryn University? They might have a better handle on the project records.'

CHAPTER 36

By good fortune one of the geothermal experts at Penryn University that Kevin had come across before, Professor Dillon, was still at work that afternoon. After his introductory phone call, Robbie and Siobhan had been given directions for finding her office. They tracked her down in a laboratory annexe, just a couple of miles from the Anchor.

'I usually come in this week to get my paperwork up to date,' she began. 'But I'm more or less clear of that now. So you two are interested in our pilot geothermal plant at Rosemanowas?'

Professor Jennie Dillon was no older than her interviewers. Introductions were made and a brief explanation offered of the reason for their interest.

'So this plant was the first geothermal site in Cornwall?' asked Robbie. 'I've got a remit to look into future mining prospects. I'd like to know what they were trying to do, how far they got, where it went wrong and how it might be done better in the future.'

Like all academics, the professor was delighted to find anyone interested in her pet subject, especially ones no longer in their first flush of youth. She also welcomed the fact that both had produced notebooks to take down anticipated words of wisdom.

'I can see you're serious,' she said. 'Let's go down to the old project room for Rosemanowas. There's lots of diagrams and models still in there. They'd make more sense than listening to me.'

Robbie and Siobhan followed the professor down several flights of stairs and finally reached the basement. She unlocked a door and led them inside.

The room was cold. The office central heating didn't reach down this far. The most striking thing on display was a huge three-dimensional model of the pilot plant, inside a large glass case. The site itself, a series of simple buildings, was on the top layer. Below a pair of vertical pipes, a distance apart, dropped down to a jumble of rocks laid out on the floor.

Jennie tapped on the case. 'This was assembled during the design phase. It shows what the developers hoped would happen. Let me talk you through this and then we can go back upstairs to talk about things that went wrong.

'The core idea of geothermal energy is there are very hot rocks not so far below the earth's crust. If we can find places where they're fairly near the surface and then drill a pair of pipes down to them, the hope is that we can pump cold water down one and then recover hot, or even superhot, fluid out of the other.'

'How far down might you need to go?' asked Robbie.

'If you could drill down far enough then you'd be bound to find hot rocks, I mean, that's what makes up the core of the planet. But there's a limit on how far you can drill. At the moment the deepest hole in the world goes down about fourteen thousand metres. But it takes much longer to drill, gets exponentially more expensive, the deeper you go. I believe that one was drilled out over a decade.'

'How on earth can you drill that far?' asked Siobhan.

'It's very clever technology. But you need that when drilling for oil so it's quite advanced. Basically you work with sections of drill each about ten metres long than can be screwed together. Every ten metres you have to stop drilling and add on another length. Even if you're only drilling down a couple of kilometres it'll take a long time – weeks or months.'

Jennie pointed inside the glass case and they could see piles of tiny model pipes, stacked up outside one of the plant huts.

'You wouldn't want to spend all that money drilling and then find you were in the wrong place,' observed Robbie. 'That's why the location is so important.'

'Yes. The trouble is you can never be certain. Geology's never that precise. How far down do you need to go? And how fractured are the rocks between the pipes you're putting down? After all, it can only work if the water is able to pass from one to the other.'

'Is that what went wrong at Rosemanowas?' asked Siobhan.

Jennie turned to her and nodded. 'It took a long time to sink each of the pipes and to force water down one of them. Then it took even longer before they could recover any hot water from the other.'

'But they got some hot water eventually?' asked Robbie.

'Trouble was, though it was warm it wasn't that hot. Not superheated enough to drive a steam generator, anyway. They tried and tried, all sorts of variations, but they could never produce electricity from what they got out. In the end they got plenty of hot water, which they piped down to the nearest village

250

as communal heating so it wasn't entirely wasted. But sadly, they never got any power.'

There was silence for a moment as this reality was absorbed.

'But Jennie, they'd need some power to extract the water in the first place. So, you mean, it was a net sink of energy?'

Jennie sighed. 'That's right. Not easy to admit but the place was too expensive to run.'

'And what lesson did the team learn from that?'

Jennie sighed again. 'Views differed, to put it mildly. Some of the team thought that if we'd managed to drill down further in the first place then the rocks we'd accessed would have been a lot hotter. Others thought we'd just been unlucky in the way the rocks fractured between the two pipes: there just happened to be no easy route from one to the other.'

Jennie picked up a large cardboard box. 'These are records of the various arguments. Let's go upstairs, back to the warmth. Then I can go into as much detail as you want.'

Ten minutes later they were seated in Jennie's office with mugs of coffee, starting to warm up.

'Looking back, what's your opinion?' asked Siobhan. 'If geothermal is ever to be routine in Cornwall, what else needs to be done?'

'It's still a matter of debate,' the professor replied. 'We had our biannual geothermal conference here last week. It's pretty well advertised. There were experts from all over the world, but still there was no consensus.'

There was a pause for a moment.

'Can I ask a different question?' asked Robbie. 'Is it true that the plant was never stopped by a major accident? Nothing, say, like the collapse of the man-riding ladder at Levant?'

'That's an interesting point. There was one operational incident in 1980 that caused some disruption. Let me try and explain.'

The professor paused to recall the key facts.

'By this stage the plant had run for several years. Operational control was in the hands of a few relatively junior engineers, two in the daytime and one at night. Their main task was to adjust the input flow so as to maximise energy output.'

'You mean, vary the pressure and the flow rate?'

'Also the direction it was pumped out at the bottom. By this stage there were various levers you could juggle.'

'Whereas energy output would combine the temperature and flowrate of the energy recovered?'

'That's right. These days we'd have some sort of automated control using Artificial Intelligence, but back then that was in its infancy.'

Jennie glanced to check that she was being understood.

'The other thing you need to understand,' she said, 'is that the fluid that came out from the deep wasn't pure, it contained all sorts of impurities. To make sure the water that left the site was safe, a heat exchanger was installed. The recovered flow transferred heat to clean water, ready to be pumped away. Meanwhile the recovered flow, still warm, was pumped back down to the rocks far below.'

'It sounds quite complicated,' said Robbie.

'What made this more difficult to manage,' said Jennie, 'was that there was a lag of hours between any deliberate change to the input and the effect it had on the output. The water had to go down two thousand metres, across fractured rocks and then back up the other side. But worst of all, the situation two thousand metres down wasn't steady. There would be variation in the temperatures of the rocks themselves.'

'So only a junior engineer was on duty when something happened?'

'That's right. Just the one, as it was the night shift. Looking back you can see that the rock temperature at the foot of the pipe started rising. Of course, the operator couldn't see that at the time, had no warning anything was amiss. So the output temperature started to rise too. Then, as that flow went back down again, the temperature rose further and the whole situation got worse and worse.'

'You mean, the designers hadn't allowed for a rapid temperature rise in the rocks below?'

'By today's standards control at the plant was rudimentary. Glorified trial and error. The risk of adverse feedback loops hadn't been thought through. And what made it worse was that the night operators would always go for their tea break at three in the morning, which by sheer bad luck was just after the massive heat-rise began.'

'So the poor bloke came back half an hour later . . .'

'And found the temperature was approaching 100° C. But no-one had ever reported seeing that sort of temperature before, so the operator assumed the meter was faulty and ignored it.'

'You mean, the temperature went on rising and he took no notice at all.'

'For several hours. Until the first of the morning shift arrived. One of the first tasks was always to check the pressure inside the heat exchanger. That had come to mean loosening a valve and making sure there was no steam in the system.'

'Crumbs. So he got the whole impact?'

'He did. He was scalded down the entire front of his body. He was in agony. One of the operators shoved him in his car and drove him to Truro Hospital, where he was rushed into intensive care. He pulled through in the end but it was a close thing. Almost brought the plant to final closure.'

'So was there a massive inquiry?' asked Siobhan.

'There was. It took months. But of course it wasn't easy to assign blame. Lots of things had combined to make it happen. The core problem, a sudden rise in rock temperature, was unprecedented. How you might design a control system to respond well to such events was the subject of several future PhD's here at Penryn.'

'What about the tea break?'

'Having just a single operator on duty at night was found to be illegal. You couldn't expect one person to go through the whole night without a break so nothing was said about the tea break itself.'

'What happened in the end?'

'The plant was closed for six months and then brought back into service with better control. Multiple independent systems were put in at all the key points. Less skilled staff members were laid off and the new ones were better qualified and given much better training.'

There was a pause. The professor had reached the end of her narrative. 'It was, after all, a pilot plant. It was intended to allow designers and operators to make their mistakes. And to be fair, this was the only time that the plant was stopped for any length of time. In itself that incident wasn't enough to stop geothermal energy for good.'

Robbie glanced at his watch. It was nearly six o'clock. No wonder it was dark outside.

'Jennie, you've been very generous with your time. Thank you so much.'

'Thank you both for coming. I've enjoyed sharing.'

'By the way, that geothermal conference you mentioned earlier. Is it possible to have a list of the delegates? I might try and get in touch with some of them.'

Professor Dillon went to her desk. 'Here you are. It's a spare delegate list and a list of titles and speakers. You could borrow my incident report too if you wanted. I haven't looked at it for twenty years.'

CHAPTER 37

Although Esther had set the time for the rehearsal as six thirty, most of the key participants were there early.

It had long been dark in St Just but the church was well lit. Esther noted, though, that no-one had thought to switch on any heating. It was a good job they were all wearing thick coats.

Father Giles came in from the vicarage and stood at the back as Esther started to pull the group together. Strictly speaking he wasn't needed, but he wanted to meet the participants.

Another newcomer appeared. This turned out to be the organist, Oliver, a wiry man in his late thirties. He seemed cheerful enough. 'I know I'm only playing the opening and closing items, Esther, but those are the bits you'll want music to process with.' He crossed to the organ console and switched on. A low hum showed that something was happening.

Esther moved to the front of the church and stood on the first altar step. She didn't have a microphone but the low roof made for good acoustics.

'Good evening everyone. One aim of the next hour is for everyone to have chance to meet one another. Some of you only got here this afternoon, some of us lucky ones have been here for days. Tonight is mainly a positioning rehearsal and I want us to go through the key movements.

'First I want to tackle the opening bridal procession. Those of you not in that – yes, that is you Peter – can sit down for a few minutes, please.'

Most of those present spread themselves on either side of the main aisle. Maxine, George, Shelley, Frances and Katrina – Peter Travers' niece – gathered at the south door. After a shove from his wife, Alex joined them.

'Right, girls. Now, d'you know who's going to come in first?'

Maxine was confident now. This was her event and she wasn't going to be overshadowed. 'We've decided to come in Australian style. All the bridesmaids first, then Dad and I'll walk in last.'

'Great. Let's do a first walk through without any accompaniment. Then when we're happy we'll try it with Vivaldi. Remember, girls, there's no hurry. Take your time. Everyone in the church will be agog to see you all.'

The first attempt was fairly chaotic. George set a slow pace down the aisle but Katrina, behind her, was nervous and closed the gap. Maxine's cousins had to choose between keeping up with Katrina or sticking to George's pace and falling behind. But by the third go it was fairly tidy.

'Right. Let's do it with music. Oliver, you've seen the pace they go. Can you play the Four Seasons at that tempo? If necessary go round it more than once. Girls, you'll need to listen hard and start at the right point.'

Steadily the rehearsal inched forwards. Esther made sure the bridal couple knew where to stand for the wedding ceremony and where they would sit for the sermon, on the special seats at the front. Robbie was to read the lesson but for some reason he wasn't there. 'It's not a problem, he's done that sort of thing lots of times before,' said George loyally. Inside she was seething.

Finally they came to the closing procession. There was some confusion over who was in the main procession itself. But Esther patiently but decisively guided them into a sensible pattern. It was as well she'd had a few days down here, so knew who they all were and their foibles.

When she'd finished, Maria went forward and stood on the step beside here. 'Right, everyone. You're all invited to have a meal with us this evening at Chy Brisons. Most of you know where we live and the rest can follow. Leave your cars in the village car park, please. The invitation's to Father Giles and Oliver as well. Oliver, you might like to meet The Slaters. They'll be leading the singing in the middle part of the service.'

There was cheerful confusion over setting out on the walk down to Chy Brisons. Everyone was coming but no-one was in any hurry. Maybe they were just being polite.

Peter was glancing round, working out which newcomer he needed to spend time with, when George accosted him. 'Peter, I've got something to talk about. Could you and I could go back a longer way?'

Peter was mindful of his wedding responsibilities. But he was still uncomfortably aware that the Ding Dong case was completely unsolved. He'd been thinking about it all day. In any case, there were plenty of other people talking. Soon he and George had slipped away and were heading for the Star. He didn't really need a drink but he didn't fancy having an important conversation out in the cold.

'No, I don't want anything alcoholic,' she said. 'Ok, maybe a cup of tea to warm me up. This doesn't need to take long.'

Peter ordered a pot of tea and they found a table in the far corner. 'Right, George. What gives?'

'I spent today learning about geothermal energy. From a book in Alex's study. After a couple of hours I decided I needed a break, so Maxine and I went for a stroll down to Cape Cornwall.'

'It's spectacular, isn't it?'

George smiled. 'Almost as good as the cliffs in North Cornwall. Anyway, this time Maxine and I went down onto that rocky bay at the side – Priest Cove, I think it's called. The wind was biting cold so we were the only ones on the beach.'

'Yes?'

'Well, one thing hidden among the boulders is a rocky pool, a short walk from the jetty. It was low tide when we were there and most of the water had drained out. Maxine and I were scrambling around it when we noticed something snagged in the bottom.'

Peter looked at her. He hated the wait but the girl deserved her moment of anticipation. He had no idea what was coming next.

'Guess what, Peter. It was a rope ladder. Looking like it had been abandoned.'

Peter drank some tea as he pondered.

'Was it a old relic - broken, say, or with missing rungs?'

'It didn't seem to be, looked bang up to date. We didn't touch it, of course. It might once have been part of a crime scene.'

'Well done for thinking of that. Mind, if it's been in the sea for a week there won't be any DNA left.'

'No. But it looked more or less the same size as the one you and I climbed down on Tuesday.'

The policeman mused for a moment. 'If it's a working ladder then it's an odd place to leave it. It must be worth a hundred quid.'

'What Maxine and I thought was that someone might have driven down to the car park and put it the pool at low tide, assumed the next high tide would wash it away. It would have been an easy way of getting rid of it. Safer than leaving it in a skip, or setting it on fire. But the seas haven't been too rough this week so it's still there.'

'OK George, that makes sense. But there can't be many rope ladders round here that need throwing away. Other than one from Ding Dong.' He had a further thought. 'You've no idea how long it's been there?'

George gave a shrug. 'You'd only see it at low tide. It might have been there for a week.'

There was another pause.

'It's something else to tell the Penzance police,' he said. 'I'm planning to send them a note setting out our findings before Maxine and I go on our honeymoon. Actually, there is one other thing which you might be able to help on.'

George relished being needed. She wouldn't admit it but was feeling sore over Robbie. 'Tell me.'

'Well, when I was out with Kirstie yesterday, we drew in at a different point near to Ding Dong. She wanted to take pictures of the landscape. There was a muddy path leading over to the mine. I noticed a pair of bicycle tyre tracks on it, they should be

260

on one of her pictures.'

'Yes?'

'Well it occurred to me that any recent bike tracks leading to the mine might be significant. I've no idea how, at this stage. But if you could get Kirstie to show you the picture, you might be able to tell something.'

'I'll have a look if you like, Peter.' She glanced at her watch. 'But don't you reckon we should be going? It would be a shame to miss supper.'

When they got to Chy Brisons they found they weren't too late: supper hadn't started. There were lots of comings and goings, the pair had hardly been missed.

Maria had suggested that guests all swapped tables between courses to mingle as much as possible. That left plenty of intermittently vacant places and made for a jolly and sociable meal. It would make a good basis for the wedding the next day.

At one point towards the end Peter found himself seated next to Sidney Giles and Esther's comments on him came to mind.

'I wouldn't mind a chat as we walk back to St Just,' he observed.

Sidney looked at him and smiled. 'Fine. I'm not staying too long. It's great to be here but I don't want to outstay my welcome.'

Peter didn't want to stay late either. He was still bothered by the case. A short while later the two men were walking up the road.

'Esther tells me you were the first one down Ding Dong shaft

261

last week?' Peter began.

'I volunteered. Priests are used to death. I've come across many victims in coastguard duties. I didn't understand why the police weren't hustling to be first down, mind. It might have been different if you were in charge.'

'Did you recognise the victim?' Father Giles had heard this question before from Esther but now it was being asked by a policeman. A straight question required a straight answer.

'I did. It was Jeremy Hocking. We've chatted from time to time. The last time I saw him alive was at the Lunch Box at Carn Galver.'

'Did you know what his project was about?'

'It was something to do with geothermal energy.'

Peter sighed. It was good to get confirmation of his suspicions but it would have been good to learn something new. His instinct was that Father Giles knew more, but he couldn't hit on the question to unpack it.

'Peter, none of us can do everything. Your priority at this point is your wedding; and from then on looking after Maxine. Justice is God's business, not yours. You might have a small part to play in it, in His mercy, but you're not the only one. It's not all down to you. What you need most of all tonight is a good night's sleep. I pray that's what you will have.'

'Thank you, Father. You're very wise.'

SATURDAY DECEMBER 31st
NEW YEAR'S EVE

The historic church of St Just

263

CHAPTER 38

Saturday Dec 31ˢᵗ. It was just before seven that Peter Travers awoke from a deep, dreamless sleep. He felt refreshed, almost alert.

For a second he lay still half asleep, wondering where he was. Dawn was some way off. His window faced away from the lights in the square and the room was practically dark. Then he remembered: this was his last night ever in the Kings Arms. For this afternoon, joy of joys and barring an unimaginable catastrophe, he was going to be married.

For a few seconds he wondered what his fiancée was doing at this moment, down the road in Chy Brisons. Was she already up, heading for a shower or unpacking her wedding trousseau? Or more likely, was she still deeply asleep, storing up energy for all that the day would bring?

So what had woken him so early? Another hour's sleep wouldn't have come amiss. Then he heard it again, a gentle knocking at his door.

For a second he fantasised that Maxine had woken up before him and walked up to St Just to greet him. Was she fully dressed or had she simply slipped her coat over her nightdress? How many layers would she let him remove?

The knocking came a third time, now more fiercely. Whoever

it was seemed really determined. It was frustrating, he could see no choice but to slide out of bed, slip on his dressing gown and see who it was.

'Coming,' he called.

A moment later he had unlocked the door and was peering down a dark corridor.

'Thank goodness for that,' said a male voice that he dimly recognised from long ago. 'Room 6 was the right one. I was afraid I might be waking up the landlady.'

There was no doubt that whoever it was they intended to come in. And if there was to be a confrontation, he thought it would be better to happen within his room than out in the corridor.

'Oh, come in,' he said. Turned back and switched on the light.

To Peter's complete amazement his visitor was another police-man, Sergeant Percy Popper.

'What the hell are you doing here at this time of day? I'm getting married in a few hours.'

'And welcome to you too, Peter. I'm afraid I didn't come with a present.'

Peter remembered that he had a tea tray in his room. Staying on his own and always coming in late, he'd never bothered to use it. But however awkward the conversation to come, it would be improved by a cup of tea.

'Hold on a minute. I'll get the kettle on.' It was good to have something to do while he collected his thoughts.

Deep down Peter had been aware all week that he was on

delicate ground, conducting a murder investigation well away from his home turf. Goodness knows, he'd tried hard enough to hand it over. Once that had failed he'd done his best to be discreet. But it seemed clear that he had not been discreet enough.

Percy had sat down. He'd glanced round the room, seen nothing inflammatory that he could complain about. Peter mashed the pot of tea and brought the tray over to the coffee table. Then he took the easy chair opposite.

'I've got some questions and I'd like them answered,' began Percy.

'You mean, you think I might have been right in my concerns about the death at Ding Dong?'

'I'll ask the questions, if you don't mind, Peter. But if you obstruct me then I warn you, I'm quite prepared to cart you off to the police station. The powers that be might struggle to hold the wedding, though, if it was known the bridegroom had been arrested.'

Peter sighed. It was clear the man was deadly serious, though he hadn't found much sense of humour. 'Go on then, what's your first question?'

'Well, it's a good job we know one another from a long time back. And also I know, though I might tease you about it, you're a serving police officer of good repute. I'd like to assume that you didn't commit the crime yourself -'

'Hell's bells, you know I was the one trying you get you to take it seriously.'

'- but for the record, where were you in the middle of last week?'

For a second Peter was about to explode. Then he recalled that his longstanding complaint about Percy was that he cut too many corners. So he could hardly complain if the man was now working by the book.

'Last week I was on duty every day in Bude. Finishing things off, getting ready to take a fortnight's leave. Inside the police station. I can find you a dozen witnesses if you like.'

Percy considered for a moment and then nodded. 'OK. I'll take that for the time being as proof of your alibi.'

'I can't believe you've come all this way to check I wasn't the murderer.'

'That was just a preliminary, Peter. What I want to find is places where you might have found some evidence that I need, something that can tie the ends together. For example, did you find Hocking's car keys?'

Peter cast his mind back. 'That's a thought. No, I've never come across them. I borrowed Mrs Hocking's keys to bring back their car.'

Percy looked at him quizzically. 'From where?'

'From the road near Ding Dong.'

Percy blinked. 'Peter, I find that very surprising. My colleague and I drove up and down that roadside carefully, for a mile in either direction, trying to make sense of how Hocking had got there. I couldn't imagine that he'd walked. I'm telling you, there was no car there on Christmas Eve.'

Peter knew he sometimes had doubts about Percy's efficiency but this was astonishing. 'The coastguard mentioned a thick fog,' he protested. 'Could that not have hidden the Skoda? It was obvious to us on the day after Boxing Day. That's how I found the name of the victim and the address of his widow.'

A moment's silence as both men considered. The known facts just didn't make sense.

'To go back to the keys,' asked Percy, 'none of your lot saw sight of them?' Peter shook his head.

'In that case,' said Percy, 'it must have been murder. Or at least, a second person at the scene. If something had happened to Hocking on his own then he needed keys to get there. But the post mortem report showed there were none in his pockets.'

'That's not absolutely certain,' replied Peter. He was a rigorous policeman. 'True, the keys have never been mentioned in our inquiries. But . . . might not one of the coastguards that went down the shaft have lifted them out of Hocking's pocket?'

It was Percy's turn to think for a moment, then he nodded. 'Blast. I never wrote down their names. I suppose I could ask Colin Trewern.'

'I can tell you, Percy. One was my fiancée's dad, Alex Tavistock. The other was Father Sidney Giles. He's the vicar here at St Just. I've never talked to Alex about it. Maxine said he didn't want it mentioned in case it spoilt the wedding.

'But I did talk to Sidney, after last night's rehearsal. He didn't deny that he recognised Hocking when he first got down the shaft. More or less implied that was why he straightened him out.'

There was another silence. Peter poured them both a second cup.

'So what's your next question?'

'My constable did find the Skoda outside Hocking's house on Wednesday morning. We assumed it must have been there all along, see. She checked the boot but there was nothing in there. So did you lot take anything from it?'

'For the record, Percy, I wore gloves when I drove it back from Ding Dong. In case it turned out to be part of a crime scene. To be honest, we never thought to look in the boot. But we had a second trip down the mine on Thursday. And found this.'

He stood up and fetched his rucksack, pulled out the black sensor, still in its evidence bag. 'It wasn't obvious, mind. We had to go down a side passage from the bottom of the shaft to find it.'

'What on earth is it?'

'It measures temperature at the bottom of mine shafts. We reckon that was what Hocking was doing on all his trips down old mines.'

Percy's eyes had widened. 'So if there are any fingerprints on that, it might point to the murderer?'

'Could do. Be my guest. Take it with you. My team have had plenty of ideas but this is the only piece of hard evidence that we've collected.'

He mused for a second, recalling what George had told him. 'The only other thing I can think of that might be relevant is that George found a rope ladder. It had been abandoned in the cove beside Cape Cornwall.

'And now, if you wouldn't mind, Percy, I'd like to get dressed. The heating's not too hot in these bedrooms, but they do a smashing breakfast. This is the last time I'll be able to indulge myself.'

CHAPTER 39

Sergeant Percy Popper felt envious of Peter Travers. He would have liked a decent breakfast too. But he had work to do.

By now it was almost eight o'clock and dawn had broken. It was going to be a glorious winter day, very cold but bright. The sky was clear, slightly hazy now but foreshadowing a cloudless blue sky later on. He judged it was still too early, though, to call on Father Giles.

Whilst he was waiting he might as well check on this rope ladder that Peter had mentioned. It sounded bizarre. It might not be relevant but one had almost certainly disappeared from Ding Dong and the police hadn't taken it. The coastguards had brought one of their own, of course, but they'd taken it back with them.

He drove down towards Cape Cornwall, parked in the National Trust car park. He glanced back up the road but, from the far side where he'd halted, his car couldn't be seen from the houses above. So there wouldn't be any witnesses of the ladder being dumped.

'The cove beside the Cape,' Peter had said. There was only one that it might be. It had a simple concrete jetty running down to the sea and a few boats tied to the rings along it. There were a few lobster pots resting at the top but it seemed there was no-one else here.

The policeman waddled down and eyed the rocks more carefully. Yes, he could just see the hint of a small pool a bit further round the cove. It wouldn't be a bad place to hide something bulky if you had to get rid of it quickly.

The trouble was, high tide was close. The waves were lapping most of the way up the jetty. He tried to work it out. If George had been here yesterday afternoon, say, and it had been low tide then, that would make sense: eighteen hours later would be high tide. He wouldn't be able to see anything inside the pool at this time of day. It was filled to the rim in murky, icy seawater. He wasn't going to swim in after it. Not even Peter Travers would do that.

Frustrated, the policeman turned to walk back to his car. As he did so he became aware that, even at this early hour, he was not alone. A tall woman, warmly dressed in a thick purple cagoule and matching bobble hat, was walking quickly down Cape Cornwall. She waved energetically, seemed like she wanted to speak to him.

As she got closer he could see she was carrying a hefty camera. Maybe catching the early sun on the chimney above would explain her presence.

He wasn't in that much of a hurry so he paused to let her catch up.

'Hi. My name is Kirstie Conway,' she began. 'I'm a friend of Maxine and Peter, here to do the wedding photography. I've just been taking some background shots. It's glorious isn't it?' She noticed his uniform. 'Is Peter Travers a colleague of yours?'

271

"Colleague" might be overstating it but Percy was feeling generous. 'Peter and I go back a long way. I was talking to him earlier.'

'Right. About Ding Dong, no doubt? It's mysterious, isn't it?'

Percy Popper wasn't sure what, if anything, she wanted, but maybe this was a chance to learn something for himself. 'Have you been helping Peter?'

'We all have. I was the one to find the sensor.'

'So that's where it came from. Peter's handed it over to me to look after. I've got to dust it for fingerprints when I get back to Penzance. I've a few more St Just folk to see first, mind.'

'Best not keep you then. Maybe I'll see you later. We're all staying in that guesthouse at the top. I've got to start on pictures of the bride next, working up from the shoes.'

Kirstie turned and started jogging up the hill. Envying her energy, Percy walked more slowly back to his car. He glanced at his watch. Surely Father Giles would be fine for a visit by this time?

In truth Father Giles was not ready at all but his ministry led him to be courteous to all callers. He recognised the policeman from a week before, when he'd been helping him recover a body from Ding Dong.

He also remembered that the man had not been particularly grateful. He scolded himself: mustn't hold that against him.

'Good morning, Father.'

'Good morning. Still working on the death at Ding Dong, I presume? Come in. Can I offer you a coffee?'

The policeman stepped inside. 'My name is Sergeant Percy Popper. I'm from Penzance. I may have been a bit short with you all last week. It was very cold up there, wasn't it?'

Father Giles stepped into the kitchen and started fiddling with the coffee machine. The policeman could see it wasn't the fastest device on the market.

'It's cold here too. I'm afraid the only room here I keep warm is the lounge. D'you want to go through? I'll bring the coffee in a moment.'

Percy was shown into the lounge. He glanced at the book-shelves, saw several relating to geothermal energy. The policeman was about to delve deeper when Sidney reappeared, carrying mugs of coffee.

'Right, Sergeant. How can I help you?'

'A week ago the death on Ding Dong seemed a straightforward accident, or just possibly a suicide. But now it's looking far more suspicious. I'm trying to go back and double check the evidence. I regret I didn't send my constable down the shaft at the time.'

'Or even gone yourself.' The words were said gently but there was sharp thought behind them.

'To be honest, Father, I'm afraid of heights. Always have been.' He smiled. 'You might have had two bodies to bring up. You'd have found one of them very heavy.'

The policeman took a sip of his coffee.

'First of all Father, can I ask, did you know the dead man?'

'I'm sad to say that I did. It was Jeremy Hocking.'

'Why on earth didn't you tell me?'

'You never asked. As a priest my habit is never to volunteer information unless it's wanted and is not already known. But Colin had told us that we were only there because his wife had called in, so you must have known who she was worried about.'

Percy sighed. These days it was harder to be ahead of the witnesses. 'OK. In that case, did you touch the victim?'

'I did. He was stone cold, been dead for hours. The rigor had passed, he wasn't even rigid. He lay in a crumpled position, just where he'd landed. I'm afraid that offended me. Even in death I had to make him more comfortable.'

The policeman thought about it and nodded. 'Fair enough. But this is important. While you were turning him over, did anything like keys or a phone fall out of his pocket?'

'No keys. No phone. And no money either. Is any of that significant?'

'Seems so. Makes murder much more likely, in my opinion.'

The policeman paused to select his next question. 'Did you know the other volunteer – Alex?'

'I did. He's a regular member of my congregation here in St Just. He seemed to recognise Hocking as well.'

'And you were both in sight of one another all the time you were down there?'

'Pretty much. We were down for nearly an hour, remember. We each went off for a pee at one point or another down a side passage. Apart from that we were beside the body the whole time.'

'As someone who knew Hocking, have you any idea what he was doing, going down old mine shafts in the middle of winter?'

'He was keeping that secret. It was some project he'd been

recruited for. We sometimes had coffee together. From odd snippets he let slip, I'd say he was measuring temperature at the foot of all these shafts.'

'And what might that achieve?'

'Well, I don't know. But I'd guess he thought that could be translated into an estimate of the best place to start drilling for geothermal energy.'

'So did he have any opponents on this work? Anyone that would prefer to see him dead, rather than allow him to succeed?'

Sidney Giles gave a sorrowful shrug. 'He must have had at least one, Sergeant. But I have absolutely no idea who that might have been.'

A few minutes later, questions over, the policeman left. Various points had been confirmed but he hadn't learned much that was new.

The next question was what more he might learn from Alex Tavistock. Persuading the man to spend time seeing him, on the morning of his daughter's wedding, was going to be his next challenge.

Once Percy had gone, Sidney Giles went to his desk and opened the top drawer. Then drew out a small piece of paper which he examined carefully. There was a date on it: Thursday, December 22nd.

The policeman hadn't exactly asked for this so he hadn't thought it necessary to show him. It might mean nothing at all. But maybe, later on, he could make an inquiry of his own.

CHAPTER 40

L ife in Chy Brisons was hectic. Like her fiancé, Maxine had also been awake since seven holding imaginary conversations, though these hadn't included an early morning cross examination from a fat policeman in her nightdress. (Maxine in her nightdress, not the fat policeman). But hopes and dreams for life ahead were still interleaved with moments of anxiety.

Suppose there was a power cut that affected the whole of Land's End? How would Alice cope? She recalled discussion about that on the news (the power cut, not Alice). A Select Committee had cross-examined the Energy Minister before Christmas, been far from confident in her answers.

Chy Brisons would not be completely bereft. It had its own emergency generator, so the kitchen would probably still operate. With rigid door discipline, the freezers that held the ingredients for the Wedding Breakfast would probably keep going for the day, if not much longer. But the generator had not been designed to take account of the battery of heaters that Dad and Ross had been putting up in the Barn. How would the reception go if everyone was huddled in their coats? What response would there be from cold guests to warm wedding speeches?

Everyone but her, she reminded herself. She'd be like a penguin in the Antarctic that had lost its huddle. She was prepared for a few minutes standing outside the church in the biting wind, but she hadn't planned to be at that temperature for the whole reception.

Why on earth had she resisted her Mum's advice to buy a pashmina to go with her lacy wedding dress? Of course, when that had been chosen it had been autumn, with the wedding planned for the spring. It was much colder now than she had ever anticipated.

This was nonsense, she told herself. Wake up, girl. Electricity was still being supplied, someone was having a shower next door. And if the worst did happen, if it did come to several hours of bitter cold, she could face that. She'd had some training in facing discomfort. She'd be alright as long as she had Peter by her side.

Time passed and the morning hastened on, ever more hectic. There was no substantial breakfast in Chy Brisons, though there was plenty of nervous excitement as they enjoyed juice, cereals and toast. To the best of her knowledge, Maria observed, no-one had gone down with food poisoning after last night's informal banquet. At least one nightmare hadn't happened. All the bridesmaids were "bright eyed and bushy tailed", though Shelley noted that a different expression was used for that Down Under.

Kirstie returned from her photographic odyssey on Cape Cornwall and reported that she had met a fat policeman who seemed at last to be taking an interest in the mysterious death at Ding Dong. She admitted telling him where they stayed. The news brought a variety of reactions, though with Alex present making the most of his grapefruit there couldn't be much open discussion of its significance.

Maxine had checked the local forecast on her phone and reported a bright but icy cold day was expected for Land's End. The wedding guests might be wind-swept but at least they wouldn't be rain lashed.

That was just as well. There had been a mix up between Maxine and Peter over who would confirm the order for a wedding car and it was far from clear that one would come. For the bride and bridesmaids to walk half a mile through the village to church, with locals waving them on, might turn out to be one more special feature of a hastily-planned but much anticipated local wedding.

Alice arrived from the Kings Arms a few minute later and commandeered the kitchen. From now on, she said, no-one was to go in or out without her permission. She had her schedule and nothing would deflect her from it. There was still a long time to go before the Wedding Breakfast but there was a huge amount to do.

The hair stylist was due at nine and turned up a few minutes early. The road that she had driven from St Ives, she reported, was quiet. It was decided she would use the guesthouse lounge. No-one but the bride and the bridesmaids would be allowed in there from now on.

Alex wanted somewhere quiet to run through his Father of the Bride speech a few more times, well away from the Mother of the Bride. In the end he retreated to the Barn, saying that, like Captain Oates, he might be "outside for some time".

So all was as prepared as it could be for the arrival of Sergeant Percy Popper at half past eleven.

The sergeant didn't feel prepared for a guesthouse full of excited bridesmaids and the urgent anticipation of a wedding. He'd been almost tempted to pass the interview challenge by. Then he remembered, that was exactly the sort of thing Peter Travers would accuse him of.

Now he had taken the Ding Dong case by the scruff of the neck and told Peter that was what he was doing, he daren't let the case slip through his fingers. After all, given no-one had seen Hocking's keys, he was probably dealing with a murder.

He could tell it was the right guesthouse by the hubbub coming from within. He knocked hard, was pleased when it was Kirstie that came to the door. At least it was someone he recognised. She didn't even seem that surprised to see him.

'Hello again.'

'I'd like to have a chat, please, with Alex Tavistock.'

Kirstie glanced round. Incompletely dressed bridesmaids were scurrying up and down the stairs. The kitchen and the lounge had already been designated out of bounds for visitors and the dining room was still being cleared by herself and Lisa. Then she remembered the guesthouse office.

'Make yourself at home in here,' she said, showing him in. 'I'll go and look for Alex. He's busy preparing his speech. It might take a minute or two to find him.'

The policeman glanced round the office as he waited. He had no search warrant but that didn't stop him glancing at the contents of the desk.

He noticed that Alex had been working through his recent

bank statements. Diligent activity on the day of his daughter's wedding. He glanced down: the man had a healthy balance. Running a guesthouse was a lot more profitable than being a police sergeant, it seemed.

He was about to turn away when a name jumped out at him. And there it was again. All of a sudden he felt a burst of energy.

It was then that he noticed, stuffed at the back of the folder, presumably waiting to be filed away, there was a letter. It wasn't his business to be reading letters to or from Alex Tavistock but all policemen have a nosy instinct. Besides, it might help the forthcoming interview.

Especially when he noticed who the letter was from.

'Good morning, Mr Tavistock. I'm Sergeant Percy Popper. We last met a week ago. You and several other coastguards helped us recover a body from Ding Dong Mine.'

'You've not chosen a very good time, Sergeant. My daughter . . .'

'Yes, I know sir, she's getting married later today. I won't keep you long, I can assure you.'

'Good. Go on then, what d'you want to know?'

'When we first found Mr Hocking's body, I looked on his death as an accident. But since then I've had the post mortem report, which gives some cause to doubt. So I'm now doing some routine interviews that should arguably have taken place last week.'

Alex's face turned into a scowl. Admitting incompetence did not make it justified. 'Go on.'

'First of all, did you recognise the victim?'

'You've got to remember, his face was badly battered from the fall and we were working with a single torchlight.'

'So the answer is. . .'

'I think I did. I'd had dealings with the man from time to time.'

'And you didn't mention that because . . .'

'Well, you didn't ask me. By the time Sid and I got back up you'd disappeared. It took us another half hour to carry the body to the road and put it in the ambulance. After that there was no reason to hang about. I came home for a long hot bath.'

The policeman considered. It was plausible, in fact he'd done much the same himself. 'OK. Next, did you take anything out of the victim's pockets?'

Alex looked offended. 'I did not, Sergeant. I was there to help, not to act as a pickpocket.'

'No keys?'

'Nope.'

'And did you see any rope or rope ladder?'

'There was nothing at the bottom of the shaft. Hey, hadn't you removed it from the top when you first got there?'

There was a pause. The policeman had a sense that he wasn't being told everything but needed longer to think it through.

Alex, though, was in no mood to delay. 'Now, if that's all, I've got a speech to polish. All I need is a good joke to end on.' He glanced hopefully at the policeman but could see that would be blood from the proverbial stone. 'You can find your own way out, I trust?' A moment later he was gone.

281

The policeman paused before stepping into the hall. He'd hoped to move onto a discussion of the letter in the folder. Alex wouldn't need it for the next few hours, he thought. It would be best to read it sitting somewhere quiet. He slipped it into his pocket and headed for the door.

CHAPTER 41

Robbie had woken up on Saturday morning in St Ives, simultaneously happy and guilt-stricken.

On Friday evening he and Siobhan had travelled back from Falmouth, battled with end-of-week traffic, not arrived till after seven and decided to treat themselves to a meal out. 'We've a lot of meals to catch up on from the last twenty years,' declared Siobhan.

After a short wander round the winding streets near the harbour they'd found a Chinese restaurant which offered a multi-course banquet at a special seasonal price.

It had been far too dark to read any of the documents they'd been lent, sitting in the car, and they weren't going to let them spoil a fine meal. The corner to which they'd been guided had subdued lighting too. There was a lot more to talk about on their separate lives after they'd left Bristol, even a few hints, perhaps, of a less separate future.

It was halfway through the second course that Robbie remembered the wedding rehearsal in St Just; especially that he was supposed to be there, to be told when and how to read the lesson. He had rung to offer a grovelling apology successively to Maxine, George, Esther and finally to Peter, but no-one had been answering their phone.

After which he had given up and spent the rest of the evening in animated conversation with Siobhan.

Consequently it was the Saturday morning before the pair had time to read the documents from Professor Dillon properly over a sizzling breakfast.

As they ate, Robbie grappled with the outline of the mining conference that had taken place on the Tuesday before Christmas: it included the topics discussed and a long list of those attending.

'It's such a pity I missed this,' he grimaced. 'It's covering a lot of the ground that I need for my remit.'

'But you've got the names of those that were there, Robbie. You're a journalist. They'll be happy to meet you to be sure, tell you what was said. They'd value the publicity. This is a far better starting point than anything you could have imagined.'

'Yes.' His eyes scanned down the attendees and their place of origin. A few were from overseas; presumably they'd be long gone home by now. Then he came across a name that he recognised.

'There's one here, Siobhan, that's based in St Just. But he won't be actively mining these days. He's got a church to run.'

For the moment Siobhan wasn't giving him her full attention. She had the official report of the incident in Rosemanowas Quarry to read, or at least to skim.

This was where her finely-honed speed reading skills came into their own. Then, in the body of the report, she came across something that astonished her.

'Well, well, well. Can you guess, Robbie, the name of the man who was scalded at the site, nearly forty years ago?

'We'd both be small children at the time, Siobhan. I've no idea.'

'It was Jeremy Hocking.'

'Wow.' He pondered for a moment. 'That's an amazing coincidence. But even that didn't cause him to lose his passion for mining. I suppose it might explain why he was still keen on pursuing geothermal energy.'

Siobhan took another forkful of bacon and read on more carefully. Robbie poured them both second mugs of coffee and studied the topics covered at the conference in more detail.

'That's not the only name that we'd recognise in this report, Robbie. The operator who was on duty that fateful night is known to us as well.'

Robbie was still preoccupied. 'And he is?'

'It's the father of the bride. A young Alex Tavistock.'

Siobhan put down the report and concentrated for a moment on her breakfast. There was a silence but in it both of them were thinking furiously.

'That couldn't possibly have anything to do with the death at Ding Dong, could it?' she asked.

'It might not,' Robbie replied. 'But if it didn't it's an amazing coincidence. The two met at Rosemanowas, next they met at Ding Dong.'

'So d'you think the police are already aware of these findings?'

'I've no idea. But I think we have a duty to tell them. As soon as possible.' He seized a piece of toast and started to spread it with

285

honey. 'Well, as soon as we've finished our breakfast, anyway.'

In the end, as time was short, they decided to take both cars and follow the two new leads separately.

Robbie would go directly to interview Father Giles in St Just, to learn as much as he could about what happened at the conference. Meanwhile Siobhan would take the incident report to show to the police in Penzance.

'They're responsible for solving this, Siobhan. Don't let them wriggle out of it. There's no point in us bothering Peter. He's got much more important matters to attend to today.'

Though much the same might be said of Sidney Giles, Robbie reflected, as he drove along the coast road past Zennor and on towards St Just.

Father Giles was having a busy morning. A good job his wedding duties were light. He had not long seen off Sergeant Popper when there was another knock at the door.

A tousled-haired, tubby man stood there that he'd never seen before. He was wearing a suit and tie, trying to look smart. Maybe he was another one involved in the wedding?

'Good morning. How can I help you?'

'Morning, Father. My name is Robbie Glendenning, I'm a journalist. I'm also a friend of Peter Travers and the rest of the wedding crew that you'll be dealing with later on. But something urgent has come up that I need to discuss with you.'

'Please, come in. And call me Sidney. My house isn't very warm, I'm afraid. But I can at least offer you coffee.'

A few minutes later the pair were seated in a slightly-warmer lounge sipping mugs of hot coffee. From somewhere in the depths of the kitchen Sidney had also found a packet of hobnobs.

'Right, Father. This all ties in, I believe, with the death at Ding Dong. You know that Peter Travers, the man you'll be marrying, is a policeman? Well, he doesn't believe it was an accident at all. He's been desperate to solve it before he goes on his honeymoon. After all, if he doesn't there's a murderer still out there. So this week he's had us all out, looking for reasons why Hocking might have been up near the mine.'

'Yes. I'm up to speed with the death at least. I was the first one, you know, to see the body.'

Robbie helped himself to another hobnob. 'The thing is, that was the second time that you saw Hocking last week, wasn't it? Earlier you'd both been at that mining conference in Penryn.'

Father Giles looked surprised. He wasn't used to being under the microscope. 'How on earth did you know that?'

'I was talking to Professor Dillon yesterday. About the geo-thermal pilot site at Rosemanowas. Did you know . . .?'

'That Hocking was almost killed there? Yes I did. We quite often talked about it over the years. Jeremy was bitter for a long time but he was through that now. It was him that invited me to the conference, actually. It was his way of saying thank you. I'd always thought geothermal energy had lots of potential, you see. Provided you could find the right place to drill.'

'The thing is, Father, this was only a couple of days before the poor man came to an untimely death. So did anything happen at the conference that might have any bearing on that?'

287

Sidney was silent for a moment. He'd asked himself much the same question once he'd seen Hocking's body down the mine. Now the question was raised out loud he had to take his fears seriously.

'The timing of the conference, a few days before Christmas, was planned to give it a lighter tone – a sort of celebration. Most of those attending seemed to know one another. I gather the conference ran every couple of years.'

'But it was the first time you'd been? Was there anyone else there that you knew?

'There were about forty present, one or two whose faces I recognised. No-one I knew well.'

'Right. But, looking back, would you say Hocking seemed at home there? Did he get on with 'em all?'

'Hocking had been before. Even so, he wasn't a core character, more of a fringe player. And his project was so secret he couldn't say much about that. Except . . .'

Sidney tailed off. He'd obviously thought of something.

'Yes?'

'There was one point in the afternoon's discussion when Rosemanowas was mentioned. I was sitting high up on the other side of the lecture hall. I glanced across, could see that the name had brought back memories. Then at the afternoon tea-break Hocking took one of the delegates off to show them the exhibition in the basement. When he came back he was obviously quite upset.'

There was silence for a moment. 'Seeing the plant model and some of the gear might have brought back old memories, I suppose,' said Robbie. 'After all, he'd been very badly injured.'

'I don't think it was just the gear. Jeremy told me on the way home that he'd seen the model many times before.'

'Well, did you know who the delegate was?'

'I'm afraid I didn't know him by name. But I would recognise them again, I think. In the right context, anyway.'

CHAPTER 42

It was just before twelve. A smartly suited Peter Travers, wearing a brand new shirt and an expensive tie, had packed his honeymoon bag and collected his tickets and passport from the bedside cabinet. He had moved on to checking his wardrobe was empty and clearing his room when there was a firm knock at the door.

No doubt his best man, he thought, being efficient and in good time. Good old Brian. But the church was only two minutes stroll away, he didn't want to be too early.

But it wasn't Brian at all. To his amazement Percy Popper was standing there once again.

'If this is some sort of wind-up, Percy – '

'Can I come in, please, Peter. We've got a problem.'

'My problem is that my wedding is at one. And I'm not going to be late. Whatever happens I am not having Maxine get there before me.'

Percy could see it wasn't the best time. 'I'll be as quick as I can. I've been given new information about Hocking. First no-one has seen the keys. Then a whole new dossier, which opens up the whole case.'

'Good, good. Well done. It'll be a relief to go off on my honeymoon with it all sorted. You've arrested someone?'

'Not yet. But I've got strong grounds for bringing them in for questioning.'

'So what the hell are you doing here?'

Then he noticed that Percy had a hangdog look. That was odd, why wasn't he more excited? With his dismal energy levels the man wouldn't often have the chance to arrest a murderer.

Perhaps that was the problem. Such arrests had happened so seldom for him that he was lacking in confidence, needed some encouragement.

'You don't need my permission, you know.'

'The thing is Peter, it's someone you know.'

'No-one is above the Law, Percy. Remember those lectures we had at Plymouth. "The towering glory of the English legal system," they called it. However great or mighty, every man still has to submit.'

Suddenly it clicked what Percy was saying. 'Who is it?'

'It's the father of the bride, Peter. Alex Tavistock.'

Peter gave a start. 'I think we'd both better sit down.'

'I don't want to know anything about the evidence that you've now got. Who you've seen or what they've said. You're an experienced officer, I'm sure you'll assess it well. Anyway, there's no time for that now. The only question for me is, exactly when are you going to take him away?'

'In normal circumstances, Peter, I'd take him in straightaway. There's no real hurry, but I wouldn't want to give him any chance of hiding further evidence. Shredding key documents, for example. Or perhaps juggling a bank account.'

291

Peter paused for a moment. 'On the other hand, if they were standing beside the bride at the front of church, in front of a hundred witnesses, they couldn't do much at all.'

Percy looked relieved. 'That's more or less what I was thinking. But I was afraid that he might still do a runner at the end of the service.'

There was a short pause as options were considered.

Then Peter said, 'One of my best officers, Holly Berry, is coming down from Bude for the service. She's acting as one of the ushers. I'll be seeing her in a couple of minutes. I'll tell her to stay at the back for the whole service, so she can keep guard on the main door. Then she can bring Alex Tavistock to your police car before the guests start to come out.'

He tried to imagine the scene. 'But you'll need to go down to the guesthouse beforehand, Percy, and warn him that's what you're doing. Then, if he makes no fuss and walks off quietly, most of the guests won't even notice. They'll all be too busy staring at my new bride.'

CHAPTER 43

Two o'clock. The wedding service had gone splendidly. Peter and Maxine Travers, rings exchanged, the register signed and witnessed, were now officially married. The next stage was taking the photographs, outside and within the old photogenic, stone church.

It was, as predicted, a brilliantly sunny day but with a biting wind. From her early morning stroll Kirstie knew what to expect and was once again wearing her thick cagoule and bobble hat. She had been given a long list of guests to capture, sharing their beaming presence with the happy couple. As she had expected, the process seemed to go on for ages.

Peter Travers had long operational experience of standing around in the cold. From his early days as a traffic policeman in Plymouth to more recent incidents supervising cliff rescues he knew how to mitigate the worst effects of the weather. Today he seemed to be wearing only a light blue suit, but beneath that he had put on two distinct layers of thermal clothing. He planned to remove these before the reception began.

Maxine was not so wise or so fortunate. She could see now why her mother had advocated a pashmina. Even so, fingers numb and teeth chattering, she was determined to stick it out. The smile had more or less frozen onto her face. It was after all a unique occasion, one that she would never have again.

Peter's notion that no-one would miss the Father of the Bride in the scrum around the happy couple was true in general but did not apply to the Mother of the Bride. Maria was never at her best under pressure and today, even without the latest complications, had been an unusually intense day.

Everyone was agreed that the service had gone well. Father Giles had welcomed them all graciously and dismissed them all eloquently. In between Esther had led them all through the wedding ceremony. No-one had dared to offer any reason why the couple should not be married. And after declaring Peter and Maxine to be "man and wife", Esther's sermon had been gently profound, teasing Maxine and her deep analysis in a way that only someone who knew her well could have managed.

Later The Slaters had led the singing harmoniously, many of the congregation joining in with gusto. And finally, once the register had been signed by all and sundry, the wider family had processed to the back of the church and then out the south door.

At first, as she stood with her brother in law and his wife, Maria had assumed that Alex was talking to other guests some-where else around the church. There were a number of relatives invited, many of whom they had not seen for a long time. Even so, he was a long time out of her sight.

In the end she started to panic. She didn't care what Alex was doing or what old friend he had just re-discovered; his job right now was surely to stand alongside his wife. She had checked Kirstie's list carefully, there was a whole raft of photos in which they were both supposed to appear.

Meanwhile, out of the corner of his eye, Peter Travers had seen Alex escorted to the police car as he and Maxine turned in the other direction. So Percy had taken the plunge. It was what civil servants would call a "brave move".

The newlywed would love to have had sight of his colleague's new evidence, found it impossible to believe that his new father in law was in trouble at all, let alone guilty of murder. Then it dawned on him that he was the only one in a position to stop the exit torpedoing the rest of the wedding.

There was a slight lull in the photography as another tranche of guests were being gathered together. Peter took the chance to sidle off and stand next to his new mother in law.

'Maria, don't worry,' he whispered. 'I'm afraid that Alex got called away.'

It was not the message Maria was expecting. She seemed almost to buckle. Before she collapsed, or erupted, he needed to show her an excess of compassion and understanding. And to be generous in the way he presented the truth.

He leaned down and gave her a warm embrace. 'Alex wanted me to tell you he'd be alright,' he whispered. 'He'll be back before long. The thing is, he said, we mustn't let it spoil the reception. But if you and I don't say anything, the guests won't notice. They're all fixated on your lovely daughter, my lovely wife. Doesn't she look fantastic?'

As the first event after the wedding a cake reception had been organised inside the church. Alice's delicious gateaux and pastries, made over the past few days, had been brought along earlier

295

today and stored in the vestry. Now some of the church regulars, friends of Alex and Maria, were delegated to fetch them out, lay them on a large table beneath the tower and serve them to the guests. Tea was also being supplied.

Kirstie was glad of a reason to stop taking pictures outside in the icy cold wind. These new ones would be a great deal more informal than the posed pictures taken outside: cheerful guests with cake in their hands. She would rely on the bride and groom identifying the various guests afterwards. The main goal at this stage was to capture the community festive atmosphere.

Before long the background hum was so friendly that Peter decided he could go missing for a few minutes. Maxine was the centre of attention and she could manage without him at her side for a short while. He needed to know when Alex might return. Maybe prepare his next half truth for his new mother in law. He felt a pang of guilt, this wasn't an ideal way of starting their new relationship.

The policeman had no idea what Percy's new information might be. The only new facts he had gleaned from today's chats were that there was doubt over when Hocking's car had been at Ding Dong; and that no-one had seen the keys.

As he mused, he recalled the question he had set George the evening before. The bicycle tracks near the mine. That would be one way of arriving at the place without a car. Good job there were several bridesmaids; one wouldn't be missed for a few minutes.

Peter had had enough of the biting wind. It was good that George knew him well, responded at once to his murmured suggestion. A few minute later both had quietly slipped into the church vestry.

'Don't tell everyone, George, the guests don't need to know, but Percy Popper took Alex off for questioning straight after the service.'

George simply didn't believe him. Was this some sort of police joke? But looking closely she could see that her friend was far from smiling.

'So now,' he went on, 'we need to solve the case, find who really did it. Percy tells me there's an issue over how Hocking got to Ding Dong. Have you had a chance, yet, to look at Kirstie's cycle track photos?'

George recalled that Peter had been married for less than an hour. But this wasn't policing zeal, it was a response to a member of his new family being in trouble. She took a deep breath.

'It took a while to decode, Peter. There were two sets of tracks, each coming from a pair of tyres. In each case one wiggled a lot more than the other. That makes sense, though. On a normal bike only the front wheel changes direction quickly, the rear one is dragged steadily behind.'

'Right. Could you tell which direction they were going?'

'That took me a while. Fortunately, the picture showed the start of the path. You could see that the tracks weren't the same. One trailing track started near to the camera, the other was further away. So I think there was only one bike, making a journey in each direction. I can't be sure but I'd guess it went to the mine and then back again.'

'Ah. So the killer might have ridden there. Well done George.'

He turned to go back into the main church but George hadn't finished.

'There's one more thing. Kirstie's camera has a high resolution sensor, so you can focus on each part in turn. I found the mark of what must be a worn bit of tyre. The thing is, it repeated five feet later. Which means the wheel only had an eighteen inch diameter.'

Peter frowned. 'That's not right, surely?' He stretched out his hands. 'A normal bike wheel is well over two feet across.'

George had had longer to ponder. 'Exactly. So this must have been a commuter bike, like a Brompton, that are designed to fold.'

They went round the argument until Peter was convinced.

The only place near to Ding Dong he could think of to hire such a bike was the shop in Penzance, the place he'd bought pumps for the balloons.

Two minutes later he was on the phone. It was New Year's Eve but fortunately the shop hadn't yet closed.

'Good afternoon. My name is Sergeant Peter Travers. I'm a police officer. D'you hire out those commuter bikes with folding wheels?'

'We have a couple, yes.'

'Did you hire out any in the week running up to Christmas?'

'Hold on a minute, sir. I'll check.'

There was a pause. George could see Peter's fingers drumming impatiently on the table. Then the manager was talking again.

'Right sir. We hired out just the one. It was on the morning of Thursday, Dec 22nd, and was brought back at the end of the day.'

Peter nodded. That was the key day, the day Hocking had died.

'And could you tell me, please, the name of the hirer?'

'Let me see.'

There was another pause and a rustling of pages. 'Yes. I've got the name here. It was some chap called Tavistock.'

'Right. Thank you very much. Could you make sure you keep that documentation, please. I'll send someone round for it later.'

Peter Travers switched off his phone. Then he buried his head in his hands.

CHAPTER 44

I feel like I'm being torn in two,' muttered the policeman, still distraught. 'I was sure that phone call would give me another name. Once I had that I could contact Popper and get him to bring back Alex. Then I could focus on the wedding.'

'Let me go in first, Peter. I'll send out Maxine. You two can have a cuddle and then go back in together.' This was getting ridiculous, she thought. But it might be horribly serious.

George slipped into the church. Nothing much seemed to have changed in the quarter hour she'd been away, though Maria was once again starting to look panic-stricken.

As chief bridesmaid it was easy to catch Maxine's attention. 'Peter's had to go into the vestry. It'd be best if he explains. Can you go and walk him back in? If you like I'll keep an eye on your mum.'

As Maxine slipped out George sidled alongside her mother. 'This is a great occasion, Maria. The flowers and the refreshments are terrific. You and your friends have all done so well.'

'Thank you, dear. I only wish Alex could be here with us. I hope he's alright.'

'He made it through the service, anyway. Peter's been making a few phone calls but can't get hold of him. But the show must go on. We don't want to draw attention to his absence. Is there anyone else that could do a speech on your behalf? What about Ross, for example?'

'I'd rather not risk that, dear. To be honest, he's a brasher version of Alex. I'm sure he knows lots of jokes but they'll all be Australian, some worse than others. He might not go down too well.'

'Well, is there anyone else who could take the role of family friend? One of your church friends, say?'

Maria thought for a moment. 'There's always Father Giles, I suppose. He didn't have much to do in the service and he's coming to the reception. D'you think I should ask him?'

'That'd be a great idea. Tell him Alex has been called away. Promise him he won't be called on if Alex gets back in time. Just a few general words about the family and your time here in St Just would do fine. He's used to public speaking, anyway. Why not let his speech be given last, the order doesn't really matter?'

Maria headed over to Father Giles. She looked better for having something specific to do. It was the only remedy George could think of on what she knew at present.

The ordering of a bridal car was one wedding detail which had gone awry. But with the weather clear and bright, it was not a disaster. The church was only half a mile from the Tavistock's guest house. They could all walk in dribs and drabs, led by the bride and groom. A prescient Kirstie had slipped into St Ives the day before and bought Maxine a white skiing jacket, which gave some protection from the cold. The chance for informal chat on the way down was an extra bonus.

For George this was a chance to catch up with Robbie. He had appeared mid morning, contrite about missing last night's rehearsal but still eager to read the lesson. That lapse was forgivable. George was less impressed though when she realised he had spent another night in St Ives.

'What's going on, Robbie? Am I missing something? Has Siobhan taken my place?'

Robbie could see no way of finessing the situation. It would be best to be straight. George had been a good friend; that was the least he could do.

'The thing is, George, a long time ago, back in Bristol, Siobhan and I were very close friends indeed. It would have gone a lot further but there was an almighty mix up over a final meal together where we missed each other. After that we each went our separate ways. We hadn't been in touch since.

'I only contacted her this week when I wanted access to a mining expert. The trouble was, when we did meet we couldn't help ourselves, we found ourselves carrying on where we left off twenty years ago.'

There was a pause. How would George take it, he wondered? He could see from her demeanour that it had come as a shock.

'Oh Robbie, I feel so sad and so wretched. But to be honest it's not fair to complain. You and I haven't made a very good job of building a solid relationship, we always seem to be rushing past one another in opposite directions. I guess if it had been going to work then by now we'd have made sure it did.'

She swallowed hard. 'Siobhan seems a great friend for you. I've only seen you together the once, two evenings ago, but you gel so well. It's great you've found one another. I hope though that you and I can stay friends in the future. You've been a real blessing to me. It would be terrible to lose you completely.'

If there hadn't been wedding guests all around they would have given one another an all-embracing hug, but they could both see that, here and now, that might be misunderstood. Robbie made sure though that he clutched her hand and squeezed it tight. It had been good to talk.

They continued walking down the road together. George glanced behind her, noticed there was no-one close behind. It was a chance to give Robbie an update.

'I was talking to Peter a few minutes ago,' said George. 'He tells me that Maxine's dad, Alex, was taken in for questioning after the service by the Penzance police. So he may not be around for the reception. But he asked me to keep it under wraps. It's made Maria very upset.'

This was an afternoon of shocks. 'Wow.' There was a pause. 'I wonder if that's anything to do with Siobhan's visit there this morning.'

'What was that all about?'

'We haven't had chance to talk about it with you, but we had a great day yesterday. We heard about a conference in Penryn, just before Christmas. Hocking was there. Since it was only two days before his death we thought we'd better tell the police. I haven't had chance yet to find out how her visit went. I was busy visiting Father Giles. He was at the conference too, he's a friend of Hocking.'

'You've made a lot of progress, Robbie. With Siobhan's help, of course. When you get the chance it'd be worth passing the news on to Peter. As you can imagine, with Alex down at the police station, the bridegroom's not in a position to relax. It's not exactly the wedding day he was hoping for.'

CHAPTER 45

There was one picture which Maxine had especially wanted: the bride and groom, herself and Peter, standing in their wedding finery on top of Cape Cornwall. Consequently the pair did not go into Chy Brisons when they reached it, but carried on down the road.

Many of the guests, especially Maxine's old friends from college, had never been to this remote part of the Cornish peninsula and had followed the couple down to the headland. There was still a brilliantly clear sky, though by now it was mid-afternoon and the temperature was starting to fall. Maxine had warmed up a little on the walk down but she would cool again in the various poses now required.

Kirstie took the planned pictures of the couple and then several bonus ones that included many of the guests as they strolled about enjoying the view. It was a good job, she thought, that she'd taken the trouble to research the best angles and backgrounds.

'This is where I met your police colleague,' she told Peter, as she took a concluding picture of the pair, coming down the path from the headland. 'He said he'd talk to you later. Has he caught up with you yet?'

'Hey, I haven't seen my dad recently,' added Maxine. She

started to add two and two together. 'D'you know what's happened to him, Peter?'

'I'll tell you both. But for now we'll need to keep it from the guests. Why don't we turn around, have one more sunset picture at the top?'

As Kirstie settled them into a "contented couple" pose, with the ruin of Botallack Mine on one side and the grey Atlantic surging beyond, Peter summarised his various conversations over the day with Percy Popper; and also outlined the man's subsequent actions.

'My last chat with Percy was this afternoon. It was a brief phone call after I learned that the person who borrowed a small-wheeled folding bike in Penzance last Thursday – that's the day Hocking died – was called Tavistock. And that went with the cycle tracks near Ding Dong Mine that you and I spotted, Kirstie.'

The bridegroom shook his head. 'I'm so, so sorry, Maxine. I'm afraid the evidence is not looking good.'

Maxine seemed to shrink as the facts overwhelmed her. For a few seconds she was lost for words. Then she recovered her power of speech and her emotions took charge.

'But you're talking nonsense, Peter,' she protested angrily. 'My dad a murderer? He would never do such a thing.'

A pause and then cold logic took over. 'And he doesn't need a bicycle of any sort to get anywhere. I mean, he owns a car. In any case, how would that explain Hocking's car disappearing and reappearing at Ding Dong like a Land's End winter bus? Surely no-one thinks the man got there on the back of a push bike?'

It didn't make sense to Peter either. He could only trust that, against the odds, Popper knew what he was doing.

By now the informal procession was setting off in twos and threes back to Chy Brisons. This was the point at which the capacity of the building and barn would be pitted against the final size of the wedding party. Maria had been worried all week at the way Maxine seemed to be adding to their number. It was a tight fit, but as several of the guests remarked, being squeezed close together did at least keep everyone warm.

'We don't need a formal greeting. There'll be plenty of time, during and after the meal, to greet each of the guests,' she declared, 'Peter and I can go round and talk to them table by table.' Two of the ushers were instructed to take charge of all presents offered and keep them safe in the guesthouse office. For once a key had been provided.

For his part, Peter had requested that the speeches should precede the Wedding Breakfast. He didn't think he would enjoy the meal knowing that he had a speech to deliver at the end of it. It was much better to get the formalities over early. Of course, when he'd insisted on this he hadn't expected that one of the speakers would be missing, "helping the police with their inquiries".

Alice murmured to Maria that the Wedding Breakfast was close to ready. The mother of the bride responded by gently but firmly urging the guests out towards the Barn.

'Wow. Doesn't that look fantastic!' exclaimed one of the

307

guests to her partner as they stepped inside.

Alex and Ross had done a great job, laying the place out to maximise the use of space. There was just room for ten tables, each hosting six or seven guests. Shelley and Frances had gone mad with the decorations. A poinsettia adorned every table, balloons and other festive decorations were hanging down from the ceiling. The lighting was provided by multi-coloured Christmas tree lights, wrapped around every beam and window.

Many of the guests had heard the term "Barn" and feared that the place would be icy cold. They were pleasantly surprised to see heaters glowing beneath the rafters and they could see the problem, if anything, was going to be overheating. The place was already warm. Quite a few scurried back to deposit their coats in the guesthouse cloakroom.

It had been agreed that there would be one top table, set at the far end of the Barn on a dais. The same platform would later provide the stage for The Slaters. The top table was for the bride and groom, best man and bridesmaids. The rest of the guests would arrange themselves as they chose around the remaining tables.

Just one of these had a reserve notice. That was for Maria, Alex (if he turned up), Ross and Lisa and Peter's family, Tony and Celia.

Robbie and Siobhan found themselves at the same table as John and Sally from the Carn Galver Lunch Box. No doubt they'd been invited as long-standing friends of Alex and Maria. Numbers were completed by Father Sidney Giles and Esther Middleton.

It was clear that the locals knew one another, no doubt Sidney had regularly enjoyed the delights of Carn Galver. It seemed Esther was there to partner Sidney. Robbie felt he'd lost any claim on a special status as friend of the chief bridesmaid after his serious conversation earlier. Siobhan had been given a last-minute invite, recognising her role in the "case team".

There was some time to chat, between the guests starting to sit down and the next event on the schedule. Sidney seized the opportunity.

'Ah, John, Sally. There was a question I wanted to ask you. You know that dreadful death last week up at Ding Dong?'

'Awful, wasn't it,' replied Sally. 'What's your question?'

'Well, I don't know if you know, but I was one of the coast-guard team called out to recover the body. It was worse than that, actually. I had to go down the shaft to strap him to a stretcher, ready for it to be hauled up.'

'Dreadful business,' commiserated John. 'No fun for anyone.'

'The thing is, a receipt dropped out of Jeremy's pocket as we were preparing him for the stretcher. I'd put it in my pocket, forgotten about it until a policeman came to see me this morning. So I had another look. According to the receipt, Jeremy had been to your cafe just before he died. On Thursday December 22nd in fact. Is that right?'

'We get a lot of customers, Father. I can't possibly remember them all.'

Sally, though, recalled the visit clearly. 'Don't you remember, John, I said so when we heard about his death. But do the police know exactly when he died?'

It looked as though Sally would be the only one that could take this subject any further.

'If they know they haven't told me. But the odd thing is,' Sidney went on, 'the receipt is for two coffees. He wasn't on his own. So can you remember who he was with? It might be important, you see. That might be the last person to see him alive.'

Sally frowned in a way that suggested she was thinking hard. 'It wasn't anyone I knew well.'

Sidney felt frustrated. It had been a long shot, almost bound to fail. Then he had a moment of inspiration. After all, several locals of Land's End were in the room. 'I don't suppose it's anyone here?'

Sally looked slowly round the crowded room. 'It could be one of those over there.' Her hand waved towards Maria's table.

'Thank you very much, Sally. I'll have a chat with them later.'

CHAPTER 46

Tony Travers, Peter's fisherman brother from Padstow, was his only close family member present that afternoon. Their mother was very elderly, lived in a Care Home in Port Isaac and hadn't been well enough to travel. Tony was the Master of Ceremonies and relished the chance to contribute to the occasion.

Maria leant across and spoke a word in his ear. Alice had told her it was now time to begin. Tony stood up, moved onto the dais and called for silence. It was a good job he had a loud voice, it took a moment or two for the chatter to die down.

'At this wedding, friends, we are going to enjoy the speeches before we start the reception meal. That's mainly to deal with one or two speaker's nerves. I'm not mentioning any names. But without further ado I give you the bridegroom, my brother, Peter Travers.'

A few laughs and a round of warm applause as Peter stood up. He looked round the tightly packed Barn and felt a surge of pride.

'Ladies and gentlemen, family and friends, best man and bridesmaids, my wife and I want to welcome you all here on this happy occasion. This is a really emotional wedding – look, even the cake is in tiers.'

A pause, then a ripple of laughter went round the room.

311

'Before I say a little about how Maxine and I came to meet, I want to say various thank you's to everyone who has made this day possible.

'First of I'd like to say a heartfelt thanks to Alex and Maria for hosting the event so splendidly. This cosy Barn where we're gathered now didn't look anything like this a week ago. Maxine's dad, Alex, and his brother Ross, who's over from Australia, have worked tirelessly, day after day. We have them to thank for fixing the heating on the rafters and the lights to the beams. They're both mechanical engineers so we can only hope it all stays lit. You would hardly believe it but most of this stuff only reached St Just ten days ago. It's a demonstration of Cornwall's industrial potential. Bring on Cornish independence.'

A cheer from the locals. It was a popular slogan round here.

'Most of all I must single out Maria, Maxine's mum. She's worked tirelessly and been a great hostess for all who've been down to help get things ready. And thank you both, most of all, for your wonderful daughter.'

'There are others, too, who we should thank. Two of the bridesmaids are Maxine's cousins, Shelley and Frances. They've made a great job of decorating the Barn. Thanks, too, to Brian's wife, Alice, who's prepared us a massive banquet. And to friends from the church, who gave us the smashing cake reception earlier – I hope you all left space for the main meal.' He glanced across the room. 'Thank you too, Sidney Giles and Esther Middleton, who led us through the wedding service.'

He paused to draw breath. That was the thanks dealt with.

'I'd like now to tell you a little more about Maxine. She and I

312

first met in Delabole, in the house of my best man Brian and his wife Alice. So the first meal my wife and I had together was cooked by Alice, who is going to be catering for us today. You might think that's a happy coincidence but I'd say it's a mark of how far Maxine plans ahead.

'Our first walk together was a tramp round the top of Delabole Slate Quarry. I should perhaps explain, to those of you from this end of Cornwall, that while you sink deep shafts we dig massive craters. In fact our slate quarry is the largest in Europe. And after seven hundred years it shows no signs of running out.

'The Slaters from Delabole, who'll be entertaining us later, have chosen their name with care. They know so many songs. Did you enjoy their folksy rendering of "Amazing Grace"? And did you notice the last line, the talk of "Forever Mine"? Hold onto that phrase. You might consider it a good term for a geothermal mine. Once it's dug, you see, if it's located in the right place, then it will produce electricity not just for a few years or even a few centuries but for ever.'

Peter stopped again, pacing himself.

'Finally, I'd better tell you a little about myself before my best man blackens my record. Some of you may know that I'm a policeman.' He laughed. 'I can see the guilty conscience on some of your faces. Don't worry, folks, I'm off duty. I won't be booking any of you for speeding. Cornwall's roads are built to suppress speed, anyway.

'I'd say my conscience is clear. Though you might think that just means I've got a dreadful memory. Which to be honest, is one reason I need Maxine. She has a fabulous memory.'

313

He went on to recall a feat of recall that had helped solve their first case. 'That's when I started to learn what a mathematical brain has to offer.'

'So a policeman doesn't just manage traffic. He has to chase alibis. When someone is accused of a crime that happened at a known time, can they prove they were somewhere else altogether? For example, if the washing machine jams at home when I'm at work, I have a perfect alibi: I wasn't there at the time.

'Mind, if the washing machine fails for Maxine, I want to be there with her. My goal is to be part of the solution, not part of the problem.'

He spoke for a little longer and then came to the conclusion.

'So, ladies and gentlemen, I'll conclude with a toast. "To the bride, the lovely Maxine. I hope she'll be Forever Mine." '

There was a scramble as the guests seized their glasses and rose to their feet. 'To the bride: the lovely Maxine.' And then a round of applause as Peter sat down.

Maxine leant over and whispered in his ear. 'Well done, Peter. But your speech reminded me: Dad has an alibi for the time of the murder. That was the day he took the Australians over to Truro to show them the Cathedral and pick up the heaters. He was with them all the time. Mum told me about the day when I rang her that evening. Don't you remember me telling you?'

CHAPTER 47

There was a few minutes pause during which glasses were refilled. Maria noticed that Ross Tavistock seemed to be drinking enough wine for his brother as well. But then, she remembered, he was Australian. Then Tony Travers stood up once more, demanded silence and called on Dr Brian Southgate to give the best man's speech.

Brian had been looking forward to this opportunity for years but feared, as Peter remained steadfastly single, that he would never have the chance. Now it had come. In his preparations over the week he had noted down some of the mishaps which had befallen Peter in his younger days. He'd got one or two tales of the young policeman's training in Plymouth and some of the awkward colleagues he had tangled with. It was a good job Sergeant Popper wasn't in the room. He'd searched exhaustively, even gone back as far as the days they'd shared at school.

Peter, too, had been looking forward to the event, even fine-tuned some of Brian's memories. His own public speaking ordeal was now over and he could relax, listen and enjoy.

Except that, though he pretended to be attentive, the police-man could barely listen at all. His mind was working overtime, trying to make sense of the case fragments he had assembled over the last week.

315

So what was the case against Alex? Motive, for example? Why on earth should his father-in-law have done away with someone he knew, the luckless Jeremy Hocking? They had talked in their evening case reviews about someone who feared a new mining scheme on the peninsula, but would Alex hate it that much? He recalled a comment from George: she'd seen books on geothermal energy in the man's office. He probably wasn't opposed to geothermal energy at all.

So he hadn't found a plausible motive. But that might be because he hadn't seen all the evidence. He wished he knew exactly what Siobhan had shown the police in Penzance. He hadn't had chance to ask her about it yet but that was certainly something he needed to do during the evening.

On the other hand, where if anywhere was the opportunity? Had Alex really been with his wife and family for the whole of that Thursday, as Maxine had just whispered in his ear? As he'd made clear in his speech, he trusted Maxine's memory completely; but was it possible that her mother had mis-remembered, or given her incomplete information?

Perhaps, say, Alex had claimed to be away for a couple of hours sorting out the heaters? Would that have given him long enough to slip over to Ding Dong, push Hocking down the shaft and then rush back again? The policeman tried to visualise the map. Truro was in mid-Cornwall but the roads around it were good. How long would Alex have needed? It might be geographically possible; but was it psychologically feasible?

If there was strong evidence that Alex was innocent, shouldn't he tell Percy Popper right away? Well yes, but no-one would expect him to walk out of the reception in the middle of his friend's "Best Man" speech.

Anyway, what was he to make of the bike hiring on the fatal Thursday? It was the shop owner who had produced the name Tavistock, not him. Maybe there was someone else of that name living around here? Was it just a ghastly coincidence? Or did the small-wheeled bike and its tangled trail across the moor have nothing to do with the case at all?

For a few minutes Peter came back to the world around him. By now Brian had the room in stitches. It was clear there was a lot more to come. Once his friend was onto things that had gone wrong, he could talk for a long while.

'I recall one case,' said Brian, 'which started with a headless, armless torso in an old quarry. The problem was identity. Peter developed a theory that the arms hadn't been cut off to erase fingerprints but to hide tattoos. Off he went to the local tattoo parlour. The trouble was saying exactly what he was after. He'd got two tattoos on his bottom before they realised all he wanted was access to their records.'

Brian turned to Maxine. 'So that's one more thing for you to check on this evening, my dear.' There was another burst of laughter.

Peter mused on. There were other Tavistocks, of course, in fact a whole family of them, sitting on the table in front of him. In particular there was Alex's brother, Ross. So might he be the one that had hired the bike?

No, that made no sense. For a start, motive was non-existent. Ross wouldn't care two hoots about a new geothermal plant in

317

Land's End. He'd be back on the other side of the world in a week's time, years before anything was built. And anyway, he recalled, Maxine had reported Maria saying that Alex had taken his Australian family for the day to Truro. The alibi covered Ross as well as Alex.

And he was still no further forward on Jeremy's itinerant car near Ding Dong. He could imagine why the murderer might have driven off in it – even driven off with the bike folded inside. For example, that might make it less likely that a body would be found there. But if that was the case, why on earth should it be brought back a few days later?

Baffled, he tuned in again to his best man. He was now in his prime story-telling mode and had left all facts far behind.

'There was one time, I recall,' said Brian, 'when the young Peter was posted to the town of Newquay. One day he was driving down the road past the zoo when he came across a vehicle involved in a bad traffic accident. Peter, keen and diligent, stopped his car but it wasn't clear what had happened. As he got out a monkey slipped through the fence towards him.

"I wish you could talk," he muttered, scratching his head. To his amazement the monkey seemed to nod.

"So what happened?" The monkey paused for a moment and then raised his arms, mimicked someone swigging a large can of beer.

"Ah, so they were drinking?" The monkey nodded again.

"What else?"

This time the monkey pinched his fingers together and held them towards his mouth.

"And they were smoking?" Another nod. What substance wasn't clear, but he didn't think even this monkey would be that clever.

"So the driver was drinking and smoking?" Nod.

"And what were you doing during all this?"

"Driving," motioned the monkey.

More guffaws of laughter went round the Barn. Peter feared he would never live this down, hoped that his friend would have the sense to quit while he was ahead. Mercifully, a few minutes later, he did.

'But I see from the way my wife is tapping her watch, to make sure it's still going, that my time is up. So now I invite you all to stand, please, and drink another toast.'

He seized his glass as the guests pushed back their chairs and stood with him. 'To four lovely ladies: George, Shelley, Frances and Katrina – Maxine's delightful bridesmaids.'

There was still no sign of Alex. After another chance for everyone to refill their glasses, Maria nodded at Father Giles. He smiled in response, got to his feet and headed for the dais.

Tony Travers once more called for silence. 'And now, rounding off the speeches on behalf of the Tavistock family, I give you Father Sidney Giles, family friend and vicar of St Just.'

The vicar took a moment to prepare and to let his audience settle. It would be wise to leave a small space after the previous humdinger.

'Friends, I am glad of this chance to speak on behalf of Alex and Maria. They have been regular members of the congregation

319

here for many years. I am so glad they invited me to be with you all on this happy occasion.

'My only regret is that the Tavistock's did not live here when they were bringing up young Maxine. Esther, my colleague today, who knew her at Cambridge, tells me she would have asked searching questions of my Sunday School class. And later, I guess, of my sermons.

'Most questions, though, do have answers. There is a great deal of logic in Scripture. Peter talked earlier about alibis. Alibis may prove someone was elsewhere but they can confirm presence as well as covering absence. I'm sure Maxine will be able to augment Peter's analytical skills with her own, feminine qualities. Only some of which are in the mind.'

A gentle chuckle went round the room. Maxine, looking embarrassed, glanced down at the top of her lacy dress.

'So now, friends, let us stand for one more toast: To Maxine and Peter, the happy couple. We wish them both well in their lives together.'

The toast was confirmed by everyone present.

As Sidney squeezed past Peter to leave the dais he murmured in his ear. 'That wasn't the speech I'd expected to give. Standing up here gave me an entirely new perspective. I'll tell you what it is when the meal is over.'

So Peter did not have an entirely stress-free meal after all.

CHAPTER 48

At Tony Travers' invitation the Rev Esther Middleton was requested to say grace. Then the meal was served.

There had been some discussion between Maria and Alice as to how this was to be done. The idea of individual servings had been rejected as being too slow, even using her usual waitresses. In any case it was New Year's Eve. The girls were all busy, mostly enjoying themselves in St Ives.

In the end the food was brought in using piping hot tureens and served to the tables, with the current household guests acting as waiters. Kirstie put down her camera as she took hot venison casserole to the top table, though she did manage to snatch an image of the happy couple about to eat. Esther, Maria and Lisa supplied two more tables each. Even Ross "stood up to the plate".

Then a sight gladdened Peter's eye. For among the helpers was Holly Berry, his colleague from Bude. She was back from Penzance police station, evidently, and had resumed her role as usher. Did that mean . . .?

He was about to point her out to Maxine when there was a ping and all the lights in the Barn went out. A gasp from the guests, one or two whimpers of panic. There was limited illumination from mobile phones.

It wasn't a widespread power cut, as some in the media had feared when the cold spell gripped the nation. The guests could see across the darkened lawn to the guesthouse: lights were still on over there. And also up in the village.

The darkness only lasted a minute and then lighting was restored. Relief all round, there was no damage done. Tureens continued to be brought to the tables. But now, Peter observed, there was someone else carrying them in. For Alex, smiling at his diversion, was once more part of the crew.

For the next hour there was nothing that could be done to advance the investigation. Maxine forced her new husband to concentrate on the meal, the guests and the occasion.

'I gave you a free hand all this last week, Peter,' she observed. 'You've chased about the peninsula to your heart's content, mostly with my female friends. But right now you've another job to contend with. Say to yourself, "I am not on duty, this is my Wedding Breakfast." I mean, it's a unique occasion. Everyone here wants to see us enjoying it. That's why they're here.'

The policeman could see that for the moment nothing could be done. He was itching to talk to Sidney, to Robbie and Siobhan, and indeed to Holly and Alex, but all the guests were busy eating and chatting with their neighbours.

Everyone agreed that the food itself was truly delicious, Alice had excelled herself.

For some time the newlyweds were able to relax and make the most of the occasion. Maxine pointed out her friends from Bude and places beyond who had arrived earlier in the day. Peter did his best to remember the names, he'd meet them properly later on. In turn he pointed out some of his friends from Delabole: The Slaters hadn't come on their own.

It was only after the meal was over and coffee was being served that there was a chance for the top table to circulate. That was also the chance for The Slaters to quietly fold up the top table and make space for their various musical instruments. The folk group would stand there to perform later on.

Maxine, though, was not letting Peter loose. This was her wedding and she was making the most of it. 'We'll go round all the tables once both together, Peter. If you really need to, you can cross-examine your sources afterwards.'

Several of the people he was introduced to were Maxine's old friends from college. They were a similar age and presumably highly intelligent, though he didn't feel they were looking down on him. Either they trusted Maxine's judgement, or else assumed he was a top level policeman. He did his best to act out the role.

Most of Maxine's friends were well-established couples, though there was one man on his own who looked slightly disconnected.

'Hi Harry,' said Maxine, giving him a big hug. 'So glad you could make it.'

'It was a battle but they let me out in the end,' he replied.

'If you want some company, George is on her own,' observed Maxine, nodding at the chief bridesmaid who was circulating on the far side of the room.

'Ah.' Peter wasn't sure if it was his imagination, but did a glow appear in the man's eyes?

Peter was tempted to ask Harry if he'd just been released from prison but managed to restrain himself. It was more likely, he thought, given Maxine's connections, that the man was one side of a spy exchange with some nefarious country in the back of beyond.

Eventually the pair had toured the room once and Peter was left free to pursue his inquiries. It still wasn't easy. Most of those he wanted to talk to were equally busy talking to someone else.

Usher Holly was sitting by herself in a purple outfit near to the Barn doorway. She was his invite, he remembered, no one could complain if he spent time with her. She also had the latest inside knowledge. The policeman grabbed a seat beside her.

'Great occasion, guv,' she said. 'Thank you for inviting me.'

'I'm off duty right now, Holly. Please call me Peter. Thank you so much for your work earlier.'

'It was no trouble. Alex was compliant enough. Sergeant Popper must have scared him earlier, perhaps less with stick than with carrot. He might have been promised an early return if he was cooperative. As in the end he was.'

The policeman frowned. 'But you were away for hours. Was Alex being interviewed all that time?' He was desperate for full details but knew he was no longer an independent man.

Holly looked at him and grinned. She too was a dedicated police officer and knew what he was after.

'I could give you a résumé if you like?' The answering sigh was all she needed.

'Popper began by asking Alex about his relation to Hocking.

He admitted they'd known each other for a long time.

'Then Popper asked about financial relations between the two. Alex was silent for some time. Your colleague pressed him. Said he'd happened to notice his bank statement while waiting to interview him. And seen it showed regular monthly payments from Alex to Hocking.'

'Wow.' This was new information to Peter.

'Alex got quite angry, said the policeman had no business peering into his bank account. "You've neither permission nor a search warrant."

'Popper was unapologetic. He hadn't pried, he said, the folder of bank statements was open on the desk and the name of the man he was investigating jumped out. But he kept asking, why was Alex paying all this money to the now dead man?'

'Did Alex tell him?'

'Not at first. Well, not for quite a while. After a bit Popper switched tack, started talking about an accident that Hocking had suffered at Rosemanowas geothermal plant in 1980. First Alex tried to deny it. Then he said the man was fully recovered and it was a long time ago.'

'But Holly, I don't understand. What on earth would any of that have to do with Alex?'

'Well, somehow or other Popper had got hold of the official accident report. That's how he knew about Hocking being the accident victim. He turned to a marked page and thrust it forward. That showed that the operator on duty that night was one A. Tavistock.'

'Incredible. So what happened next?'

'Alex denied it, swore he wasn't on duty that night. He said the report must have made a mistake. At that point, in desperation, he gave us an alternative reason why he was paying Hocking. It wasn't any kind of blackmail payment, he said. Rather, he was sponsoring a project on geothermal energy, in which Hocking was the key worker.'

Holly paused and looked at him. 'Remember, Peter, I'm just giving you a résumé. I don't have the background to do more. All this took place with plenty of stalling, interleaved with frantic deliberation. I'm just telling you where we finally got to.'

'So Popper just accepted his word and sent him home?'

'Oh no. There was another round of questions to come. That was when Popper produced a letter from Hocking to Alex and asked him what that was all about.'

'No doubt that prompted more questions on how he'd got it?'

'Alex was past all that by now. He admitted that Hocking had sent him the letter. But he said Popper was misreading it. He'd started off thinking this was a case of blackmail and read that into it.

'In fact, Alex said, the letter was simply a warning from Hocking. It stated that he would need a bigger payment next month to process the data he'd collected. It wasn't an extra blackmail request at all.'

'Hm. What did you think?'

'To be honest, Peter, it could be read either way. Either as subtle pressure for more blackmail funding or else as a straightforward project request. It wasn't clear.'

'So that was when he was sent home?'

'Oh, it wasn't that at all. At some point late in the interview Popper claimed Hocking's death had occurred on Thursday Dec 22nd. Alex said that was wrong: he'd previously been told the man died on the 23rd.'

'Yes, that was what the police first thought.'

'Well, at this point Alex seemed to brighten. He could see a way out. "But I wasn't around on the 22nd," he said. "Maria and I took Lisa to Truro for the day to show her the cathedral. I got the barn heaters from B&Q while I was there." He took out his wallet and scrambled through some old papers. "Here, I've still got the receipt."'

'Exactly what time did it give for the purchase?' asked Peter.

'Half past twelve on Dec 22nd.'

Peter mused for a second. Was this watertight? 'But we don't know the time of Hocking's death do we?'

'Popper did. Or at least he had strong evidence for it. Hocking was wearing a watch when he fell, you see. It stopped when he hit the ground, giving the time as 12:17. So I'd say that was almost certainly when he died. Which means that, whoever gave him a push, it couldn't possibly have been Alex Tavistock.'

CHAPTER 49

Maxine tapped Peter on the shoulder. 'You've had enough "job time" for now. It's time for us to cut the cake.'

The policeman glanced at his watch and realised with a shock that he'd been talking to Holly for half an hour. 'Sorry, darling. I got carried away.'

'Make sure there's something left for me.'

His wife headed for the small table across the room where a three-tiered, finely decorated chocolate cake was waiting. Tony Travers saw the pair coming and stood to make his final announcement.

'Gather round everyone, please. Maxine and Peter are now going to cut the cake.'

By now the tables had been folded away and the chairs arranged round the walls of the Barn. That left the space in the middle ready for dancing. Some of the guests had migrated to the guesthouse for peace and quiet but they heard the call. Soon everyone was clustered together for the ceremony.

'Could Alice our master chef please provide a knife,' called Tony.

Alice heard the cry and emerged from the kitchen. Her work for the day was now almost over.

'Ladies and gentlemen, before we go any further, please can we show our appreciation to our champion chef, who has fed us so well.' Peter's call led to a resounding round of applause, a stamping of feet and a myriad cheers.

Alice looked embarrassed at the warmth of the approval. 'I'd gladly do it all again. It's been a privilege and a joy.'

After which Maxine and Peter were given the cake knife. Slowly and carefully they inserted it into the lowest layer and carved the initial slice.

Then Alice seized the whole cake and took it off to the kitchen to be sliced into sensible portions.

Father Sidney tapped Peter on the shoulder as he moved away. 'Have you a moment?'

'Of course. Why don't we go outside for some fresh air?'

Outside and fifty yards away from Chy Brisons it was cold and very dark. The sky was still clear and studded with a vast array of stars.

'Right, Father. So you've seen something the police should know about?'

'It may be nothing. But your friend Robbie started me thinking. He came to see me this morning, reminded me that I went to a mining conference in Penryn a few days before Christmas. Jeremy Hocking, he was a long-time friend, knew I was interested and took me. There were about forty present. In the afternoon Jeremy took one of the delegates to see the model of the geothermal plant that used to run at Rosemanowas Quarry. My friend came back looking rather upset.'

He stopped.

Peter assumed he had finished. 'Thank you, Father –'

'That's not all, Peter. This evening, standing on the dais for my speech, I recognised who had gone off with Jeremy. I was looking down at all the guests, you see: seated, with the men in their best suits. A bit like they were at the conference.'

Peter frowned. 'So who was it?'

'It was the bride's uncle: Ross Tavistock. It doesn't make sense, does it? He'd only been in the country for forty eight hours. Not been here before that for thirty years. It might just be a coincidence. But I was fond of Jeremy, he'd had some hard knocks but he was making the best of his later life. It would be good for his killer to be caught, wouldn't it?'

Father Giles went back inside for another drink but Peter wandered down towards Cape Cornwall, pondering deeply. The street lights didn't go down this far but by now his eyes had adjusted to the dark.

What possible motive might Ross Tavistock have to kill Jeremy Hocking? It couldn't be to end his geothermal project, surely. Ross wouldn't care much about that. In any case, Holly's account had shown that his brother, Alex, was behind the project. It couldn't be that bad.

But if not that then . . . what about blackmail?

What if . . . what if Ross had seen the bank statements that Alex seemed to leave lying about so casually in his office? Maybe he had asked his brother about it but received no satisfactory answer. It was, after all, a secret project. What if he had then made the same jump as Sergeant Popper, assumed Alex was being blackmailed by Hocking, based on memory of the incident at

Rosemanowas?

Or was it even worse? The report had blamed Alex Tavistock for the incident but he had protested that wasn't true. How hard would it be to change an operator's hand-written sign-in initial from R to A? Was it possible that it was Ross Tavistock that had been the operator duty that fateful night? Was that why he'd gone off so suddenly to Australia, and not come back for so many years?

Almost as soon as he had arrived in the UK, Ross had gone to the conference in Penryn on behalf of his firm in Australia. He'd wanted to hear what was going on in mining elsewhere. Maybe it was a pure accident that he'd come across Hocking, been shown the model and heard him talk about his injury at first hand.

But then the two strands had come together. He'd learned that the man was wandering about isolated moors on his own in the depths of winter. Ross had suddenly realised that he could deal with Hocking, end the man's blackmail on his brother for good, and be out the country altogether inside a week.

He might well calculate that, as an outsider, the chances of being caught were negligible. Would have been completely negligible, except that his niece happened to be marrying a policeman with a nose for crime.

Was it Ross and not Alex that had hired the small-wheel bike? Peter couldn't quite see why he should have moved Hocking's car away and then brought it back a few days later but maybe determined questioning might dig that out.

At the very least Ross needed to be taken into the police station for questioning. There might still be DNA traces from

331

the previous driver on the Skoda. They would need to compare these with a sample from the Australian. That might prove conclusively that Ross had driven Hocking's car. And that in turn would give him a direct connection with the crime.

Peter saw that he needed to talk to Holly. This would be best handled by her. For he couldn't do it himself: his marriage had given him a personal connection. For it seemed, horribly, that Hocking's killer was a member of his newly-acquired extended family.

CHAPTER 50

The rest of the reception seemed to go in a blur. The Slaters proved to be talented musicians with a huge repertoire of songs, old and new. Over the next couple of hours they managed to get almost everyone to dance, one way or another.

Peter and Maxine led the early dances and were hyperactive for some time. Then, somewhat hot and flustered, they stood back to let others lead the way. By now it was all free and easy. The two didn't have to dance as a couple or even be on the dance floor together.

At some point, when Maxine was locked into a Cumberland reel that might go on for some time, Peter managed to manoeuvre himself next to Holly. He was glad to see she'd only got a soft drink in her hand.

'Can we chat?'

'It's my turn next on the cloakroom rota,' she told him. 'No reason why I shouldn't take over early.' Quietly the two made their way to the guesthouse cloakroom. It was mid evening, no-one else was around.

'Here's my theory,' said the policeman. He spoke for some time, outlining his thoughts from his stroll down to Cape Cornwall. 'Ross might not be guilty of anything but he needs to be questioned as soon as possible.'

'But it's New Year's Eve, Peter,' she protested. 'I doubt Popper's still on duty, let alone at his most incisive. All police effort will be on restraining those who've hit the bottle. Can't this wait till tomorrow?'

Peter considered. Ross was unlikely to be going far tonight. After all, the wedding was what he'd come halfway round the world to attend.

'I guess you're right, Holly. First thing tomorrow will be fine. But I know Ross keeps his hire car round the back here. Why don't you park yours in front of it, stop him driving off anywhere?'

A few more details were settled then Peter slipped back into the Barn. He was just in time to catch a wobbling Maxine as the reel came to an end.

Just before ten the taxi driver that Peter had approached in Penzance appeared in the Barn doorway.

Peter wasn't sure if the man was being super-punctual, wanting to make sure bride and groom had plenty of time on their own or just creating space for late-evening bookings. Whatever it was, he wasn't going to argue.

Their suitcases were rescued from the cloakroom, farewells were made. Soon they were seated in the back seats, heading round the coast road.

As part of their wedding plan Peter had made all arrangements for the honeymoon. His bride had to trust him, didn't even know where they were going. It didn't matter, she thought, as she snuggled up beside him. It was all the start of their great new adventure.

The car headed past Geevor Mine, past Morvah and past Carn Galver. Maxine wondered if they were heading for St Ives.

But they weren't. A couple of miles after Carn Galver a large, well-lit building loomed out of the darkness. 'I've booked us in for a couple of nights at the Gurnard Hotel. After that we'll go further afield.'

Still in their wedding gear, the couple made their way into the hotel. It was obvious who they were. Keys were handed over. 'We've put you in the room at the top,' said the receptionist. 'It's not quite a penthouse but most of our honeymoon couples prefer it. It's really quiet.'

Maxine could see that this was a high-class hotel, even if it was off the beaten track. Peter had done well to find it. Soon they were being escorted to their room. For the next few hours Peter Travers gave all his thoughts to a different form of ding dong.

The weather next morning, as far as they could judge from their high bedroom window, was a continuation of the day before: bright but cold.

'At least you'll be able to dress warmly today,' Peter remarked, 'though you did look so lovely in your wedding dress. We could walk along the Coast Path, maybe go to Carn Galver for coffee.'

Most of the hotel guests had stayed up to see in the New Year so were in no hurry to rise for the rest of New Year's Day. The honeymoon couple, though, still had the adrenalin of the wedding preparations pumping through their veins and were in the breakfast room by eight.

335

Neither had over-eaten the day before so were ready for a sizzling hot breakfast. For once they could eat at their leisure.

Inevitably the conversation moved onto the death at Ding Dong and subsequent enquiries.

Peter was about to admit his latest thoughts on Ross Tavistock, reminding himself that this was his wife's rarely-seen uncle. How would she cope with the notion that he was now being questioned in Penzance? Would she mind that her new husband was the one that had caused that to happen?

But Maxine got her news in first. 'I had a good chat with Aunt Lisa towards the end of the dancing last night. We went out to see the night sky over Cape Cornwall, it was stunning. It gave me chance to ask her how she'd got on this week tracing her Cornish ancestry.'

'I thought she was a hundred percent Australian?'

'She was born and brought up there alright, same as her father; and she has an Australian passport. But it seems her mother didn't. She came from St Ives.'

'Wow, you mean she's a local. So that's what Lisa's been doing on her various trips to St Ives.'

'Well, she'd done the internet research beforehand and brought all her mother's documents with her. So it wasn't that hard. She managed to track down her cousin, anyway.'

'Good for her. Where did she find them?'

'It was a "he". He's still running the photographic shop in St Ives where her mum used to work before the war. That's why he and his wife were invited last night. He was the one in the musty looking suit.'

'D'you know, I wondered who that was. Robbie and Siobhan seemed to have come across him somewhere.'

'The thing is, Aunt Lisa knew the whole story. Her mum was a young professional photographer before and during the war. Her speciality was tin mines. She'd been to see Brandy Mine, actually been down the main shaft and knew it was hot. Later she'd helped to film it being blown up by the Army.'

'Golly. Was that the exercise Robbie told us about?'

'I think it must have been. That was how she met her husband, anyway. He was an Australian commando. Though I'm not sure "met" is the word.'

'How d'you mean?'

'Well, on their first encounter he knocked her over, stripped her practically naked, tied her up and left her on the cliffs.'

Peter frowned. 'That's no way to treat a girl.'

'No. He had the grace to come back, though, when the exercise was over. Having started, the two continued as they'd begun. He realised her gifts and got her some sort of official role filming commando manoeuvres. Then whisked her away to Australia as soon as the war was over. She never returned.'

'That's an interesting tale, Maxine. But how does it impact on the death at Ding Dong?'

'It's like this. Lisa told me that she and Ross had gone looking for the remains of Brandy Mine. She found the word "Brandies" on the map, it's the name of a group of rocks just offshore. The nearest place was Carn Galver so they went there for coffee. Somehow or other they got involved in an altercation with the owner, he's called John.

337

Peter was hooked. 'Please, carry on.'

'Ross started to talk about his work in Australia. It turned out John was seriously opposed to geothermal energy. Especially any developments close to Brandy Mine. "Drilling it would desecrate the coastline," he pleaded. "Destroy tourism, ruin our teashop."'

Peter mused for a moment. 'You mean, you've found us one local man that would strongly disapprove of Hocking's project?'

'I think so. Lisa had got several drinks inside her by now. She said Ross let slip to John that this was what Hocking was aiming to do.'

Peter decided now wasn't the time to present his theories about Ross to Maxine. He wasn't as sure about them as he had been. There was something new here crying out for investigation.

'How would you feel about us walking over to the Carn Galver cafe? Maybe we could ask some questions of our own.'

'We've got to go somewhere. Sounds fine to me.'

The pair had brought their walking gear. Half an hour later they set off. Peter reckoned an hour would be enough to reach the teashop via the Coast Path.

This part of the path was fairly level. As they walked Peter outlined his anxieties about Ross.

As he feared, Maxine was sceptical. 'I'm not saying Ross couldn't do it,' she said. 'I mean, I've only known him for a week. And he is now an Australian, some of them are quite rough. But your theory seems to start by assuming he's guilty and then trying to explain why.'

Peter cleared his throat to defend himself but Maxine swept

on.

'For example, you seem to assume there was no way Ross could have had contact with Hocking before he got to the UK two weeks ago. But that's not true, is it? After all, my dad hired him. Ross and Jeremy could have been email friends for years.'

Peter had to admit that was true.

'And nothing you've said so far explains why Hocking's car disappeared and then reappeared three days later.'

'No, but –'

'Peter, can we develop a scenario that includes Lunch Box John and maybe assumes Ross and Hocking were friends?'

The policeman was silent for several moments.

'Alright,' he said. 'Let's assume that Ross got a lift into Penzance with Alex and family, on their way to Truro. He was hoping to look up Hocking. But when he rang, Hocking said he was away, starting his day in the cafe at Carn Galver.'

'Ross is a fit man, could cycle seven miles. So he hired a foldable bike to bring back later. Then cycled from Penzance over to the Lunch Box.'

'We know the two met there, Maxine: Sidney told us. Or at least, he reported that Sally had said so. Maybe John saw the two together, had another row with them about geothermal energy.'

'Maybe something was said, Peter, that made him think he was running out of time if he wanted to stop it.'

'Right. Hocking set off to Ding Dong in his own car, pursued by John in another.'

'Uncle Ross cycled along too, but took longer to get there.'

'Hocking parks his car, humps the rope ladder over to Ding

339

Dong. He doesn't realise there's any danger.'

'It was really foggy all last week, remember.'

The newly-weds covered a short distance along the path in silence as they each projected the next stage.

'Hocking gets onto the rope ladder, Maxine. It's just as John arrives and gives him a huge shove. He falls down the shaft and is killed.'

'John doesn't realise there's anyone else around. Not only is it foggy but Ross is coming on a bike; and bikes don't make much noise.'

'John hasn't time to haul up the ladder, wants to get away. Can't do anything about Hocking's car since he doesn't have a key, maybe hopes it won't be seen in the mist. Drives back to Carn Galver, where he pretends to Sally that nothing's happened.'

'Meanwhile my uncle pedals up to Ding Dong and sees the rope ladder. He assumes Hocking has already gone down the shaft, so he goes down after him. When he reaches the bottom he finds his friend crumpled and dead but still warm – he's only just died. So what does my uncle do?'

'If he's an honest citizen, Maxine, you'd expect him to climb out and ring the police. Wouldn't you?'

'He might. But he realises police are always suspicious of the first man on the scene. Especially as he's an outsider. But that cuts both ways: he'll be gone in two weeks. He wonders, is there any way he can keep the whole thing hidden until he's back in Australia?'

Peter knew how plots evolved. 'That'd be obvious. First he

searches Hocking for his car keys. Then he climbs back out, hauls the ladder up and takes it back to Hocking's car.'

'I suppose, if he'd left it dangling over the edge that would have been a dead giveaway.'

'Yes. He might have needed a second trip to bring his bike, but that didn't matter, he wasn't in any hurry. Finally he sticks his folding bike in the boot and drives off.'

'Remember, Peter, there's no reason why he should know that Hocking has a disabled wife that he rings every night. As far as Ross knows, there's no-one to miss him. And today is a good day for skulduggery: all Ross's family are over in Truro. Crucially, they're not in St Just.'

'So he drives back to the village and down to the Cape Cornwall car park. There's no-one around and in any case it's foggy. He takes the ladder out of the boot and lugs it down to the shore. There he spots a rock pool that he reckons will fill up at high tide. An ideal spot to dump a rope ladder, he thinks. The tide will wash it away, or at least remove any traces.'

'But Peter, he can't leave Hocking's car on its own in the Cape Cornwall car park. Someone will see it. Someone from Chy Brisons, perhaps even his brother. So what does he do?'

Peter knew the answer. His own car had been parked in St Just for most of the week. 'Well, the simplest thing is to put it in the St Just car park. It could sit there for weeks before anyone noticed that it hadn't moved. He parks it, swaps the bike into his own car and drives to Penzance. Where the now-unfolded bike is returned to the hire shop. Then . . .'

'Well, he'd just drive home. He'd be back at Chy Brisons long before the rest of his family came home.'

They plodded on in a silence, content. Carn Galver came into view. As a thought experiment the crime had been resolved. Or had it?

'Peter, we've shown a possible reason why Hocking's car might have been taken from Ding Ding. But why on earth would it be brought back again?'

The pair might have the broad outline of the case but they did not yet have the whole solution.

CHAPTER 51

They were almost at the Carn Galver cafe by now. It was just after ten. Peter had doubted the place would be open this early on New Year's Day but Maxine spotted a "Welcome" sign.

She had been brooding over their analysis. 'The only thing is, Peter, I can see a huge hole in the theory.'

Peter shrugged. 'Bound to be a few things we got wrong.'

'It's Hocking's phone. We know it was used for the text sent to his wife after he died, to make it seem he was well on that Thursday evening. His killer must have had it. But how?'

'Well, was it taken from his pocket?'

'Yes but think about it. If Ross had taken his keys, he could have grabbed the phone as well. But assuming he's not the murderer, that'd leave it with the wrong person.'

The policeman was in a buoyant mood. 'We'll think of something.'

The two were the first customers in the teashop. Sally was in attendance, her newly-ironed cream apron as smart as ever.

'You've done well to be in business this early in the year,' said Maxine as they sat down.

'New Year's always a good day for us,' Sally replied. 'There'll be plenty of walkers in here later. What'll you have?'

Coffees were ordered. Peter wondered, now he was here, what

he could actually do. His warrant was in his pocket but he was, after all, off duty. Not just off duty but on annual leave.

But his wife was on full alert. When Sally returned with a tray holding a cafétiere, milk, sugar and a pair of mugs, plus a plate of bourbons, she had a subtle but perceptive question.

'Sally, do you keep track of the lost property that's been left here?'

Sally smiled. 'Oh yes. There's a locked drawer of things that have been forgotten, right over here.'

'Is my phone in there by any chance? I mislaid it in the run-up to the wedding.'

'Dunno. Let's have a look.'

Sally produced a ring of keys from her pocket, opened the drawer and peered inside. 'Yes, there's one in here. Is this yours?'

Maxine hesitated. Sally was about to reach for it when Peter leapt from his feet. 'Can I take that, please? It might be a vital piece of evidence.'

Before the hostess could respond he produced a plastic bag from his cagoule and used it to scoop up the phone, then laid the resulting bundle on the table. A quick glance showed that it was the only device in the drawer.

Sally, though, did not look annoyed at the uninvited interruption. It had revived a memory. Rather, she looked distressed.

'Is this . . . is this anything to do with the death at Ding Dong?'

If Sally was willing to talk then Peter was more than happy to listen. 'Can't tell until it's been examined. It might be.'

Fears from the previous week gnawed at her. 'It's John, isn't it?'

He gave her a sharp glance. 'Why d'you say that?'

'He was behaving very oddly last Thursday. Went off straight after poor old Hocking had settled his bill and walked out. Then he came back half an hour later, muttering that it was all dealt with. I asked him what on earth he was talking about but he just shrugged, said it didn't matter.'

She sighed. 'I'd just found a phone, you see. That one. It was under the chair where Hocking had been sitting. I remember, John watched me find it. But I slipped it into the Lost Property drawer and forgot all about it.'

She looked at them sadly and then at the parcel. 'It is the one, isn't it? It's not yours, Maxine, I'm afraid. It was Hocking's.'

There was a pause.

'Where is John?' asked the policeman, simulating indifference.

'He's gone for a run. He goes off for an hour or so every morning, hopes it might help him lose weight. It was one thing they suggested on his anger management course. He should be back by eleven.'

'Right. In that case I think I'll just make a phone call.'

The policeman drew out his mobile. Then he walked over to the doorway and called a number.

A female voice answered. 'Peter! It's the first day of your honeymoon. What –'

'Holly, have you done anything with Ross yet?'

'No, I'm downstairs at Chy Brisons but the poor man's still asleep. The party didn't stop just cos you two left us, you know. It was New Year's Eve after all.'

'Well, forget about him for now. He's not been very forthcoming and he'll need questioning but he's not the murderer. I need you at the Carn Galver cafe, just past Morvah, as soon as possible. There's an arrest to be made here. And a witness waiting to give a statement.'

'You'll wait there for me?'

'Sure. And while I'm waiting I'll ring Popper. Let him know what to expect.' He gave a laugh. 'I hope he's got some space left in his cells.'

The policeman came back to the table and turned to Maxine. 'I've just called Holly. She'll be here in a few minutes, she can take charge. After all she's the one on duty. We'll wait here for John to finish his run, if you don't mind.

'After that, my darling, we can continue with our honeymoon. Maybe go and explore Gurnard's Head. You'd hardly believe it but I am supposed to be on annual leave.'

It was twelve days later when Maxine and Peter flew back to North Cornwall after a glorious, relaxing time in Italy. It was cold there but not as cold as Land's End. A recorded message awaited them.

'Maxine, we're driving back from St Just to Heathrow on Saturday Jan 14th. Could we drop in, say, around eleven? It'd be good to see you before we go.'

The newlyweds had just enough time to put away the many wedding gifts and to make the house tidy.

The Australians arrived in Delabole full of enthusiasm. 'I'm afraid we can only stop for an hour,' said Lisa. 'Just long enough for coffee, really.' Shelley and Frances were keen to see the famous Slate Quarry and set off after being shown its location on a village map.

'So what's the news from Land's End?' asked Maxine.

'The local police solved the Ding Dong killing,' said Lisa. 'Without any help from you two. Guess what, the killer was the man who helped run that cafe in Carn Galver.'

'Great,' said Maxine. 'A bit of a shock but at least Mum and Dad can relax now. Did you ever meet him?'

'Oh yes. We went there the day after we got to St Just,' said Lisa. 'It was the first stage of my ancestor hunt.'

'You're not related to John or Sally, surely?' asked Maxine.

'No. But my mum had filmed a special mine near there, just before the war. She told Ross and me about the place: it had to close, she said, because the shaft got too close to the hot rocks down below.'

Ross took over. 'I told the Lunch Box owner, his name was John, that that made it an ideal spot to sink a geothermal mine. I even offered them consultancy to take the idea further. I mean, that's the kind of work my firm does. The remit would give me chance to come back here for longer.'

'Hm. How did that go?'

'Badly, Peter. They didn't want to know. The woman was polite enough but it caused a fierce argument with her husband. He said that any drilling would ruin the coastline. But I said it wouldn't.'

'Why ever not?'

'Well, Lisa's mum had made some enquiries, you see. There

was a zawn cut into the cliffs next to the mine. And there was a huge cave formed at the back of that. Once you got the drilling gear installed there, properly muffled, I reckon the sound would hardly be heard from the cliff top.'

'And that was the end of it?'

'Oh no. I met an old friend, Jeremy, who was working for Alex, at a conference in Penryn – that's the one my firm had sent me over for. We agreed to meet again at Carn Galver. I wanted to encourage him to delve into this overheated local mine at Brandy Cliff. I could see it had real promise for geothermal. But seeing us together talking about it, Jeremy starting to get really excited, seemed to knock John off balance completely.'

'You mean . . .'

'My friend set off to Ding Dong as he'd planned and John disappeared. I followed on my hired bike as fast as I could but it's quite a hill. By the time I got there my friend was out of sight but I could guess where he'd gone. There was a rope ladder in position, you see, so I climbed down after him. When I got to the bottom I found that poor Jeremy had fallen down the shaft and was dead.'

'But you didn't report this to the police?'

'To be honest, I didn't trust the local police. It would be easy to blame the death on the one who told 'em, especially if they were an overseas visitor. I'd had one or two tangles with law down under, I wasn't entirely blameless.'

Ross shrugged. 'To be honest, I panicked. So I pulled up the rope ladder and found somewhere to dump it, then I moved Jeremy's car down to St Just. I knew the body would be found eventually, but I planned to be long gone by the time it was.'

'What happened next?'

'On Christmas Day Alex told me about being called out to recover the body. He didn't realised I'd been there earlier and of course I didn't tell him. He asked me to keep it quiet so it didn't spoil the wedding. And said he'd been told by the police that the death had happened on Friday, which was a day later than it really did. That changed the whole thing.'

'Why?'

'Well, I had an alibi for the Friday. I'd spent the day with my family on St Michael's Mount. So now I wanted the crime solved. I still wasn't going to report it but I tried to restore the clues. I drove Jeremy's car back to the roadside near Ding Dong, then walked back to Chy Brisons.' He shrugged. 'It's not far and mostly downhill.'

'And the police put it all together?'

'It took 'em a week, including several hours interviewing Alex. But every cloud ... well, it got him out of doing a speech, and the rest of us out of having to listen. But the Penzance plods got there in the end.'

'And were you involved?'

'Once they asked me I gave them a full statement, which seemed to be decisive. Somehow they'd found Jeremy's phone at the teashop, containing the final message to his wife. Fingerprints showed that'd been sent by John. It was all fairly watertight. In the end John broke down and confessed.'

A satisfactory ending. Peter thought it was probably better for family relations that his part had been entirely obscured. And a good job he hadn't had Ross taken in for questioning. Was there any precedent, he wondered, for a police officer detaining two members of his new family within hours of the wedding?

By now Shelley and Frances had returned from the Slate Quarry. It was almost time for them all to drive on to Heathrow.

'You must come and see us in Australia,' instructed Lisa.

'There's plenty of unsolved crime over there, Peter,' added Ross. 'Hey, you could ask for a transfer.'

'There's enough still to do here,' smiled Peter. 'It can't all be left to Percy Popper.'

AUTHOR'S NOTES

The remote Cornish mines which form the backcloth to this story have existed for hundreds of years and may have fresh life in the future. Even as I started to write there came news of a consortium to explore the chances of mining Cornish lithium.

St Just, Zennor and Cape Cornwall are as described. Operation Brandyball was a Commando exercise in 1943 which led to the demolition of one old mine. The geothermal plant at Rose-manowas ran in the 1970s (although the accident in Chapter 36 is made up). The overheating of parts of Wheal Jane Mine by rocks far below did happen.

The history and artefacts of the ancient church of St Just are taken from the church guide. Ding Dong Mine does exist; one Chief Engineer later ran a silver mine in Peru. How any of these events might prompt fresh activity today is a matter of conjecture.

The Mining Museums at Geevor, Levant and Camborne are well worth a visit. As is the Coast Path, running round the Land's End peninsula.

In short, the story has a real context, but the characters are all made up.

There are photos of Land's End on my website. Please use this to send me your comments; or ideas for further Conundrums.

David Burnell   *www.davidburnell.info*
May 2018

DOOM WATCH describes George Gilbert's first encounter with crime as she helps Padstow plan an upgrade.

A body is discovered behind the Engine House of the old quarry at Trewarmett; but identification proves tricky.

It takes the combined efforts of George and local Police Sergeant Peter Travers to make sense of a crime which seems, simultaneously, to be spontaneous and pre-planned.

"A well-written novel, cleverly structured, with a nicely-handled sub-plot..." Rebecca Tope, crime novelist

SLATE EXPECTATIONS begins as George Gilbert buys a cottage overlooking Trebarwith Strand.

The analyst finds herself part of an outdoor drama based on 19th century events in the Delabole Slate Quarry – a drama heightened when one of the cast is found dead in the opening performance.

The combined resources of George and Police Sergeant Peter Travers are needed to disentangle the past and find out precisely how it relates to the present.

*"Slate Expectations combines an interesting view of an often overlooked side of Cornish history with an engaging pair of sleuths who follow the trail from past misdeeds to present murder."
Carola Dunn, crime author*

LOOE'S CONNECTIONS finds George Gilbert conducting a study of floods in Looe when, without warning, her colleague disappears.

Without really trying George is drawn into a web of suspense and foul play. But when her personal and professional lives begin to overlap, is she the unwitting suspect or the next victim?

The trail covers ways of reducing the flooding in the town and events over many centuries. Even the Romans have a part to play.

"History, legend and myth mixed with a modern technical conundrum makes this an intriguing mystery." Carola Dunn, *crime author*

TUNNEL VISION begins with a project to turn the old North Cornwall Railway into a cycle trail. Then journalist Robbie Glendenning, exploring the only tunnel on the line at Trelill, finds first a peculiar side chamber and then a skeleton.

Making sense of a death half a century ago is a huge challenge. Who were they? When and why did they die? Who had reason to intend them mischief? And who intends more now?

It takes George Gilbert's late arrival to rescue Robbie and move the case to a dramatic conclusion.

"Enjoyable reading for all who love Cornwall and its dramatic history." Ann Granger, crime author

TWISTED LIMELIGHT is the tale preceding Forever Mine. It begins with George Gilbert in Bude for the Limelight Exhibition, acclaiming Goldsworthy Gurney, the man who discovered lime-light and hence lit the Houses of Parliament for half a century.

Meanwhile Peter Travers battles to assert his authority in Bude police station. The missing chimney sweep and the escaped convict are only the latest cases attracting his team's attention.

But it is only when Maxine Tavistock tells George her disturb-ing tale of abduction that the various strands can be woven together.

Can the three untwist this web of confusion?

"The plot twists will keep you guessing up to the last page. This is a thrilling Cornish mystery." Kim Fleet, crime author

Made in the USA
Lexington, KY
04 May 2018